WASHOE COUNTY LIBRARY

3 12                P9-DWX-311

───────────── ★ ─────────────

It's a man's kind of murder," Koepp said. "Women don't like to kill with that much gore."

Margaret paused and looked out at the corridor to make sure no one was close enough to hear. "I think you have to consider a woman as a possibility, and particularly Karen Merrick."

Why her?"

Because she's good at manipulating men."

Koepp caught her inference; Karen Merrick was manipulating him. Resentment flared up and died deep inside him, chilled by the unpleasant truth that Margaret might be right.

───────────── ★ ─────────────

"Intelligence and implication...brighten this book."
—*Milwaukee Journal Sentinel*

NORTH VALLEYS
LIBRARY

Forthcoming from Worldwide Mystery by
C. J. KOEHLER

PROFILE

NORTH VALLEYS
LIBRARY

# C.J. KOEHLER

# MIND GAMES

# W☉RLDWIDE.

TORONTO • NEW YORK • LONDON
AMSTERDAM • PARIS • SYDNEY • HAMBURG
STOCKHOLM • ATHENS • TOKYO • MILAN
MADRID • WARSAW • BUDAPEST • AUCKLAND

If you purchased this book without a cover you should be aware
that this book is stolen property. It was reported as "unsold and
destroyed" to the publisher, and neither the author nor the
publisher has received any payment for this "stripped book."

**MIND GAMES**

A Worldwide Mystery/May 1999

First published by Carroll & Graf Publishers Incorporated.

ISBN 0-373-26309-0

Copyright © 1996 by C. J. Koehler.
All rights reserved. No part of this book may be reproduced
or transmitted in any form or by any means, electronic or
mechanical, including photocopying, recording or by any
information storage and retrieval system, without permission
in writing from the publisher. For information, contact:
Caroll & Graf Publishers Incorporated, 19 West 21st. Street,
Suite 601, New York, NY 10010-6805 U.S.A.

All characters in this book are fictitious, and any resemblance to
actual persons, living or dead, is purely coincidental.

® and TM are trademarks of Harlequin Enterprises Limited.
Trademarks indicated with ® are registered in the United States
Patent and Trademark Office, the Canadian Trade Marks Office
and in other countries.

Visit us at www.worldwidemystery.com

Printed in U.S.A.

To Lynn and Mike

# ONE

EVEN NOW, as the county pool car spun out of the freeway traffic and down an exit ramp, Sergeant Ray Koepp expected to be recalled from this murder investigation. If that happened, and the department sent him back to vice for good, his career was finished; it would be tantamount to forcing an actor to be a street mime after he had played *Hamlet*.

His partner, Margaret Loftus, swung the car onto a street lined with imposing Colonial homes, deep-set on sprawling, tree-covered lots. Old-money territory.

"You've been watching that radio like it'll bite," she said. "Stop worrying. It's our case."

"I keep expecting Lieutenant Tarrish to call us back. I had to grovel to pull this homicide. He reminded me I came up empty on my last three cases." What he didn't say was that he had now been a cop for six years, the same length of time it took him to fail as a priest. A strain of superstition ran through his soul; maybe he was doomed to fail every six years.

"Those cases were drug-related," Margaret said. "They don't count. Every user in the county is a suspect. Besides, who else could he send to this neighborhood? These people read Proust and raise dahlias."

They both laughed. "You're good for me, Margaret," he said. Her optimism had always been infectious; he was beginning to get his confidence back.

Margaret's cheeks colored. She tried to change the subject. "You should be driving, then I could rubberneck."

Koepp studied her smiling profile. "You know I've been

hounding Tarrish to put us back together. He's sticking his neck out with the chief, but he knows you bring me luck.''

She glanced at him. "Don't take all the credit. I told him you were my partner again or I'd transfer to Metro.''

Koepp turned toward the car window so she couldn't see his wry smile. Margaret made a hard right turn into a woodland setting with a tastefully unobtrusive sign announcing "Friars' Close.'' Koepp caught a glimpse of the condominiums. The stately Williamsburg architecture reawakened his sense of irony; people who chose to live here had expected an island of order and tranquility in a sea of urban violence, but violence had followed them inside.

The area between the two nearest buildings, consisting of a matrix of walkways and parking lots surrounding a grass-covered central mall, was jammed with vehicles and people. Some sort of bazaar had been in progress, and its participants were hurriedly boxing their merchandise.

Not everyone was anxious to leave, however. A crowd had formed at the entrance to one of the buildings. Margaret parked and they began threading through the onlookers.

A fat woman in a billowing print dress, as if cued by their arrival, emerged from the building closest to the access road shrieking, "Oh, God, he's dead, Oh, God!" She stopped just outside the double glass doors, crying theatrically. A blond woman in her early twenties, waif-thin next to her charge, was trying without success to propel the woman to the asphalt parking lot.

As the detectives broke free of the crowd, the grieving woman emitted loud sobs that reminded Koepp of someone trying to start a car. A few times, lack of breath caused her to break off in midsob, as if her starter drive-gear had jammed in her flywheel.

Although Koepp was anxious to get rid of her, he had no idea how to do it; hysteria rendered a woman impregnable to males. Margaret wasn't cowed, however. She put a hand gently on one of the woman's massive arms—it reminded Koepp of a Tootsie Roll—and told her, "Madam, I'm a police officer. I order you to leave immediately."

Fresh sobs greeted this command, but the woman began to move unsteadily forward. The spectators made an aisle for her, curiosity giving way before lamentation.

Inside, a uniformed county patrolman barred their way until Koepp held up his gold detective shield. The cop, young and sullen-looking, jerked a thumb over his shoulder. He nodded Margaret through. At an intersecting corridor another patrolman was talking to two men and a woman. When he saw Margaret his face lit up and he greeted her by name. Margaret had that effect on people, even suspects; they were genuinely glad to see her. She introduced them.

"Let's pay our respects," Koepp said. They followed the patrolman past a dining hall and stopped in front of an open doorway.

"Victim's name is Issac Steiner, Dr. Issac Steiner," the cop told them. He stepped aside so they would have an unobstructed view of the crime scene.

Issac Steiner's body was portly, with short, wiry hair and a neatly trimmed mustache and goatee. Attired only in crumpled tan slacks, brown oxfords and a dark-brown knit sportshirt, the corpse lay on the right side with its legs curled up beneath the torso. A dark stain of blood covered the victim's mutilated chest and stomach and spread like the fingers of a hand across the floor tiles, as if it were reaching for something.

No knife was evident.

Koepp glanced at Margaret and was reassured by her studied intensity. He had trained her in her rookie year and watched with satisfaction as she developed into one of the county's best investigators. She was thirty-two and, like him, single.

Standing in the doorway, Koepp made a quick sketch of

the room, then handed the notepad to her. She added a few details to the diagram. As he watched her draw in a precise hand, he wondered if she had heard the scuttlebutt that he'd be transferred to vice if he messed up another case. Probably. She didn't miss much.

Koepp felt vaguely apologetic as they bestowed on the corpse the final courtesy, a moment of deferential silence. The two of them would be the last human beings to treat Issac Steiner as a person; he could hear the technicians down the corridor and their business was with cadavers, not people.

It was hard to imagine this thing alive; violent death extracted the essence of spiritual humanity. The room also exuded the stench of excreta and urine, confirming physically the metaphysical reality.

The scene of the crime, an antiseptic room filled with gray computers and gray metal cabinets, yielded its sparse gray information. He was struck by the orderliness of everything, the sterility. Even from the doorway Koepp could see that there were no helpful, out-of-place objects like a cigarette butt or a button lying around. He seldom found such convenient physical evidence at murder scenes, but he felt cheated all the same.

"Who called it in?" he asked his partner.

"A Mrs. Merrick," Margaret answered.

"She find the body?"

"No." This reply came from the county patrolman. Margaret had introduced him as Roger Somebody. He stepped forward now and flipped open his notebook. "Guy named Charlie Tirquit found the body a few minutes..." He paused, unsure of himself. "Must have been about quarter to four."

Koepp made a mental note to verify when the body was discovered; the officer's uncertainty might be significant.

"Where does the victim live?" Koepp asked.

"Upstairs," Roger said.

Koepp and Margaret had passed a squad car parked at the

entrance to the parking mall. Two officers from the Hillside police department had been asking each departing driver for his license and auto registration.

"How'd the Hillside cops get involved?" Koepp asked.

"Hillside picked up the call from our dispatcher and sent a couple of uniforms to help out. We put 'em to work checking people out of here to keep them out of our hair." After consulting his notes for a moment, the patrolman advised them that the medical examiner and a scene-of-the-crime team were on the way. He closed his notebook again, signifying that in his judgment those were the significant facts. Pleased with himself, he looked at Margaret for approval. She nodded and smiled.

Koepp tried to remember what he had read in the ads in the real-estate section of the newspaper about this place. It went something like: More than a condominium, Friars' Close provides an on-site accredited day-care center, a university-sponsored school and full meal plan for active two-income families...

Roger had done his own research. "Besides the dining room, they have their own grade school and high school," he said. "You better get that Merrick woman to explain."

The three policemen joined the trio of strangers whom Roger had been interrogating when Koepp and Margaret arrived. Roger performed a stilted introduction. He began with Mrs. Merrick, a small woman in her early forties, then identified her husband and Leon Jaroff. The policeman used the title "Doctor" for both men but not for the woman. Koepp asked them to wait nearby. Oddly, he could feel the woman's scrutiny; he made a conscious effort not to look at her again, but his eyes were drawn back to her face. Her large, luminous brown eyes registered a disconcerting, surprising empathy. As Koepp turned away, he noticed that Margaret was watching him also. Her face was blank, always a bad sign.

Although Roger tried to direct the three residents to separate offices in the east wing, Dr. Jaroff refused to go. Instead, he followed the policemen toward the crime scene. His voice betrayed considerable agitation as he demanded of Koepp, "Can't you do something about that crowd?"

"Do what?" Koepp asked, stopping.

"Get them to leave—obviously," Jaroff cried.

The detective noticed perspiration droplets on the man's forehead; they reminded him of rosary beads. "How much do they know?" he asked.

"Only that someone is dead," Jaroff said. "Their curiosity is grotesque, grotesque."

Shooing the onlookers away wasn't going to keep the world from knowing a murder had been committed in this "sanctuary." The media were on the way already, Koepp was certain. But he sympathized with Jaroff, who probably counted Steiner's demise as a defeat for Friars' Close.

Koepp reluctantly accompanied him to the entrance, where he advised the crowd that they would have to leave. But his admonition was probably unnecessary; the silent men and women, their morbidity unquenched, had already begun to drift away. Jaroff, mollified, agreed to wait nearby for Koepp's interrogation.

Even though the investigation had barely begun, it had a bad feel to it. First of all, the victim was a prominent man, at least in academic circles, which presaged intense media interest in his murder. Pressure from the media usually generated impatience and irrationality in the offices of the district attorney and the chief of detectives, compromising the work of the investigative teams.

Suddenly, more professionals appeared in the hallway outside the crime scene. Koepp recognized Tom Sturmer, a pathologist from the medical examiner's office, and a photographer whose name he couldn't remember. Another man, balding, middle-aged Russ Kalmbach, shuffled past the others and entered the computer room on his hands and knees. An evidence technician from the county lab, he began to dust the floor with black powder between the doorway and Steiner's body. He not only searched for latent prints but was responsible for bagging physical evidence. He was looking for prints on the floor because murderers sometimes knelt to rifle a victim's pockets.

The fingerprint man advanced beyond the body far enough so that the photographer felt safe in entering the room. Sturmer followed him, knelt behind the corpse's back and placed a stethoscope against the dead man's bloody chest. The photographer took stills of the room and the body from various angles, then duplicated his effort with a video camera. Using a tape measure, Koepp and Margaret determined the dimensions of the room, then recorded their findings on their crude diagram. By triangulation, they fixed the exact location of the victim's head in relation to the doorway and the computer terminals which lined the two longer walls.

Kalmbach tied plastic bags over each of the victim's hands. Later, in the lab, he would get fingernail pairings and prints from the corpse. Fingerprinting the victim was essential so that his prints could be differentiated from those of his attacker. Kalmbach looked at Koepp. "Weapon?"

Koepp turned to the two patrolmen.

"We didn't have time to look for a murder weapon," Roger said. His partner nodded assent.

Koepp told them to start searching.

Roger asked, "What kind of knife are we looking for?"

Sturmer heard the question. "Big butcher knife is my guess," he said. "I'll help you look once I finish up here." When he returned to the forensics lab, Sturmer would squeeze a barium/sulphate paste into the wound until the cavity was filled, then X-ray it. That would tell him the shape, width, and thickness of the knife blade and whether it was single-or double-edged. If the killer had driven the weapon in up to the hilt, bruises on the victim's skin would betray that fact; this would reveal the exact length of the knife.

Sturmer gently touched the dead man's eyelids, then grasped the jaw and attempted to move it. He sighed, checked a rectal thermometer and made some notations in his ubiquitous notebook. He rose stiffly to his feet and joined Koepp and Margaret in the hallway.

"Time of death between two and three o'clock," he said, consulting his notes. "Maybe as early as one-thirty at the outside. His stomach contents will tell us more."

Immediately, Koepp's mind cycled back to Roger's vagueness about when the body was discovered. If the murder occurred before three, either no one noticed the body for a long time or a lot of time had elapsed between the discovery and the call to the sheriff's department.

"Shall we get some answers?" Koepp asked his partner.

As they walked to the dining hall, Koepp tried to remember what else he had read about Friar's Close. Unlike many co-op projects, this one was being co-sponsored by the university and a private foundation as a research project.

With sponsors like that, the project's leaders had clout, which they'd use if his probing threatened any reputations.

Koepp's sigh was audible.

They sat at a table near a window washed in orange and pink from the late-afternoon sun and motioned for Mrs. Merrick to join them. Margaret pulled a tape recorder from her handbag and placed it on the table between Koepp and herself. Mrs. Merrick wore a white blouse and a blue skirt secured by a white cord belt, which accentuated her slimness. She still had a name badge, imprinted with the words *Hello, my name is,* stuck to her blouse. Beneath the lettering, in block printing, was the name *Karen.*

She sat down directly across the table from Koepp. Her brown hair fell neatly in a shoulder-length permanent wave curl. Her face was triangular—a narrow jaw resolving into a small but prominent chin. Something in the woman's expression, her frank curiosity perhaps, challenged him, and made him uneasy. Six years ago another woman had looked at him that way. Diane. Was this her legacy, that he would meet women who reminded him of her?

"Who killed him, Mrs. Merrick?" Koepp asked as casually as one might inquire about the weather.

She glanced down at the tape recorder, smiled faintly at Margaret as if acknowledging her presence and answered, "I've been asking myself that question ever since—ever since it happened. I don't have any idea."

Margaret picked up the recorder, but set it down again without pushing the start button. "Sergeant Koepp wasn't being facetious when he asked you that question, Mrs. Merrick" she said.

"I realize that," the woman answered. "I suppose in most investigations everyone knows who the murderer is." She addressed her remarks to Koepp, not to Margaret.

"Could you explain exactly what this place is?" Koepp suggested. "For starters, who's in charge? You?"

She laughed outright at that, a genuine, unaffected laugh. "Nobody's in charge. We're a co-op." She smiled again when she saw him frown. "Forgive me. I'm not being obtuse deliberately. This is just a condominium that offers a few more services."

"I've read about something similar in Denmark," Margaret said. "Didn't somebody write a book about it?"

"That's right," the woman answered. "There's a book titled *Co-housing* which describes the basic concept.

"Friars' Close—which is the name the real-estate people came up with, by the way—is a sociology lab. My husband, Dr. Jaroff, and Dr. Steiner are all social scientists working on grants involving different aspects of community living. The residents have agreed to cooperate with them in their research. That's a condition for either buying or renting here. When you leave, you have to sell your property back to the condo association.''

"That's how you keep your mission pure," Margaret commented.

"Yes," the woman said. She studied Margaret with interest. "Most people don't mind the special covenants. They like being part of an effort to find a way to replace the extended family, to help people deal with problems like day-care, meal preparation, latchkey children—''

Through the window Koepp saw two more squad cars on the access road. Reluctantly, he excused himself and went back to the corridor, irritated that he had to miss any of the interview. Another team of detectives, Markowicz and Neves, was waiting for him at the police barricade outside the computer room. After briefing the pair, he sent them to the adjacent building to interview the occupants. Then he went outdoors to meet the newly arrived patrolmen. He assigned one to guard the crime scene once the medical examiner left and the rest to look for the murder weapon.

Rapidly the full force of the county's law-enforcement resources descended on Friar's Close; the meat wagon from the ME's office pulled into the parking lot and disgorged two burly, taciturn males, a gurney, and a body bag. Without speaking to anyone, the men went inside in search of their grisly cargo. Nobody spoke to them either. Two more detectives arrived. Koepp assigned them to Building C.

When he returned to the dining room, Margaret was reviewing a list of names she evidently had extracted from Karen Merrick. She handed the list to Koepp with the explanation that it identified everyone who had been in the Administration Building about the time of the murder. Koepp counted nine names, including, unaccountably, Steiner's; Margaret was nothing if not thorough.

He noticed that Mrs. Merrick's name was on the list, as

well as the name Erin Merrick. "Your daughter?" Koepp asked, pointing at it.

She nodded and briefly explained who the other people on the list were.

"You're the business manager, condo president, what, Mrs. Merrick?" Margaret asked.

"Please call me Karen. We don't use titles here—even something as innocuous as Mrs. and Ms."

"I wasn't thinking of joining up, Mrs. Merrick," Margaret said.

Her sarcasm surprised Koepp. Across from him, a crooked smile had formed on the dusky, angular features. The woman's eyes were riveted on his and he could see the conspiratorial laughter in them.

Margaret noticed the eyes, too, unfortunately.

Koepp intervened quickly. "Tell us what you did during the day."

The woman explained that they had held a Starving Artists show and that she had assisted exhibitors in finding their booths and registering during the morning.

"Are the artists from this community?" Margaret asked.

"No, we have our own show in August."

"What did you do next?"

"We had brunch in this room, then the public started to arrive at about twelve-thirty. From then on I was doing whatever I could to make the show a success. I was in and out of my office—that's down the hallway on this floor—getting cash to make change. I also made announcements on the PA from time to time—you know, helping kids find their parents, that sort of thing."

"Could you account for your whereabouts between one-thirty and three?"

"If you mean, could I construct an alibi—and I'm sure that's what you mean—the answer is no. That's probably true

of all one hundred and seventy-eight members of Friars'
Close. The day was too unstructured.''

Margaret tapped her fingers restlessly on the table. The
long, hard nails made an annoying clickety-click sound. Finally, she asked, ''You've only talked about alibis for your
members, so you must think one of them killed him?''

''I don't think that at all,'' the woman answered, alarmed.
''None of *us* would do such a thing. We abhor violence.''

They concluded the questioning and asked Mrs. Merrick to
locate Charlie Tirquit, the young man who had found the
body. Margaret also inquired whether they should hold their
interviews elsewhere so dinner could be served.

''Normally that would be necessary. Tonight we're having
a cookout—cleaning up the leftovers. You're welcome to join
us.''

Koepp declined, surprised that he wanted to say yes.

After she left, they called Dr. Jaroff to their table. Margaret
kept the tape running. As soon as he had given his name and
address, she asked, ''Who do you think killed Dr. Steiner, Dr.
Jaroff?''

''First off, please call me Leon. We don't use titles here,
only first names. We're trying to foster a family atmosphere.
As to who killed Issac, I can't help you.''

''Please describe your movements earlier in the day.''

''This morning I helped get picnic tables out and scattered
around the grounds. All of us find manual labor cathartic on
occasion. I did lunch in this room from about noon until just
before one o'clock.''

Beginning at one o'clock, Jaroff had been meeting in a
nearby conference room with Paul Merrick and Elizabeth
Maklin. Each time Margaret asked a question, he paused before he answered; Dr. Jaroff was a cautious man. He called
the meeting a ''Planners'' session.

''Planners?'' Margaret asked with interest.

"We're condo association officers really. But because of the services we offer, we have a great many responsibilities."

"So someone *is* in charge," Margaret exclaimed with evident satisfaction.

"Not in the sense you have in mind," Jaroff replied. "Each Planner serves only three years, and all of our decisions are subject to review and rejection by two-thirds of the members of the community."

Koepp broke in. "How long did the meeting last? Dr.—Leon."

"Until about three-thirty or so. We don't meet that often. We had a lot to discuss." Jaroff settled back in his chair—he had chosen to sit opposite Margaret—arms folded. Whether by intent or not, his posture conveyed an attitude of passive resistance. While he considered some other tack, Koepp studied his subject. The man was bald except for a trimly cut fringe of fine blond hair. He wore thick, rimless glasses and a khaki one-piece jump suit. The suit suggested the air of an outdoorsman, but his pallid skin and scrawny frame contradicted the image the clothing tried to create. Koepp noticed that the man was uncomfortable in the absence of questions. He decided to let the silence work.

After a while Jaroff said with some impatience, "Don't you think you should be addressing your efforts toward tracking down Issac's murderer instead of talking to me?"

"Are the two activities mutually exclusive?" Margaret asked.

"Yes," Jaroff said. "I can't help you. None of us can. The murderer was some sort of transient—one of the artists, someone in the crowd…"

"What motive might such a person have?" Koepp asked.

"How should I know? I do know that the people who live in this community reject violence, and in addition are in Issac's debt. More than anyone else, he is responsible for our crucial support from the Grayson Foundation."

"Is that so?" Koepp said, leaning forward to encourage the speaker. "Mrs. Merrick and you both say people here wouldn't kill. Have you found a way to change human nature?"

Jaroff's expression didn't change; he treated the remark with complete seriousness. "Establishing stable family and community relationships will eliminate the need to commit crime. That's why it's so important that your investigation not compromise our work." His penetrating eyes were fixed on Koepp as he added, "This tragedy is the work of an intruder. None of our people is involved. This is a violence-free environment."

Margaret turned off her recorder. "From the look of the dead guy," she said, "you haven't worked out the bugs yet."

# TWO

In the shallow, grassy valley below the dining-hall window, the few remaining artists were packing away their pictures into vans or station wagons. To Koepp they seemed unhurried, hesitant, as if they were thinking about other matters. Paper napkins, stirred by a gusty east wind, made their way among the artists, dropped to the lawn, then rose without warning, like waterfowl disturbed by an intruder.

As the interview with Jaroff ended, a young woman came to tell them that several reporters were demanding interviews. Jaroff nodded grimly and asked, "In the main office, I assume?"

The young woman nodded.

"I don't think you should talk to the media," Koepp told Jaroff. "At least not today. Let me handle it." The man looked relieved.

Teams representing the city's Channels 2 and 11 and reporters from the major morning metropolitan paper, the *News*, and the local suburban paper were waiting. After some negotiating, he agreed to one on-camera interview, which would be followed by a question-and-answer session with the two print journalists. Koepp disliked this part of the job intensely because the results of the interview were out of his control. He limited himself to the few facts which were currently in their possession and resisted the impulse to sarcasm that had occasionally gotten him in trouble with the department in the past.

Throughout the interview he tried to imagine that he was talking in front of J. L. Vorhees, the chief of detectives and his principal department critic. Following this discipline resulted, happily, in a dull taping session.

Koepp had asked Margaret to interrogate Paul Merrick alone because she could often disarm an unwary male suspect. While she was thus engaged, he collected the names of the art-show visitors from the Hillside police officers and then dismissed them. In the parking lot, several policemen were emptying bags of trash from a dumpster onto a gray tarpaulin under the supervision of Roger Somebody.

When Koepp reentered the community center, he began looking for Mrs. Merrick. He found her in a small office on the ground floor. She had put on a white cardigan sweater and sat behind a large desk piled high with unopened mail, file folders, and correspondence. She waved him toward a chair.

"Making progress?" she asked. She smiled warmly, not enigmatically as she had earlier. She leaned forward and placed her arms on the desk; the change of posture seemed to suggest that her other work was no longer important.

"Not so far," he admitted. "I could use your help."

"I'll do whatever I can." She pulled a yellow notepad from a desk drawer to underscore her commitment.

"Can you supply a complete roster of all the people living here, with their phone numbers?"

"Yes, in fact I have a computer printout I can give you right now." She found it after a brief search through her "pending" file basket and handed it across the desk to him.

"How about diagrams of all your buildings and the names of the occupants?"

"The office staff can get that for you. Do you need it tonight?"

"Morning's okay," Koepp said.

"Good. Ask for Elaine or Gwen. Gwen is the blonde you saw when you came in. One of them will be in the office where you met the press. Around eight-thirty in the morning. I'll leave a note asking them to run a copy for you."

"The woman who was crying when we arrived was the victim's wife, I assume?" Koepp asked.

His question appeared to surprise her. "Why, no. That was Dr. Jaroff's wife." Her features softened into a slow, oddly compelling smile. "She's inclined to be a little hysterical. Dr. Steiner was single—divorced, actually." Mrs. Merrick had trouble getting the word "divorced" out.

"We also want Mr. Tirquit now," he said. "And, is there a place to talk privately to people in the morning?"

"Yes, the office directly across the hall. There's a phone. We can get you a key."

"I also want to see Elizabeth—"

"Maklin?"

"Yes."

"She's probably at the cookout. I'll find her."

"Tell her to come to the dining room in, say about thirty to forty minutes."

"Of course. I doubt if Liz can help, though. She was at the Planners' meeting with my husband—"

"I know. However, she can verify the alibis of both your husband and Jaroff. They seem to be the only people with alibis, so at least we can eliminate three of—I believe you said one hundred and seventy-eight?"

She nodded but made no comment. Koepp suspected that she knew he wasn't interested in checking out alibis for everyone. She could readily see how daunting that was. Elimination of suspects by checking alibis seldom proved useful early in a homicide investigation. In this circumstance it would be futile. Hundreds of people had both the opportunity and means to kill Issac Steiner. Unless an eyewitness miraculously appeared, solving the murder would depend on motive.

That suited Koepp. Ferreting out a killer's motivation required logic and an understanding of human nature, skills in which he felt he excelled. Divining a killer's motive also lent an intellectual elegance to the process of keeping order. It's what had attracted him to police work.

When he discovered the motive, he'd prove Vorhees wrong, prove to all of them he could solve the big cases.

KOEPP RETURNED to the dining room just as Margaret was asking Paul Merrick how long the Planners' meeting lasted.

"Until about three-thirty" was the reply. Once again Koepp's suspicion about testimony involving time was aroused. Merrick's response exactly echoed Jaroff's earlier answer to the same question, which smacked of collusion. He was curious to hear how the third participant in that meeting, Elizabeth Maklin, would answer the question.

He shook hands with Paul Merrick, sat next to Margaret, and listened in silence as his partner continued her interrogation. Merrick was a lithe six-footer with regular features, curly black hair that was beginning to gray at the temples, and large, powerful-looking hands. The hands were clasped and rested on the table. While he thoughtfully answered the questions, he studied them intently, as if they contained the answers he needed.

"When did you last see Dr. Steiner alive?"

"About twelve-thirty or so. We ate lunch with him."

"We?"

"My wife and thirteen-year-old daughter were with me. Issac sat with us."

"Did he frequently take his meals with your family?"

"No more so than with anyone else," Merrick said. "I can see where you're headed, so let me explain something. My family often does not eat together. My son, for instance, had lunch today with friends. We encourage that. One of our aims at Friars' is to lessen emotional dependence on the nuclear family. We think it's important for members to enjoy each meal with different people. Ideally, we'd like everyone to spend some social time with everyone else in the community—irrespective of age."

Koepp could see that Margaret was caught up in the pragmatic aspects of community living, yet he was disinclined to force the conversation back onto the murder. Letting a person talk without asking him specific questions sometimes gave them a productive line of investigation to pursue. So far things weren't going well. For one thing he was worried about the murder weapon; perhaps he had made a mistake by not getting more policemen to help with the search. Still, even if they found it, what would it tell them? The murderer would undoubtedly have wiped off his fingerprints before disposing of it. The fact that the killer had taken the knife with him suggested that the weapon was traceable to him. Then again, perhaps he had no means of wiping it off.

Koepp noticed that this witness, unlike the others, had not invited them to use his first name. "Dr. Merrick," Koepp began, "you and Dr. Jaroff did research as a team—"

"Not here," Merrick corrected him quickly. "Dr. Jaroff and I are recipients of separate grants."

"Did you and Steiner ever collaborate?" Koepp asked.

Merrick paused. The hesitation was brief but too long for his simple affirmative answer. Koepp filed away Merrick's delay in his memory; exploring the relationship between the two scientists might prove fruitful.

Margaret resumed her questioning. "What was Dr. Steiner's mood at lunch?"

"Jovial, as he usually was," Merrick said without hesitation. "Issac was very funny and affectionate with my daughter. He enjoyed the company of young people like Erin."

Margaret looked at Koepp and shrugged, in effect asking him if he had any more questions. Koepp shook his head. They thanked Merrick and told him he could go.

Someone had brought a pot of coffee and two cups to their table. Koepp filled his. Tirquit hadn't arrived.

"Let's review what we've got," Koepp suggested. "You go first."

She straightened up, took a deep breath and grinned uncertainly, in the manner of a schoolgirl about to recite for a favored professor. Because Koepp had been her first partner in homicide, she tended to idealize him at times. "It's queer the killer took the knife," she told him. "Smarter to leave it in the corpse. He couldn't go out of the building with it. Too many people around, someone would have seen it." Koepp nodded, encouraging her to continue. "There also must have been a lot of blood. Probably the killer washed the knife off and got rid of any bloodstained clothes before he went outside. Or maybe someone who lives in this building did it."

"There couldn't be many apartments upstairs," Koepp said. "This seems to be a common building."

"Single people mostly, like the deceased. And—Paul Merrick."

"Merrick lives alone?"

She grinned. "Crazy, huh? If I lived here he wouldn't be sleeping by himself." She feigned lasciviousness, but the attempt drowned in a sea of wholesomeness.

"That is odd. They don't seem estranged. They ate lunch together—"

"The rest of the Merricks live in Building D, the one directly across the footbridge from this one. Merrick let it drop that he and his wife are thinking about a trial separation."

"What else?"

"Something about that Planners' meeting doesn't add up," she said. "Merrick was evasive when I pressed him about what was discussed."

"It may not have ended when they say it did, either," Koepp added. "Pretending it lasted an hour or two longer gives them convenient alibis—"

"People don't volunteer anything," Margaret cut in, excited by their give-and-take. "They seem to cooperate, but it's like they're circling the wagons to protect the group. I can't prove they're holding out. Just a hunch."

Koepp had learned to respect his partner's hunches. This one made sense because the murder of the community's founder, with its attendant bad publicity, posed a threat to the very existence of the experimental community. What, for instance, would be the attitude of the magnanimous Grayson Foundation? Would it withdraw support from Friars' Close?

They heard Mrs. Merrick in the hallway talking earnestly before she appeared in the doorway with a gangling young man. He was in his late twenties and had a round, moonlike face which contrasted humorously with his slender frame. Mrs. Merrick had to pat him on the arm reassuringly to start him toward the detectives.

After the usual preliminary questions, Margaret asked the man to describe the circumstances of finding Issac Steiner's body.

"My job was to take bags of ice from the big freezer in the kitchen out to the concession stands," Charlie Tirquit said. "I'd drive the perimeter road till I got as close to the concession stand as possible. They were supposed to send someone to the truck to get their bags. They didn't always do it though..." Koepp noticed that the young man—he was little more than a boy—spoke in a phlegmy voice, which in many people signified nervousness.

Margaret prodded him. "Explain about finding—"

"I come in for some ice and had to walk right by the computer room. I saw Issac and all the blood. I knew he was dead, so I didn't go in. I went to find Karen. She called you guys."

"When did you first notice Dr. Steiner's body?" Margaret asked.

"Not sure. I don't have a wristwatch." He raised both bare wrists to prove it. "But it was just before Karen called you. If you know that time, you can figure it out." He watched

Margaret with a mixture of fear and hostility, which surprised Koepp; most people liked his partner.

"The call was made at three forty-five," she said. "Doc says Issac died before three o'clock. That means the body was lying there for close to forty minutes. Sound right?"

"I don't know. I guess—"

"Maybe he was killed as early as two o'clock. In that case the body was in plain sight an hour and forty minutes."

"If you say so."

Coldness had crept into Margaret's voice. "It's what the facts say. The door was open, wasn't it?"

"Sure, how else would I have seen him?" Tirquit's pitch was rising to a whine. "I never would have gone into the computer room if the door had been shut. I'd never have seen him."

"Was the computer-room door usually left open?" Margaret had switched to a soothing tone.

"No, it was always shut." He cleared his throat as though he was aware of his unnatural pitch. "Because of the computers—they didn't want anyone fooling—"

"Why do you think the killer left the door open?"

"Huh?"

"It makes no sense," Margaret said slowly. "Put yourself in the killer's shoes. You've just killed a man. Your only thought is to escape as fast as possible. The most dangerous thing you can do is leave the door open as you leave. Someone could come along in five seconds and see the dead body. On the other hand, if you shut the door, maybe no one will discover what you've done for hours." She studied his youthful, freckled face for a moment. "Do you see my point?"

"Yeah, I'd have shut the door—no question. He must have been too scared to think."

"Maybe," Margaret said, staring steadily into his eyes. "Or maybe the killer shut the door and someone else—someone who went into the computer room to look for Issac—

found him. And maybe that person for some reason didn't want to be the one who reported the murder. So he left the door open so somebody else—you, for instance—would find the body.''

Charlie Tirquit blinked dumbly once or twice. Margaret's speculation seemed to confuse and disturb him. He looked apprehensively toward Koepp as if he wasn't sure if he could expect more of the same from him, or rescue.

Koepp chose to rescue him. ''That's all for now, Mr. Tirquit, except for getting a set of fingerprints.''

Even though the man seemed determined to cooperate, he was visibly upset by the process of having to surrender his fingers one by one to Margaret. His eyes were wide and gelatinous as he watched her roll each of his fingers on the print pad; Koepp was reminded of a small boy submitting to his mother's probing for a splinter with a needle.

At last, with a grateful sigh, the man escaped into the gathering gloom of the corridor. They heard him speak to someone, then a thirtyish woman they both assumed was Elizabeth Maklin appeared. She turned on a bank of ceiling lights over the heads of the two detectives. As soon as Koepp saw her clearly, he could appreciate why she wanted ample light. She was quite beautiful in a severe, understated way, with shoulder-length, straight blond hair, unblemished white skin, and electrifying light-blue eyes. Even Margaret was impressed, judging by her quick inhalation of air when she first saw Elizabeth Maklin.

Usually, Koepp liked to have Margaret conduct the questioning, because this enabled him to concentrate exclusively on the witnesses. He felt that the way the person responded was as important as the response itself. But he took the lead in the Maklin interrogation because he sensed the woman's vulnerability.

Without any preliminary questions, he asked what time the Planners' meeting had ended.

"About three-thirty."

Koepp felt Margaret kick his shin none too gently. "No, I'm sorry," he said. "I meant the first time." He thought he saw something, uncertainty perhaps, in the cool blue eyes, but it faded to impassivity.

"I'm afraid I don't understand," the woman said. Koepp waited in silence for a long time; often a witness who pleaded that she didn't understand was stalling for time. She refused to fluster.

He kept trying. "I thought Jaroff said there was a recess." He produced a notebook and pretended to consult it. "Well, never mind," he said. "Instead, it would be useful if you could tell us what occurred at the Planners' meeting."

"I don't see the relevancy—"

"Leave relevancy to us," he told her.

She studied Koepp with silent animosity for a few moments, then said, "We discussed various long-range problems, such as the vacancies we still have in some of our buildings, whether to change rules for our car pool—"

"Keep going."

"Anything else we discussed is confidential. I'm not at liberty to disclose the rest of it," she said.

Koepp snorted. "Bull."

Elizabeth Maklin's alabaster cheeks were suddenly suffused with red. But she managed to hold her temper in check.

"Being evasive won't help matters," Koepp said. "We have a suspect. I think you know who it is."

If Margaret was surprised by his inexplicable lie, she disguised it well.

The woman's passion startled them both. "If they're telling you garbage about Paul, that's all it is—garbage. They hate him—they're jealous—they—"

No, Margaret, Koepp thought, Paul Merrick doesn't sleep alone. He sleeps with this brittle lady. The satisfaction of knowing this curled up comfortably, like a well-fed cat, inside his head.

KOEPP CALLED Lieutenant Tarrish, at his home in the city's modish Old Town. He could hear party hubbub in the background before Tarrish noisily kicked a door shut. Koepp briefed his boss on their progress, answered several cryptic questions, then made his request, which he knew was not going to be well received. "I want a lab team to go through the building and check the drains for blood traces as soon as possible in the morning."

"For Chrissakes, that means some more overtime. How many drains?"

"A whole bunch."

"Have you got a suspect?" Tarrish was an optimist.

"No."

"Have you got a particular drain in mind?"

"No."

"Then the judge will say you're on a fishing expedition. He won't give us a warrant."

"It doesn't matter. We'll get everyone's permission. They're very cooperative here."

Tarrish finally growled his assent to the lab team. He told Koepp that an assistant DA named Tom Styles had been assigned to the case. "Call him tonight, right away," Tarrish said; he hated to get complaints from the district attorney's office. He gave Koepp the phone number. He also agreed, after Koepp's prodding, to send another team of detectives to search Steiner's office at the university.

Koepp phoned Tom Styles and explained to his answering machine who he was. He dictated his home phone number.

As he left his temporary command post, Koepp noticed a sliver of light beneath the door of Mrs. Merrick's office. He decided to tell her they were leaving and tapped lightly on

the wooden door. He heard what sounded like a chair being
moved, but no voice responded. He opened the door.

To his surprise, he encountered Elizabeth Maklin, not Mrs.
Merrick. The woman stood next to a metal cabinet with four
file drawers. In her hand she clutched a tan file folder, which
she replaced in the second drawer from the bottom. She did
it deliberately, making certain he saw her put it back, and
shoved in the lock at the top of the cabinet, which secured all
four drawers.

Her voice resonated with defiance as she said, "Good
night."

# THREE

SUNDAY MORNING. Rainy.

Koepp was up earlier than usual, having spent a restless night. He scrambled two eggs, made himself some toast and looked around his refrigerator for orange juice. Out again. He made a cup of instant coffee, collected the Sunday newspaper from the hallway and settled into the breakfast nook at the back of his apartment. From there he always enjoyed looking at the courtyard below. A small concourse in the center surrounded a birdbath on which a single forlorn robin perched. The geraniums at the edges of the intersecting walkways were a luminous red, their brilliance somehow enhanced by the morning mist and rain. Perhaps they weren't brighter, maybe it was just the contrast they presented to their dreary surroundings. Rousing himself from his daydreams, he picked up the newspaper and found the murder story immediately. Steiner's prominence as a psychologist and academician rated front-page placement. He was pleasantly surprised by the story's accuracy. He tore it out; the brief biography it contained might be useful later.

He found a lined tablet and ballpoint pen and began making notes about the Steiner homicide. After writing the first question, *Was murderer a resident or a chance intruder?* he stared at the paper for a long time. He wanted the killer to be from the community because then they would be able to determine a motive eventually. If, on the other hand, Steiner had been surprised by a thief, then a defined motive was nonexistent. In that event, absent a set of fingerprints at the crime scene or an eyewitness description of the interloper, this would be another unsolved case.

*What does the absence of the knife suggest?* He decided it
was neutral in helping provide an answer to the first, critical
question. A breaking-and-entering perpetrator would take his
own weapon with him. But so would a resident who feared it
might be traceable to him. Because Tom Sturmer had theo-
rized that the murder weapon was a butcher knife, Margaret
had quizzed the kitchen staff to learn if any knife was missing.
None was. Still, if Sturmer finally concluded that it was in
fact a kitchen knife, they'd search more thoroughly for it.

Following the seven-o'clock mass at Holy Angels church,
Koepp went to the medical examiner's office to pick up a
copy of Sturmer's preliminary report. Two items on the doc-
ument caught his attention: Sturmer estimated the time of
death at between two-thirty and three o'clock; the murder
weapon was likely a common butcher knife with no serra-
tions. Of considerably more interest was a note appended to
the medical examiner's report, which advised him that a peaty
clod of soil had been discovered stuck to the victim's trousers.
The scene-of-the-crime team concluded that the soil had been
on the floor of the computer room and that the victim had
fallen on it. The soft, moist soil had adhered to Steiner's right
buttock.

The note's implication was obvious: the peaty material had
been scraped from the killer's shoe. The lab technician who
had written the message, advised him to *look for low-lying
areas where prolonged water saturation was likely. Color of
material is mottled gray with rusty-colored spots.*

Sundays didn't stop murder investigations. Koepp arrived
at Friars' Close just before nine and parked near the stone
bridge on the boulevard at the south edge of the co-housing
property. From the bridge, he studied both banks of the stream
which meandered through the property, concluding at once
that the soil on Steiner's clothes had not come from here. The
banks were grass-covered and the little soil that was evident
appeared to be black loam. More importantly, the water was

carried underneath the boulevard by two culverts which were too small to encourage human passage.

The entry point at the northwest corner of the property was more promising. Another bridge on Ridge Road accommodated the creek, but unlike the downstream structure, this one was high enough to permit pedestrian traffic alongside the stream. Koepp scrambled down an embankment and began to survey the ground directly under the bridge. Most of the soil was damp, indicating the stream had overflowed recently. The ground was mottled gray with rusty-colored spots and covered with footprints. Too many prints to give them any hope of identifying the killer's.

Koepp dug up three samples with his hands from separate locations and put each of these in plastic evidence bags. Then he rinsed his hands in the pool of water beneath the bridge. He was confident that trace elements in his samples would match those in the soil particle found at the murder scene. A fence along the northern boundary of Friars' Close would make entrance from that direction all but impossible, except for this relatively commodious egress beneath the bridge. The numerous footprints proved it was well used. Koepp considered the implications. The killer had been here recently. But then, that was probably true of every teenager in the neighborhood, and any number of adults as well.

Still, if he came up with a suspect, and the suspect had this peaty material on his shoes, it was a useful piece of circumstantial evidence.

He went to the Friars' Close office.

The blond woman who had assisted the grieving Mrs. Jaroff the previous evening was alone in the office. She told him her name was Gwen and that she was at his disposal to help find people he hoped to interview. She handed him a set of diagrams. "Karen said you wanted these."

He glanced at the papers and saw that they consisted of a

map of the property and detailed floor plans of the main buildings.

"Thanks," he said. "Is she around?"

"In the dining room. She asked to speak to you as soon as you arrived." Koepp was surprised at the flush of pleasure the request gave him.

In contrast to the night before, the dining room was jammed with people having breakfast, people of all ages, including fifteen or twenty children. As he entered the room, the noise, which had been very intense, subsided perceptively. He noted that numerous diners were either pointing or nodding their heads in his direction, calling the attention of their companions to his arrival.

Karen, at a table in the center of the room, stood up so he would notice her. He hesitated for a moment, then saw that she had started toward him. He noticed that the table she had vacated was occupied exclusively by teenagers of both sexes.

She greeted him with a warm smile and put a hand on his elbow to direct him away from the serving line and toward the kitchen. The smells of institutional cooking reminded him of his seminary days; queer, he thought, that the sense of smell triggered memories more quickly than the other senses. Karen led him through a set of café doors into the kitchen and beckoned to a stocky, mannish woman with short gray hair. The woman appeared to be about fifty-five. She wore a loose, shapeless dress the color of her hair that was gathered around her ample waist with a cord. Despite her sex she looked like a thirteenth-century monk. Karen took her hand from his arm, slowly, letting her fingers brush the back of his wrist. She introduced the woman, who shook his hand, as Helen Kusava.

"Back here," she said, wheeling immediately and striding off toward a section of cabinets which stood next to a pair of dishwashers, Koepp noticed a knife rack on the counter.

"They said they couldn't find any knives missing last

night," the woman said. "That's what they told you people, right?"

Koepp nodded. Mrs. Kusava then turned and opened a cabinet drawer. She stepped aside to reveal a bewildering array of kitchen utensils. Even at a glance Koepp could see numerous knives that fit Sturmer's description of the murder weapon.

"I think you get my drift, Sheriff," Mrs. Kusava said, looking pleased with herself. "Nobody could tell if a knife is missing because we don't know how many we got."

"I can see that," Koepp said.

"Next time you want information about the kitchen, come to me," she said. "Anyway, it doesn't matter."

"What do you mean?"

"Nobody around here would murder Issac, so it doesn't matter whether a knife is missing. It proves nothing."

Koepp disagreed, but he saw no benefit in challenging her. Instead, he asked Mrs. Kusava about the hours when the kitchen had been occupied the previous day.

"Dish washers finished up about one-thirty or one forty-five. Then nobody was here until I came in about four o'clock to set out some condiments for the cookout: catsup, bottles of relish, diced onions—that sort of thing."

"So the place was empty from, say, two to four?"

"Pretty much. Charlie Tirquit came and went getting ice from the freezer in the corner. That's all."

Koepp asked for permission to take one of the knives from the drawer. He planned to make some Polaroid shots of it for posting on the bulletin boards on the premises. He also arranged with Mrs. Kusava to interview the kitchen help. "When you're ready, I'd like to begin with you," he told the older woman.

Mrs. Kusava started to speak, but thought better of it.

"What is it?" Koepp asked.

"I don't mean to tell you your business, Sheriff, but you're going to beat your gums to death and get nowhere. If I was you I'd get some cops up on Ridge Road. Find them junkies. That's where you'll find your murderer.''

When it became evident that she was not going to elaborate, Karen explained. "We had some youngsters come onto the property from Ridge Road to smoke marijuana. Issac—Dr. Steiner—ran them off a couple of times and called the Hillside police down on them a few weeks ago.''

"Issac said they might be into something heavier—like crack,'' Mrs. Kusava said.

"We don't know that, Helen,'' Karen said.

Although the woman was unaware of it, one piece of circumstantial evidence supported her suspicions. The peaty material that the lab had found on Steiner's trousers undoubtedly came from the shoes of someone using the creek bed beneath Ridge Road. "What is the view on drugs at Friars' Close?'' Koepp asked. "And Dr. Steiner's view—''

"Out,'' Mrs. Kusava said emphatically. "You use drugs of any kind, other than medicine, you're out.'' She stared at Karen belligerently, as if daring her to challenge the answer. Karen nodded her assent. Mollified, Mrs. Kusava said, "I'll be there quick as I can, Sheriff. Here, take some coffee with you.'' She grasped a fresh pot and two cups and saucers. Koepp relieved her of the pot; Karen took the dishes, then led the detective back out through the dining room and down the corridor to the purchasing manager's office. Koepp noticed a hot plate on top of a credenza and set the pot on it. It was an austere office which revealed little effort at decoration except for a large Impressionist print on the wall above the credenza. Koepp recognized it as one of Boudin's familiar views of the beach at Trouville. Aesthetically it mocked the room.

Karen saw him looking at the seascape and laughed softly. "A *sheriff* with an interest in art?'' she commented. "Things are changing in the outside world.''

Koepp grinned. "Is that what you call us—outsiders?''

Her mood remained playful. "Among other things." She plugged in the hot plate, poured coffee for both of them, and sat in a chair facing Koepp.

"Mrs. Merrick—"

"Karen, please."

"Karen, when a lab team gets here, I want them to examine all the drains in this building. There'll be crews going into all the rooms; we'll be opening sink traps and in general making a mess. We'll need to have each occupant sign a consent-to-search form so we can check the drains and search their private possessions. Will you alert people so they know what to expect? They can refuse to let our people in, of course. We don't have search warrants."

The playfulness had fled from her eyes, but she appeared unperturbed. "Warrants aren't necessary," she said. "We have nothing to hide."

"Someone does. And nobody can allow a search of a person's room without that person's permission."

"I'll contact everyone as soon as I can. What do you expect to find—the knife?"

"I'll know when we find it."

While he waited for his coffee to cool, Koepp went to the window that looked out on a narrow driveway. The only people in sight were two of their suspects, Charlie Tirquit and Elizabeth Maklin, who were standing close together beside a green pickup. The woman was talking earnestly while Charlie listened with a crestfallen expression on his boyish features. Suddenly, the woman struck him on the cheek with her open hand.

It was an impulsive act, yet the expression on Elizabeth's face signaled calculation, not anger. A behavioral lie. Koepp's skill in discerning untruths, which had served him badly when he was a priest, was invaluable in his role as a detective.

Almost at once Elizabeth embraced Charlie and looked at the building to see if anyone had been watching.

Koepp edged back from the window before she saw him. As he turned toward Karen, he saw that a piquant face was staring nervously at them from the doorway. The face had a timeless quality about it.

"Erin! Please come in, dear," Karen said, her tone gentle but carrying a subtle uneasiness. "Detective Sergeant Koepp, my daughter Erin."

"Hello," the girl murmured. Koepp waved. Her father had said she was thirteen. For that age she looked awfully small, Koepp decided, although, considering her mother's petiteness, perhaps it was understandable. She had long black hair, her mother's pointed chin, and deep-set eyes. Her eye sockets reminded Koepp of the way he looked when he hadn't gotten enough sleep. The girl stared at him with the unflinching, cold expression children reserve for adults who intrude unexpectedly in their lives. Kids knew that strangers usually caused trouble.

"Did you bring some homework, dear?" Karen asked.

The girl nodded. "It's in the office. What do you want me to do?"

"Sergeant Koepp needs to talk to some people. If Gwen can't get them on the phone, she'll ask you to track them down. Will you do that?"

Another nod. The girl's attention was focused on Koepp. "Do you know who killed Dr. Steiner?" she asked. When he shook his head, she said, "Somebody must know. Somebody must have seen who the murderer is. People were everywhere. Someone must have seen."

He assured her that nobody had come forward to name a suspect.

She was silent for a moment, but her penetrating stare declared she was having trouble believing him. Finally, she said, "There's a whole bunch of cops outside."

"Well," Koepp said, lifting himself from the chair, "I have to go back to work."

The girl had not exaggerated, as Koepp discovered the moment he saw the parking lot. Police cars, marked and unmarked, were everywhere; a knot of officers, also marked and unmarked, surrounded Margaret. She extricated herself when she saw Koepp.

"Where'd you get the army?" Koepp asked.

"Lieutenant's overreacting to that twit of an assistant DA. The guy is hacked off because we don't have the murder weapon. Told Tarrish we're harassing university faculty when we should be looking for a transient." She didn't amplify on Styles's unsettling complaints. "I have two lab teams—one a loaner from Metro—to do the drains, two patrol cars, and some recruits from the police academy."

Koepp explained the situation to the group of policemen, gave some general instructions to the senior uniformed officer who was to head up the search for the weapon, and led the technicians into the Administration Building. Inside, he briefed them in more detail.

"There had to be bloodstains. Check the halls and every room in the building where you can get the occupant's permission. Check out the sink traps, including the basement. The killer carried off the knife, or cleaned it. Look for evidence of washing or destroying clothes."

"Why just this building?" one of the lab technicians wanted to know. His partner groaned.

"There were a lot of people around yesterday—they had an art fair—so it wouldn't have been smart for the killer to go outside without tidying up. Forget the computer room. Kalmbach checked that."

After Margaret and the technical teams departed for the basement, Koepp took four shots of a knife he had obtained from Mrs. Kusava. The young woman in the business office typed captions for the pictures in which Koepp made his plea for anyone who found a similar knife to call him. He arranged for lunch for the policemen with Mrs. Kusava, who was waiting for him when he got back to his temporary headquarters. They settled on a rate of four dollars a head.

Then the woman gave him a concise but complete description of her movements on the day of the murder up to about one-thirty, when she went to her apartment to rest.

"I have trouble with my back sometimes," Mrs. Kusava explained. "It helps if I lie down for an hour or two."

"Did anyone come by your apartment during that time? Was anyone with you?"

"No to both questions."

Again, no alibi, Koepp thought. She could have come back to the computer room and killed Steiner. "What happened next?" he asked.

"Like I said, around four o'clock I went back to the kitchen to start getting ready for the cookout. I saw Charlie. He was getting a load of ice out of the freezer."

"And you were in your apartment until four?"

"No, I started to feel better, so I went outside to look at the show. About three-fifteen I saw Karen. She said the Planners' meeting was running late and asked me to take soft drinks to them. It gets warm in that meeting room."

"Did you?"

"Karen asked me to," she said. Koepp took that to mean that if Karen asked, of course she did it.

"Who was at the meeting?"

She seemed surprised by the question but answered readily enough. "The Planners: Paul, Elizabeth, and Leon."

Koepp's interrogation was interrupted by a phone call from Lieutenant Tarrish. His supervisor told him that the team assigned to search Dr. Steiner's office at the university had uncovered a small quantity of cocaine in a file cabinet. Tarrish said a receptionist in Steiner's office felt the psychiatrist had entertained some very disreputable visitors. She was at the Safety Building looking at mug shots supplied by the narcotics squad to see if she could identify any of them.

"Let me know if she comes up with an ID," Koepp said. He hung up. He stood next to the phone for a few moments, waiting for the queasiness in his stomach to subside. The dismal odds against breaking drug-related homicides floated through his consciousness. Whenever drugs were involved, motive—the key to solving most crimes—became universal.

Turning his attention back to Mrs. Kusava, he asked what she knew of the Grayson Foundation.

"Not much," the woman answered. "They put up money for some of the work that Issac, Paul and Leon do. I guess for the school and day-care center, too."

"Without the Grayson Foundation, Friars' Close might not be able to operate?"

"I don't know, Sheriff," the woman said. She looked at him with baleful eyes.

She was one of those unimaginative souls, Koepp decided, who would no more engage in conjecture than she would board a bus whose destination she did not know. Although Koepp spent the remainder of the morning interviewing a steady stream of community members, he learned nothing that was helpful in identifying Steiner's killer. After a while each new interrogation became a dreary composite of the interviews that had preceded it. No one saw anything suspicious or unusual. No one had an alibi that would eliminate him or her as a suspect.

The policemen ate lunch at a table reserved for them in the cafeteria. Nobody had found the murder weapon, reported the patrolman in charge of the search. They had combed the grounds and the stream bed with metal detectors and had rechecked the Administration Building.

It fell to Nils Johnson, a big-boned, middle-aged pathologist from the county medical examiner's office, to provide the first encouraging clues of the investigation. He was a quiet, likable man who had made enough of a reputation as a linebacker in college to get a pro contract with the Eagles. He had five kids and a sixth on the way.

"We found what I think is blood on the doorjamb and the steps of the stairwell down the hall from the computer room," Johnson said. "Could be the murderer touched the jamb with the knife blade."

"What about upstairs?"

"The lab found some rust-colored fibers on Steiner's shirt last night," Johnson said. "Several items of clothing we collected look like they might match the fibers. Lucky we're here on Sunday. Everyone is home."

"Any trouble getting permission?" Koepp asked.

"No, there are only eight private rooms, and everyone is anxious to cooperate. Trying to avoid getting in your crosshairs, I expect." He emitted a tentative chuckle as if he were experimenting with new style of laughter, and didn't quite have it right. "We still have some sinks to do. Caretaker fellow named Tony is helping us."

"How'd you find him?" Margaret asked.

"That little lady who runs this place—the one with the sexy voice—volunteered his services."

"She doesn't run it," Margaret informed him. "She's just the business manager."

After lunch, the county lab team, Koepp, and Margaret opened Steiner's apartment. While the technicians worked in the bathroom, Koepp and Margaret began searching through closets, dresser drawers, and desks. It quickly became apparent that Issac Steiner was a man who kept his possessions to a pragmatic minimum. Except for pictures of two women who appeared to be in their twenties and whom they tentatively identified as daughters, there was little of a personal nature in the apartment. According to the story in the morning paper, the psychiatrist had been married and divorced twice. No pictures of the former wives were in evidence. They also failed to locate either a diary or an appointment book, two immensely valuable resources in homicide investigations which seldom surfaced; like cops, Koepp thought whimsically, they were never around when you needed them. Margaret did find an address book, which she began thumbing through. A desk drawer also yielded some file folders with correspondence in them. Most of the letters were from one of the daughters, chatty but unrevealing. Suddenly, Johnson appeared in the doorway of the bathroom. "We've got blood traces from the sink trap."

Koepp and Margaret exchanged glances. Margaret spoke first. "Makes sense. You've just killed somebody and you've got a bloody knife to wash. Why not use the victim's apartment? That's the one place you won't be surprised by the occupant."

True enough, Koepp thought, which suggested that either the killer was unbelievably cool-headed, or that he knew for certain nobody was on the second floor. Once again the evidence pointed toward someone intimately familiar with the routine of Friars' Close, yet Koepp had trouble reconciling that fact with the presence of muck from the creek bed on the back of the victim's trousers. Why would the killer have come on the property underneath the bridge? Was it one of Mrs. Kusava's drug users from Ridge Road?

He realized that Margaret was watching him quizzically, so he explained about the lab finding the soil.

"You want us to keep going," Johnson asked, "or go back to the lab and see what we've got?"

"Are you sure you've got blood?" Koepp asked.

"Absolutely."

He wondered if the lab team's discovery would make the Friars' Close community less cooperative; the possible collusion about the time of the Planners' meeting, Elizabeth Maklin slapping an obvious suspect, and the delay in reporting the murder hinted they might be protecting their own.

Koepp decided the lab teams should discontinue searching;

he urged Johnson to call him as soon as they matched the blood. Nothing of value was found in Steiner's apartment, nor in the computer room. The neatly stacked racks of computer disks might all have to be checked later; the labor content of an unsolved homicide case expanded exponentially after the first day.

While Margaret went outdoors to send the other policemen home, Koepp walked to the purchasing manager's office in search of coffee. Someone, probably Mrs. Kusava, had brought a fresh pot. As he settled behind the desk, Karen appeared in the doorway. He beckoned to her.

"Your daughter's been very helpful," he said. "I understand she posted those pictures of the knife for us and tracked down some of the people I talked to before lunch. Tell her thanks."

"Have you solved Issac's murder yet?" she asked. Although her tone betrayed nothing, Koepp had the sense of being mocked. The question had been put so casually that it sounded vaguely indecent.

"No."

"I read where most homicides get solved in the first forty-eight hours, or they don't get solved. Is that true?"

"Yes, but we're going to solve this one."

She studied him thoughtfully for a few seconds, then asked, "But if you have no physical evidence—"

She's not just making conversation, Koepp thought. I'm being pumped. "Right now we don't have real evidence, that's true," he admitted. "But our investigation is unfocused. The key to Steiner's murder will be motive." He bit the word *motive* hard for effect. "When we find the motive, we'll know the killer. When we can focus on the killer, we'll find the physical evidence. We'll make an arrest and everyone will be safe."

Koepp was sure he sounded like he was babbling.

"There won't be a second killing," Karen said with conviction.

"I'm glad to hear that," he said. "How do you know you and your husband and Jaroff aren't on the killer's list?"

"Why us?"

"You started this place. Maybe the killer has it in for cohousing. Maybe he hates the cuisine."

"There won't be another killing, Ray, so even if you didn't find the killer, there won't be any lingering threat to public safety—any threat to anyone else." That was the first time she had called him by his first name.

Margaret chose that moment, unfortunately, to come in. Karen, perhaps anticipating Koepp's next question, used Margaret's arrival as a means of departing gracefully. Piqued, Koepp frowned at his partner.

She ignored his sour expression. "Johnson called," she said. "The blood type in the trap is Steiner's." When he made no response, she added, "So the murderer went upstairs to wash it off—and maybe washed a bloody shirt or blouse—"

"Blouse?"

Margaret nodded emphatically. "We don't know it's a man."

"It's a man's kind of murder," Koepp said. "Women don't like to kill with that much gore. No matter. I wish we knew for sure why the killer took the knife along."

"He—or she—panicked about wiping off fingerprints," Margaret said. "He took the knife so he could make sure it was clean."

"Maybe. Or the killer was afraid the knife would be recognized as something that belonged here. After all, he could have wiped fingerprints off on the victim's shirt."

"I wouldn't be cool and detached enough to do that. I don't think most people would." Margaret paused and looked out at the corridor to make sure no one was close enough to hear.

"I think you have to consider a woman as a possibility, and particularly Karen Merrick."

"Why her?"

"Because she's good at manipulating men."

Koepp caught her inference; Karen Merrick was manipulating him. Resentment flared up and died deep inside him, chilled by the unpleasant truth that she might be right.

# FOUR

On Monday, May 20, the apex of the investigation into the death of Issac Steiner came to rest on the second floor of the county sheriff's office, a gray stone building built during the Great Depression that still exuded a redolence of that grim period in its stern, grimy facade. Pigeon droppings stained the windowsills and fascia, effectively countering the impression of forbidding authority which the designers of the building had tried to foster. The county detectives referred to the place as "the dung heap," whether because of the bird droppings, the quality of the clientele, or the intransigence of the senior management, Koepp was unsure. The place was actually called the Public Safety Building and housed fire department bureaucrats as well as law-enforcement officers and laboratories.

In any case, this was the place where Detective Koepp interacted with his fellow pilgrims. It represented what he was now; it was home.

Koepp had started officer Mary Jo Riley on a project to find out everything she could about Dr. Steiner. She was one of the young police officers who had been raised on computers, and she had shown a knack in past investigations of uncovering important facts that detectives had missed. Koepp recognized her intense ambition early and had cultivated her to the point where she would steal time from other projects to go to extra lengths for him. It was an insight that he had discovered while he was a priest, that he could get women to do things for him, and he used it ruthlessly; the benefits outweighed the associated guilt.

Mary Jo was sure she was going to secure her future by

helping him crack a major homicide; Koepp did nothing to dispel that conviction. His only fear was that his eager protégée would not be around long because she had incited the lust of Lieutenant Tarrish. The young woman was soft and round, and she had full lips and large expectant eyes—"a Botticelli cherub," Margaret called her. Tarrish, no respecter of Renaissance fragility, had confided to Koepp that he wanted to stretch her out on her desk and "bang her until her eyes bug out."

Margaret, having overheard the remark, now waited with a mixture of trepidation and puerile curiosity for Tarrish's suppressed sexual violence to erupt.

Narcotics had sent over a mug shot of a man named Roman Weber, whom the receptionist at the university had identified as an occasional visitor to Issac Steiner's office. The photograph revealed a white male about thirty-five to forty years of age; he had a long, sensitive face with a bushy beard and mustache. The man was an artist who had been busted twice for possession.

Koepp put the photo and rap sheet in his pocket.

The two detectives worked up a list of names of people who played major roles in Steiner's life. The list included Caroline Steiner and Grace Wallace, the doctor's first and second wives respectively. Wallace still lived in the city, while Caroline Steiner resided in Ann Arbor. The latter was a professor now at the University of Michigan. They left word for Mrs. Steiner to call them and set up on appointment with Mrs. Wallace at her real-estate office. They also made appointments with several faculty members at the state university where Steiner had been teaching.

They briefed Tarrish, then went downtown to the county courthouse. Margaret had to testify in a robbery-homicide case; Koepp went with her so he could meet the assistant DA on the Steiner case, Tom Styles.

THE ATTORNEY was making a court appearance when Koepp arrived at his office, but his secretary estimated he'd be back soon. She encouraged him to wait. "I'm *sure* he'll want to see you," the woman said ominously. Koepp, who had learned that secretaries often unconsciously complemented their boss's excesses, began to dread the interview even more.

Waiting gave him a chance to review and organize his salient facts. He knew from experience that attorneys liked verbal presentations well organized and limited to what was important and supported by evidence. Koepp set about eliminating from his outline anything that smacked of conjecture, which was the curse of prosecutors. Unfortunately, once he had completed his weeding-out process, there wasn't much left. As yet, they had established no motive for anyone. They also had no murder weapon, a deficiency which the young attorney apparently had noted with some asperity to Tarrish on Saturday night. Prosecutors relished physical evidence, especially a murder weapon; it was a priceless prop in a jury trial during summation. Finally, the suspect list embraced about a million and a half residents of the metropolitan area.

The conjectural aspects of the murder, on the other hand, were both interesting and promising. Why did it take so long to either (a) discover the body or (b) call the police? And which of the alternatives accounted for the delay? Why was the door to the computer room left open after the murder? If it was open all the time, why did it take so long to discover the body? Was the door closed by the murderer and opened by party or parties unknown so that the body could be discovered by Charlie Tirquit? Was a conspiracy of silence being forced on the Friars' Close community by its leaders? If so, for what purpose? Or whose benefit?

Within half an hour an attorney who might have been a few years less than Koepp's thirty-seven came back to the office. He set his bulging briefcase on the corner of his secretary's desk and shook hands with the detective. He was a

stocky man with thick glasses embedded in the folds of a
bulbous nose. Styles talked with a faint lisp, a curious burden
for a prosecutor, Koepp supposed.

As soon as they were seated in his office, Styles commanded, "Brief me." He made it sound as if that were all
but impossible but Koepp was welcome to try. Koepp sum-
marized the murder itself and described the investigative efforts so far. He included Steiner's cocaine involvement.

When he had finished, all too soon, the attorney asked, "Is
that it?" Koepp nodded. "Sweet Jesus!"

"This one will take some time," Koepp explained. "Detection will rest on motive. So far we haven't been able to
establish—"

"When do you expect to make an arrest?"

"It's too early to think about that." He remembered then
about the fibers found on Steiner's shirt and told the attorney
about them. "So far we don't have the report on whether there
is a match."

Styles muttered something inaudible, then said, "You guys
in homicide ever read the newspapers, or watch the ten-
o'clock news? This isn't some doper from the ghetto. This
man is very prominent, not just locally, but internationally.
And he was part of the university faculty. Those people have
big-time political friends, and some of them don't like the
way you're conducting this investigation. Sweet Jesus!"

The rest of the conversation continued in the same vein;
mercifully, it was soon terminated by a phone call from the
district attorney. Koepp took advantage of the opportunity to
escape and went in search of Margaret. She was still waiting
to testify and suggested that he leave without her. "I'll get a
lift from somebody," she said.

Koepp checked in with the dispatcher once he was back in
his car, and was told that he had received a call from Mrs.
Merrick.

"Have you got her number?"

"Negative. She said she thought you ought to get on out there right away."

THE MIDMORNING traffic was light, so he had no trouble getting to Friars' Close in half an hour. In stark contrast to the previous two visits, the place was nearly deserted. He could see a groundskeeper at work, and several figures were evident in the vegetable gardens on the rim of the horseshoe-shaped terrain. At this distance, or because of Koepp's developing nearsightedness, the gardeners reminded him of those color daubs in Claude Monet's landscapes. He remembered then with a chill that the celebrated eyes of the French Impressionist finally had failed him altogether.

As Margaret had correctly observed, Karen had Friars' Close in the palm of her hand; she gave further evidence of it by greeting him in the parking lot the moment he stepped out of his car.

"You're hard to sneak up on," he said.

"I hope I did the right thing asking you to come up here. It's strange. I didn't know what to do."

"What happened?"

"One of our staff workers here is a man named Tony Divito," she told him. "Tony does odd jobs, runs errands, fixes things—he's very comfortable with mechanical things.

"After breakfast, one of the kitchen staff, Mary Ann Bauer, was trying to slice some meat for lunch. She wasn't having any luck because her knife—which she took from that rack you saw yesterday—was too dull. She asked Tony to sharpen it. But he brought it to me instead."

She opened a plastic bag she had been carrying and handed the knife to Koepp.

He ran his index finger lightly along the cutting edge. "He's right. It's dull. So what?"

"Tony says it's not the knife that normally goes in the

rack," Karen said. "It's the same manufacturer and the handle is identical, but it seems somewhat duller than the others."

"Maybe it just gets used more," Koepp suggested. "Where is he? I want to talk to him."

"In my office with Helen," she replied. "Ray, there is something you should know." She paused for several moments, trying to find the right words. Her search proved unproductive. "He's retarded," she said finally.

Retarded and very agitated, Koepp concluded when he saw the wiry little man in the gray coveralls. He remembered that the workman had helped the technicians remove the sink traps. He called Divito by his first name, which he realized guiltily was the way everyone addressed the retarded.

"Tell the sheriff what you saw, Tony," Helen prodded.

Koepp reminded her that he wasn't a sheriff.

Divito looked desperately at Koepp with large brown liquid eyes. "Sheriff, Sheriff, the good knife is gone. Somebody put a bad knife there. It was dull wasn't it?" he implored of Karen.

"Yes, it was, Tony," she replied. "It wasn't sharp like you keep the knives." She gave him a quick hug, which seemed to reassure him.

He repeated his story for Koepp's benefit from the time that he arrived in the kitchen, halting now and then to look at either Helen or Karen for confirmation.

"You're saying that someone took a knife from the drawer and put it in the rack?" Koepp asked gently.

Divito became quite alarmed at that; Helen had to make soothing sounds to settle him down. He insisted that he knew the difference between the knives, that he was very familiar with their blades. Despite his excitability, he was convincing.

Koepp dismissed him. After he was out of earshot, Koepp addressed a question to both women. "Is he reliable, generally?"

They thought about it. Not surprisingly, Karen answered him. "Yes, he doesn't lie." Helen nodded confirmation.

Koepp walked to the open counter drawer and stared down at a jumbled array of kitchen utensils. Eight or ten knives looked like the ones in the display rack.

"It's possible he's imagining things," Karen said.

"Why did you call me if you think he's confused?"

Karen studied his face for a moment. "I thought you'd want to know about it so you could make up your own mind. I didn't want you to accuse us later of withholding evidence."

While this sounded reasonable enough, Koepp couldn't help putting himself in Karen's position. She wouldn't like to admit Tony was right because this confirmed that the killer lived in Friars' Close; only someone who was familiar with the kitchen's contents would have known where to find a lookalike knife. That argued against a casual thief or a drug runner as the murderer.

Koepp decided that, for the moment, he would assume Tony's story was true. It did bring some coherence to his deliberations. Someone had grabbed a knife from the rack, then gone to the computer room to kill Steiner. For some reason the murderer disposed of the murder weapon, yet went to great risk to replace it. The only reason for doing that was to divert suspicion from the members of the project.

The obvious question was why the murderer had not simply returned the weapon, cleaned, to its usual place.

As they walked back to Koepp's car, he decided to bring up the issue of interviewing the children.

At first she objected strenuously.

"But maybe one of them saw something," he protested.

"Well, I suppose I can't stop you. It's up to the parents in any case. Still, I don't think it's wise." She stopped suddenly, her face animated by an idea. "There's a better way—for the children, for you—and that's the posttrauma session Paul is planning this afternoon. It's important that we help the children deal with this. I'm sure no one would object if you listened in. Maybe you could even ask questions. I'll talk to Paul, but I'm sure he'll agree.''

Koepp nodded, although he didn't know what he was agreeing to.

In the parking lot Leon Jaroff and Paul Merrick were loading luggage into a station wagon that Koepp recognized as one of the co-op's pool cars.

"Where are they going?'' Koepp demanded. He added, "Without telling me.''

Karen looked genuinely concerned. "To Boston, to see the Grayson Foundation people. They're nervous because of Issac. Leon and Paul will be back tomorrow night.''

Before he could say anything else, a heavyset woman with a shrill voice began dispensing instructions to the two men on how to squeeze their bags into the vehicle; most of the storage compartment was filled with cardboard boxes. After a moment Koepp recognized the woman as the one he had seen leaving Building A in tears the day of the murder. She was Jaroff's wife.

Karen introduced them.

"It's a terrible thing,'' Mrs. Jaroff said. "Friars' Close is devastated. You'll catch him, won't you?''

"Yes,'' Koepp assured her. For some reason he instinctively didn't like her. Maybe she was one of those people whom nobody liked, but equally, a person whose unpopularity nobody could explain, either. Koepp felt guilty; his mother had raised him to like everyone, even the undeserving, so he felt badly letting her down again.

It turned out that Gwen, the young woman who had been managing the office Sunday morning, was to drive the two sociologists to the airport, not Mrs. Jaroff. Gwen jumped into the car and sped away almost before Dr. Jaroff could climb into the rear of the wagon and shut the door. Koepp wondered if the haste was stimulated by a tight schedule or a desire to escape from Jaroff's wife.

"Well, let's hope they're successful," Mrs. Jaroff said, fixing a penetrating stare on Karen. "Without the Grayson moola we're going to lose the whole enchilada."

Karen visibly tensed. Before she could form a reply, Mrs. Jaroff went on. "Issac pulling out like that was bound to jeopardize—"

Koepp's heart began to pound harder. "When did Dr. Steiner decide to pull out, Mrs. Jaroff?" he asked.

Karen looked as if she were ready to interrupt, then fell silent. She knew she was too late.

"The Planners' meeting," the woman said. "Issac had them call a meeting—" At that point Mrs. Jaroff realized that she was on the verge of saying more than she was supposed to. She clamped her jaws tightly.

This was the first indication that Steiner had requested the Planners' meeting. Whatever his reason, the co-op leaders weren't anxious to talk about it.

Mrs. Jaroff's great cow eyes filled with sudden pain and confusion. She looked helplessly at Karen. The younger woman also was silent. Her eyes, however, were as expressive as ever; they were bright with anger. Mrs. Jaroff seemed to shrink under Karen's unspoken reproof. Her heavy jowls were suffused with red; she pressed two buck teeth into her lower lip.

Koepp wanted to kiss the woman. For the first time he caught the scent of motive.

"I think it's time to have another chat with Elizabeth Maklin," Koepp said. "What building is she in?"

"F," Karen said. "Ground floor." The throaty, soothing tone of her voice was noticeably absent. "I'll take you there if you like."

Mrs. Jaroff used this verbal exchange to excuse herself. She lumbered into the administration building.

"I wouldn't like, Karen," Koepp said. "You tend to intimidate witnesses. I'll find her myself."

The color rose in the woman's cheeks at the same moment that the curious lopsided smile reappeared. "As you wish," she replied.

Luckily for Koepp, Elizabeth Maklin answered his ring. She wore a faded man's sportshirt and bluejeans. Her lustrous hair was partially wrapped in a scarf. Although she civilly invited him in, she clearly was not pleased. The woman was painting her living-room ceiling, so all the furniture and carpeting were covered with drop cloths. A paint-spattered stepladder stood in the middle of the room.

"I know the meeting Saturday was requested by Dr. Steiner," Koepp began, "and I know the Grayson Foundation grant money was in jeopardy if Steiner left." He didn't know that, of course, but he hazarded little if he made a bad guess; his persistent wrong-headedness irritated people so much that they often revealed the truth just to confound him. In either case, he got the information he wanted.

This time his guess bore fruit. "Issac told us he was dissatisfied with his research, and planned to terminate his involvement with Friars' Close," the woman said.

"How did the three of you react to that?"

"We were shocked—and upset. Paul and Leon tried to talk him out of it. He was adamant. Once Issac made up his mind he rarely changed it. He claimed that even if he left, Grayson would still support us. None of us believed that."

Koepp tried another bluff. "How long did the meeting really last?"

"Issac left after about forty-five minutes. The rest of us maybe fifteen minutes later," she answered.

Koepp relished his triumph for a moment before he pointed out, unnecessarily, that all three of them had lied. "You said the meeting ended at three-thirty," he reminded her. "Since

Helen saw you together when she brought Cokes, you obviously reconvened. When was that?''

"A little after three.''

"Whose idea was it to reconvene the meeting to construct the alibi for each of you?'' Koepp asked.

"I don't intend to answer any more questions. Please leave.'' She seemed surprised when he moved toward the door.

Koepp crossed the shallow valley and the footbridge en route to the Administration Building. It was warm for May, and he kicked up tiny clouds of insects as he strode alongside the stream. He was angry. Everyone had lied to him.

He found Karen in her office pecking away industriously at a personal computer. She turned to face him. Koepp spun a chair around and straddled it with his arms folded on the back.

"I don't know why you thought you could get away with it,'' he said. "You're smart enough to know it wouldn't hold up very long. A shared lie is always a weak lie.''

"If that fool Ina hadn't opened her mouth—''

"We'd still have found out. It just would have taken longer. You took too long to report the murder. That suggested that you needed time to get some alibis organized, or get rid of evidence, or take a key witness to the airport with a one-way ticket to São Paulo. Eventually the lie would have fallen apart.''

"What are you going to do now?''

"Reconstruct for you what I think happened. Then ask for your comments. Or your creative improvisations perhaps. Let's see. The Planners' meeting started at one o'clock with Issac dropping the bombshell that he was going to abandon the project. A forty-five-minute argument ensued. Issac left. Fifteen minutes later the others left as well, probably with one of them assigned to try to reason with Steiner. It was either Jaroff or your husband. In short order Steiner is stabbed to death. Somebody—either the murderer or somebody who found his body—spread the alarm, after first closing the door to gain more time to deal with the problem.''

He paused, anticipating an objection, or at least a question. But Karen said nothing. She gave the impression of rapt attention, as if she were memorizing his scenario.

''The Planners' reconvened,'' he suggested, ''either on their own, or because you were now in command and told them to. You then sent in Helen with soft drinks. That little stratagem provided an independent witness to testify that the meeting was still in progress at three-fifteen. Somebody, probably you, opened the door to the computer room so poor Charlie Tirquit could wander by to see what Steiner's rebellion cost him. He came by around twenty to four, yelled murder, and you, good citizen that you are, summoned what are laughingly referred to as 'the authorities.'''

She watched him silently with expressionless eyes. The funny little half-smile was perched on the edge of her jaw, as if waiting for the opportunity to fly away.

''Comment?'' he asked.

''None of them did it. Paul—my husband—discovered the body. But he didn't kill Issac. None of them did. They aren't capable of killing anyone.''

''From a policeman's perspective, your husband is a first-class suspect. So are Jaroff and Maklin. They all had the means. None of them has an alibi now, so it's clear they all had the opportunity. And all of you had a motive: you were afraid if Steiner abandoned Friars' Close, your sponsors would pull the plug.''

When she remained silent, Koepp took the photograph of Roman Weber from his pocket and showed it to her. ''Have you seen this man before? He might have visited Dr. Steiner. They may have been friends.''

She stared at the photograph for a long time. ''Yes, I've seen him,'' she answered. ''He's—a friend of mine.''

It took Koepp a few moments to recover from his astonishment. "Are you aware that he'd been arrested for possession of narcotics? Also, Dr. Steiner may have been his source. Did you know Weber was a cocaine user?"

She responded immediately. "Yes, I knew Roman used drugs sometimes. And Issac did sell it."

"Weber's a dangerous friend, Mrs. Merrick," Koepp said. "Drugs have a way of leading to homicides. Maybe Weber decided to take over Steiner's trade. Maybe you helped your 'friend' eliminate the good doctor."

"You don't believe I'm capable of killing anyone."

He really didn't think her capable of it; he resented her knowing that. He put Weber's photograph back in his pocket. The two of them shared an awkward silence for a while. Koepp noticed a second photograph, a color shot in a frame at the corner of Karen's desk; it showed the four members of the Merrick family standing on a dock with a northwoods cabin in the background. Someone had written "Granite Lake, August 9, 1990" in the corner of the picture.

"Have you had lunch?" she asked.

*"Lunch?"*

She stood up, walked to his chair, and took hold of his upper arm. "C'mon, you've got time for a bowl of soup and some crackers at least," she said. She tugged gently at his arm and led him into the dining room. They each took a bowl of beef consomme-to a table near the windows, where two teenaged boys were consuming ham sandwiches in large bites.

"This is John Jaroff and my son Phil," she said. "Ray Koepp." Both boys stood up to shake hands. Koepp only paid attention to Phil, a wiry, dark-haired youth who favored his father. When they were all seated, Karen engaged the boys in a casual conversation about school. Koepp learned that designated public rooms in each of the residential buildings served as classrooms during weekdays. Teachers from the university with certain specialties supplemented the staff of three teachers who held most of the classes. That morning Phil and John had been struggling with calculus under the benign tyranny of one of the college professors.

"Calculus," Koepp said. "I'm impressed. What year are you guys in?"

"We don't have years like junior and senior," John explained. "You go at your own pace. I go fast and Phil goes slow—" He wrenched back in his chair to avoid a slap at his forearm from his companion. "And when you finish you go take the ACT, then you go to Harvard or Princeton."

"Everyone goes to Harvard or Princeton?" Koepp asked, feigning incredulity.

"Well, some of us go to Cal Poly or the University of Chicago." He laughed uproariously at his own joke. An inside joke, Koepp concluded. He looked at Phil. Karen's son stared out the window, studiously oblivious to his companion's forced joviality.

"The students do well under the school program," Karen said. "John's father and two faculty members at the university designed the regimen. Our students average about fifteen percent higher grades than the rest of the state."

"It's not Father's system," young Jaroff said. "It's all in the genes. We're all eggheads." His voice had taken on a harsher tone. Karen watched him with weary disfavor.

Young Merrick turned his attention to Koepp. "You're the detective?"

"One of them," Koepp answered. "The good-looking one is in court."

"Do you know whodunnit yet?" Jaroff inquired.

"Not yet. Maybe you can help. Who uses that creek path underneath the Ridge Road bridge?"

"All the kids use it," the Jaroff boy said. "If you don't, you have to go down to the end of the block to get to Ridge Road. Gwen and Elaine go that way to the super and Walgreen's. Tony Divito, Charlie Tirquit—they both go to the hardware store. By the way, Charlie's a prime suspect."

"John," Karen said, "that's unkind and unfair."

"But he's weird," the boy protested.

Karen sighed but said nothing further. Koepp had the impression that Karen and young Jaroff were distinctly at odds with each other and that their hostility was of long standing. He assumed their differences stemmed from John's friendship with her son, yet it could reflect conflict between the Jaroffs and Merricks. Despite its avowed community sentiments, Friars' Close harbored a surprising amount of animosity.

To some extent, young Jaroff was right about Charlie. The man was single, dull-witted, and poorly educated; he didn't fit into the elitist framework of Friars' Close.

After the two boys excused themselves suddenly and departed, Koepp said, "You don't like young Jaroff any better than you like his mother, do you?"

"I dislike his competitiveness. You saw an example of that. He hurt Phil with that remark about going slow."

"Is he? Slow, I mean."

"No, Phil's above average, his teachers tell me, but he's slow compared to John. The pleasure John got from bragging dissipates in seconds, while Phil's pain will last for hours or days. Things like that corrode a community."

"Speaking of the community," Koepp said, "what will happen now? Can this place make it without Grayson money?"

"We'd have to make changes," she said, "but we'd survive. However, we don't think the foundation will abandon us. That's what Paul and Leon are trying to prevent."

They ate in silence for a few minutes before Karen adopted a more intimate tone. "Ray, there is something you should be aware of," she said, looking rather uncomfortable. "Being sponsored by the university—and with our Grayson relationship—we're pretty political. The university board has some powerful members and they're concerned about your investigation focusing on university-connected people."

"But that isn't necessarily—"

She put a hand on his arm to silence him. "They're being guided toward that conclusion by someone here. I want you to know that it's not me. I'm not responsible."

"Cops always have critics," Koepp said.

"They're going to exploit your record. Claim you're not competent. They know you're vulnerable."

"If I don't look outside Friars' Close for our killer, then political pressure will be applied to get me off the case. Is that it?"

"Yes." She looked genuinely unhappy at the prospect.

"I'd look elsewhere," Koepp said, "if you people didn't do suspicious things, such as setting up a phony alibi for your husband and the other Planners."

"That was foolish of me," she said. "I panicked."

Koepp chuckled softly. "I find that hard to believe."

"I was afraid of the publicity, what it would do to the project if one of the leaders was a suspect. I knew none of them could kill anyone, so I saw a way to keep them out of it. It was a mistake. I'm sorry."

Although she sounded contrite, Koepp felt uneasy; her apology had a calculated quality, as if she was admitting the obvious to divert his attention from some subterfuge.

He pulled Margaret's list of suspects from his jacket pocket. "I want to review once more who was in the Administration Building at the time of the murder," he said. "The Planners, of course, now *sans* alibis. Gwen in the front office, you and your daughter. That's six. Charlie Tirquit makes seven. What was Ina Jaroff doing there?"

"She was helping Elaine with a charity raffle. She came in to get more raffle tickets. Elaine had called ahead, so I had them ready."

"And your daughter was running errands and studying?"

"Yes." She waited for him to ask another question. When he didn't she reminded him of the children's debriefing session at five o'clock.

"I'll be there," he said, "if I'm still on the case."

# FIVE

MARGARET was hunched over a desk in the squad room when he arrived at the Safety Building, studying photographs from the scene of Steiner's murder. She beckoned to Koepp, who circled behind her and peered over her shoulder.

She pointed to Steiner's body, curled up like a question mark. "You'd expect the victim to be in his chair. He wasn't. So he must have risen to meet his killer. If so, logic suggests he was killed between the door and his work station. But he wasn't. If you drew a line from the door to his computer, his body was ten feet away from it.

"He was moving around the room to avoid the killer."

"No way. He didn't have defensive cuts on his hands. The killer surprised him. The ME says the body wasn't moved. But he didn't fall where he should have. Why not?"

Koepp tried without success to fashion an explanation while they drove to the university medical center to interview some of Steiner's colleagues.

They were greeted by the chief of the psychiatric unit, Dr. Don Newhouse, in his office. He told them that two of Steiner's colleagues, Drs. Abrams and Syrk, could be interrogated as well as soon as their classes were over.

Newhouse, a short, cherubic man with thinning red hair, gave them some biographical information, the kind of facts that defined the subject's chronology but said nothing about the man. Margaret made desultory notes and chewed on the end of her pencil, a sure sign of impatience. Steiner taught few classes, being occupied primarily with research. He had been very successful in obtaining grants and had attracted some distinguished associates. He was well respected, but inclined to be somewhat acerbic, so his friends on the faculty were few.

Koepp and Margaret exchanged glances, remembering Merrick's comment that Steiner was usually "jovial."

"Did he have a private practice?" Margaret asked. "Practice therapy, I mean."

If he did, Newhouse was unaware of it. He thought it unlikely because Steiner was devoted to research. "Clinical work is beneath researchers. They're inclined to be impatient with their patients." He chuckled at his pun.

"Doctor, you described him a moment ago as acerbic," Margaret said. "We were told recently that he was usually jovial. That seems a contradiction."

"Issac was never jovial," the psychiatrist said.

Later, they interviewed Abrams and Syrk in the lounge outside Newhouse's office. Both also expressed surprise that anyone would describe Steiner as jovial. Dr. Jane Syrk, a gaunt, raw-boned, quintessential academician in her fifties, did supply one revealing fact. "Dr. Steiner made light of psychoanalysis. He particularly enjoyed making sport of psychiatrists' couches and how they weren't designed to relax the patient, but rather were a means of making the patient vulnerable. 'Get a woman on her back for half an hour, and you can put your hands—'" She stopped and looked at Koepp without evident embarrassment. "You get the picture. He was very unprofessional at times."

Neither professor had any idea who would kill Steiner.

"Anything else you can tell us?" Koepp asked.

"I really didn't know him that well," Syrk said. "He was a very private man."

"Did you see him outside the work environment?"

"Once a month at the chess club," she answered. "He was a brilliant chess player."

After the doctors had gone, the detectives sat in the empty lounge for a while. Koepp had told Margaret about everything that had occurred earlier in the day at the murder scene. He expected her to review the implications of the fabricated alibi by the three Planners. Instead she said, "What do you make of that women-on-their-backs stuff?"

"It might work," Koepp said. "I'll have to try it."

"You're not the type. If you were going to seduce a woman, you'd tell her about your anguished past, your path to disillusionment. That dissolves most of us. We want to prove we can restore a man's urge to live."

"I'll keep that in mind," Koepp said. "About what Steiner said—I don't make anything of it. Men talk dirty. If Steiner didn't treat patients, it has no significance."

"Suppose he *did* treat patients?"

"Everyone says he didn't."

"Yes, but suppose he did?"

"Then it might be significant. He might have messed with a woman—she or her boyfriend might want to kill him. That sort of thing leaves hellish scars on the soul." He lifted himself wearily from the chair. "What do you make of the fact that the killer got rid of the murder weapon, then substituted another knife just like it in the kitchen rack?"

Margaret stood up. They began walking slowly toward the elevator. "Maybe the killer got rid of the knife, then realized its absence would be noticed," she said. "Which points to someone in the project. The fact of the Planners faking an alibi is a real breakthrough; it puts three good prospects in play. Have you considered a conspiracy? Maybe the three of them decided Steiner had to be dispatched."

"There wasn't much time. It takes longer than fifteen minutes for three people to decide to kill someone."

"Maybe they knew about it days or weeks before."

"No," Koepp said. "It surprised them when Steiner said he was stopping his research project. I'm sure of that."

"How about Lady Macbeth? Maybe she knew what he was going to do, waited for him and stuck the knife in him."

"I suppose you mean Karen—Mrs. Merrick."

"So it's Karen now, is it? In a week she'll be darning your socks and telling you Steiner was hit by a train."

An elevator filled with orderlies, wheelchairs, and dashed hopes arrived to carry them to the ground floor. The artificial silence imposed on them by the full elevator gave Koepp a chance to consider Margaret's supposition. What if Steiner did treat somebody? Might his sexual indiscretions be the motive for his murder?

"Let's go see Grace Wallace, the former Mrs. Steiner," Margaret suggested.

"Do you really think she'd darn my socks?"

THE SECOND Mrs. Steiner rose with fluid grace and a trace of hauteur to greet them when they entered her office. Koepp sensed the attitude of superiority right away, and assumed she was one of those people who took seriously the notion that cops were servants of the people. The woman ran an obviously successful real-estate agency in the pricey western suburbs. She was a tall, elegant woman who gave the appearance of working hard to keep her fifty-plus years in recession inside a thirty-five-year-old body. He had seen her kind before; they dieted so rigorously and trained so hard that their bodies took on a stringy look.

Her name was Wallace now, and she was very wary. That became obvious almost from the time Margaret opened her notebook. After fielding some of the preliminary questions, she began to summarize her relationship with Steiner. It sounded as if she had memorized a prepared speech. Their divorce had been quite civilized, almost amiable. He had not contested it and his settlement was quite civilized, almost amiable. Since the divorce they had rarely seen or spoken to each other. Both of them had gone on with their lives, neither of them harbored any rancor or recriminations. As divorces go it had been, well, almost amiable—

"Would you say he was acerbic or jovial?" Margaret asked.

A long pause, allowing Koepp time to examine the woman. She had the disconcerting habit of not looking directly at the person she was addressing. Koepp didn't count this as evidence of deceit, but it made him nervous all the same.

"What?" said Mrs. Wallace.

"Acerbic. You know, it—"

"I know what it means, miss," Mrs. Wallace said. She sounded huffy. "I don't think I'd use either term to describe Issac."

"Was he religious?" Margaret wanted to know. "Did he participate at temple?"

For some reason Mrs. Wallace took this curious question in stride. "No," she said. "It was one of the things that I think contributed to our differences. My religion is important to me. Issac wasn't much of a Jew. That didn't help."

"What were the other differences?" Koepp asked.

"His strange...associates—people from outside the university who came and went for God knows why. I didn't know what that was about. It bothered me. He wouldn't talk about them."

"Were they patients?" Margaret asked.

"No, they were *not* patients," Mrs. Wallace said. "I don't know what they were."

Koepp broke in with a question of his own. "How were Dr. Steiner's relations with his professional colleagues? I understand he was admired for his work, but what kind of personal contact did he have?"

The woman hesitated only for a second or two. "They were civil but aloof," she said. "Except for Paul, Paul Merrick."

Koepp nodded encouragingly.

"Issac had something on Paul," she said. "He knew that Paul had falsified data on a research project—one that got him a lot of acclaim. So Issac held that over his head. Paul knew what those strange people were into, but he couldn't object, you see. Paul hated my ex-husband, understandably. He was a bastard.''

So much for "jovial," Koepp thought.

# SIX

BEGINNING AT five o'clock, a group of eleven adolescent residents of Friars' Close and one thirty-seven-year-old sergeant of detectives gathered in one of the larger "common rooms" of Building A to begin a "debriefing" session intended to neutralize the posttraumatic stress disorder brought about by the homicide of Issac Steiner.

Karen Merrick, wearing a gray skirt and a pink pleated blouse that heightened her femininity, greeted the participants at the door, offering them a smile and a few words of encouragement. Koepp, seated unobtrusively in the back of the room, observed that she found something different to say to each of the children. When a lull in the arrivals occurred, she sat next to him but kept the door in view.

"I was afraid you might not come, Ray," she said, fixing her steady gaze on his eyes.

The mistress of Friars' Close (as he had begun to think of her) sat tensely on the edge of her wooden chair, her abundant energy, like that of a compressed spring, under severe but obvious control.

"Maybe I'll learn something," he replied. A strained silence lapped around them. The room served as a lounge normally, but all the comfortable furniture had been replaced by a circle of wooden chairs at the end opposite Koepp. The circular arrangement made him think of a seance or a coven.

Karen explained that posttraumatic stress disorder was common among children after they had been exposed to violence. Her husband and Leon Jaroff had been meeting individually with the younger children ever since Steiner's body had been discovered, but they felt a group session would be more beneficial for the teenagers.

"Kids carry the scars of these things around with them, and you can't always tell if they're dealing with it," she told him. "We've seen signs that some of them aren't."

"Such as?" Koepp asked.

"Some of the children are having trouble sleeping, others complain of nightmares," she said. "And the Evans's daughter came into her parents' bedroom and tried to get in bed with them. Some of the older kids are afraid what happened to Issac is going to happen again. And some are exhibiting hyperactivity—"

She rose suddenly and returned to the entrance to greet three girls, one of whom was her daughter Erin. As he watched Karen talking to the youngsters, a miasma of guilt settled over Koepp again. Mary Jo had been busy picking through Karen Merrick's past, attempting to link her to Steiner in some way that would suggest a reason for her to resort to murder. That hadn't produced anything of substance, but Koepp knew a lot more about her. Born in Cincinnati on April 13, 1954, father a city employee, mother a homemaker with three older children. Moved to Albuquerque at age six because of father's asthma. He died there in 1960. Mother supported smaller children as a bookkeeper. Mother remarried, to a man who seldom held a job. Attended the University of New Mexico on a full scholarship, majoring in business administration. Worked for IBM in Connecticut until 1978. Attended Columbia University to obtain an MBA, where she married Professor Paul Merrick. Two children. Moved to Ann Arbor in 1983 when Merrick joined the faculty of the University of Michigan. Moved to the city in 1986 where Professor Merrick continued his academic career at the state university. Met Dr. Issac Steiner.

Mary Jo's research on the other academicians was similarly bland. Steiner and Merrick had won acclaim for papers they had written; Leon Jaroff had been a consultant to two Federal cabinet members and a Congressional subcommittee.

Ever since Margaret had learned about how the Planners' meeting had been reconvened, she had put Karen Merrick at the top of her suspect list. At first her heightened suspicion of the project's business manager had not been apparent to Koepp because of her noncommittal response when he told her about the clumsy attempt by the Planners to establish an alibi. But Margaret had put Mary Jo to work examining Karen's past in detail; if the woman had a motive, she was determined to find it.

Margaret may have been right about something else, which at the moment worried Koepp more than he wanted to admit. She thought Karen was trying to manipulate him to influence the outcome of their investigation.

Paul Merrick arrived with his son Phil, stopped for a moment to talk to his wife, then went to the circle of adolescents. He and Phil occupied the two empty chairs. The assembled teenagers, who were silent for the most part, watched Merrick warily as he balanced a clipboard on his knees and withdrew a ballpoint from his shirt pocket. From the standpoint of communal ethnicity they gave the impression of having been handpicked for this exercise, embracing among their number two African-Americans, an Hispanic, and an Asian. Aside from the two Merrick children, Koepp recognized only John Jaroff.

Merrick began to speak in a conversational tone, outlining several ground rules that everyone would be expected to follow. Whatever was said was confidential and not to be repeated after the debriefing. It was understood that each person would speak only for himself, not for anyone else in the room. And finally, the group would not allow put-downs or interruptions of other speakers. He asked for their agreement. Several heads nodded barely perceptibly.

"First of all, I'd like someone to tell the others in the

group—that's who you should talk to, each other, not to me— tell the others what you saw the afternoon that Dr. Issac died.''

He glanced around the circle, but perceiving no volunteers, he turned his attention to the Hispanic student. "Enrique, why don't you go first? Tell us what you saw."

Now that someone had been singled out, the tension eased and the others moved about on their chairs. All of them focused on Enrique.

"I was coming up the driveway on my bike with John when the police car passed me and parked at the top of the driveway," the boy answered. "I knew something real bad had happened because of the way the cops looked when they went into Building A."

"How did they look?" Merrick asked.

The boy shrugged.

"They were scared," John Jaroff said. "The cops looked scared."

"Did anyone else see the police arrive?"

One of the black teenagers raised his hand.

"You saw them, too, Thomas?"

"Yeah, I was working in the refreshment tent. I saw them talking to Mrs. Merrick and Dr. Jaroff by the front door."

Merrick worked his way around the circle, gently inviting each youngster to share with the group what he or she saw or heard. The young people's reticence gradually began to dissolve; comments became more animated, less guarded. The only exceptions were Merrick's daughter Erin and a girl named Susan, who appeared to be about fifteen years old. Both girls elected to "pass" after the discussion leader told them it was acceptable to do so.

"Jason, how did you feel when you heard what had happened?" Merrick asked.

A chubby boy in a sweatsuit stared at Merrick for a few

seconds, then blurted, "I was scared. I wondered who else was going to get murdered."

"Did anyone else think about that?"

Several students raised their hands, including Merrick's son Phil. Merrick invited them to elaborate on the theme.

"I thought maybe the murderer would come back," said the black girl. "I thought he might kill my dad or mom."

Although Koepp was surprised by her remark, he noticed that several of the children nodded their heads, suggesting they had experienced identical concerns.

"Why did you think that might happen, Julia?" Merrick asked the girl.

"Because, because—I don't know why," she answered. "I just had the feeling—"

"Maybe we should talk about our feelings," Merrick said. "Most of us didn't see anything or hear what happened until later. How did you feel when you heard about Issac's death?"

"I was angry," Phil Merrick said.

"Because the murderer came here?" his father asked. "Because the murderer came right into Friars' Close?"

"That's right," Jason said, nodding his head vigorously. "Outside you expect murders, but not here. It proves you can get killed anywhere."

"The police can't do anything to stop it," Enrique volunteered.

Several heads swiveled about to look at Koepp, to see how he was taking this declaration of police impotence.

"Does anyone else care to tell us how he or she felt?" Merrick asked.

John Jaroff said rather sarcastically, "Everyone wants to think the killer was somebody off the streets, but that's not true. The police think someone who lives here is the guilty one."

This time none of the children bothered to study Koepp's reaction. His effort to remain impassive must have worked, he thought. He wondered where the boy had picked up the information that an "insider" was suspected. From his father Leon?

Several of the children commented on the theme of having their sanctuary violated, then the girl named Susan took the conversation in a new direction. "I felt sorry for Dr. Issac," she said. "It would be terrible to die like that."

"Yeah, it would hurt bad," Jason agreed. "Having a knife stuck into you. Ugh." He pretended to stick a knife into his stomach.

A few of the youngsters laughed nervously.

"No, I don't mean that," Susan protested. She hesitated. "Well, yes, that's terrible, but I meant not just that physical part, but having someone who hated you that much. I mean, the last thing that another person does to you is kill you. That's the last thing he knew. Who could hate Dr. Issac that much?"

Her question smothered all conversation until Julia asked shyly, "Is it all right to talk about him?"

"About Dr. Issac? Yes, if you want to. We can talk about anything we feel, as long as it has to do with—what happened."

Everyone in the circle looked expectantly at Julia, whose back was toward Koepp, but she evidently conveyed to them that she was not going to risk anything further. She remained silent.

The spirit of the dead man had entered the circle, though, chilling everyone in the room. Koepp edged forward on his chair; he didn't want to miss anything.

Finally, Susan asked, "Do some people deserve to die in a bad way?"

"People just die," Enrique said. "There's no plan."

"I don't mean just about dying in a painful, frightening way," she said. "I mean having someone hate you enough to kill you."

"To be hated to death," said a short, plump girl named Tessie.

Susan nodded. That's what she had meant; hated to death. Nobody continued on that theme, but Koepp could almost taste the tension.

Merrick must have sensed it, because he didn't ask another question immediately. Like Koepp, he expected something dramatic to occur.

They didn't have to wait long.

"Dr. Issac deserved to die badly." This startling assessment came from Thomas.

Even at a distance Koepp could see several young faces light up with excitement. The victim's character was something they wanted to talk about.

"Why do you say that, Thomas?" Merrick asked gently. The group leader had grown tentative; he reminded Koepp of a trial lawyer who wasn't sure how a witness was going to answer the next question.

Enrique interrupted before Thomas could respond. "They just die. There's no plan." He was sure of this point.

Tessie was still ruminating on the idea of being hated to death. "Mrs. Kusava wouldn't be killed by hate. Or Mrs. Merrick."

Enrique's silence implied that her point was well taken. Several others nodded agreement.

Attention was focused back on Thomas. "Why do you think Dr. Issac deserved to die badly?" Merrick asked. The circle of young people became more constricted as the participants leaned forward to make sure they didn't miss the answer.

"Because he was a phony," the boy said. "He pretended to be everybody's friend, but he wasn't. He was always putting his arm around you, or patting you on top of the head—"

The girl who had come in with Jason and who was sitting next to him raised her hand before she spoke. "When he touched you it was like being touched by a snake. You could feel that he wasn't what he pretended to be. Thomas is right. All the kids tried to stay away from him.''

"Is Angie right?'' Merrick asked. "Did you all try to avoid him?''

Assent rattled around the circle.

Karen shifted restlessly in her chair, as if it was difficult for her just to listen.

One little boy, who appeared to be the youngest child there, also raised his hand.

"Ryan?''

"I hid in the closet where they keep the brooms once when I saw him coming from the office,'' he informed them. He giggled. "I was so scared he saw me. I thought he was going to open the door and grab me.''

"Did anyone else hide from Dr. Issac?'' Merrick asked. He appeared to have lost his paternalistic calm and seemed unsure what to do next.

His daughter volunteered something for the first time. "I did. But sometimes I had to go where he was.'' For a moment it appeared that was all she had to say. But suddenly she added, "I had to go see him that day—''

Merrick was startled. He didn't have to ask for clarification; his daughter had made up her mind to talk.

"He was in the computer room,'' Erin said. "Gwen got a message on the phone in the office—because his calls ring on the office phone if he doesn't answer. I mean, the person calling has to dial 0 if they get his message recorder and don't want to leave a message.''

"So Gwen got a message for him?'' Merrick prompted his daughter.

"Yes, she wrote it out on a message slip and told me to take it down to Dr. Issac in the computer room. I didn't want to do it but she made me—''

"Did you give him the message?''

Koepp could see the girl in profile. He thought he saw a tear glistening on her cheek. He wasn't sure, but he felt the little girl's mother coil in tension on the chair next to his. But when he looked at Karen's face, he couldn't decipher her emotion.

After a hushed interval of eight or ten seconds, the girl must have answered "yes."

Merrick realized they had said what they needed to say. The tension evaporated. After inviting more comments twice, and getting none, he reiterated the ground rules and let them go.

They trooped out in one large, silent cluster.

Merrick trailed behind them like an afterthought.

Karen and Koepp sat in an uncomfortable silence for a while, then she asked if the session had been helpful to him.

"It told me something," he said, "but I don't know whether it's useful or not."

"I suppose you mean the fact that they didn't like him, that they were afraid of him?"

"Yes. Did you know that?"

"I never realized the intensity of that dislike until now," she said, "but I knew the children tried to avoid him. I saw evidence of that from time to time."

"Didn't that worry you?"

"Not particularly. Some people don't relate well to children. Children sense it."

"Did you know that Erin had to deliver a phone message to Steiner just before he died?"

"Yes," she answered. "I met her in the hallway as she was coming back to the office." Karen rose then and stood looking down at him.

"We didn't find the message slip," Koepp said. "If she delivered it, where was it?"

She took her time in answering. "That's odd. I guess I don't know why."

"Would there be a record of who the caller was?"

"I doubt it, but you can call Gwen from my office. She is probably still here, although I think she has a dinner date. She may remember something about him."

"I'll try her," Koepp said.

"Do you have time for a drink before you leave? You can stay for a pizza. Erin and Phil and I will probably order one in."

"I'll pass on the pizza, but if you've got any Scotch, I'd like that."

"You're in luck," she said, leading him toward the door. Back in her office, she sorted through the paperwork that had accumulated on her desk, while Koepp called Gwen.

After a little prompting, the young woman remembered the phone message and asking Erin to deliver it to Issac Steiner. "When she got back from the drugstore. She gave me a bad time, but she did it," Gwen said.

"Do you remember who the caller was?" Koepp asked.

The young woman paused for a long time before she said the caller was a man. "He said his name was Neil. He sounded fairly young. Had kind of a high-pitched voice."

Koepp put his hand over the phone for a moment and asked Karen, "Who did Steiner know named Neil?"

She thought about it for a moment, then answered, "Neil Erickson. He taught here occasionally. And he came over to Issac's apartment to play chess now and then. Both of them were members of the university chess club, I think."

Koepp thanked Gwen and put the phone back in its cradle.

"What else do you know about him?" he asked Karen.

"He lives on Kensington, I think, but I don't know him well," she said, looking up from the pile of mail in front of her. "Issac said he was a teaching assistant who was working on his master's in—chemistry, maybe?"

Koepp called his office and asked for Sergeant DeMoss or Detective Alfanti. DeMoss came on the line and listened with his usual patience as Koepp relayed what he knew of Neil Erickson. He asked DeMoss to find out if he had a record and to leave any information about him on his desk. "I'll check what you've got in the morning," Koepp said.

Once again he was looking at a member of the university as a possible suspect, Koepp thought with real regret, but he had no choice; the chemistry instructor had visited Steiner at his apartment, so he knew its location. And while he was teaching at Friars' Close he probably had been in the kitchen.

And may have come across the drawer filled with knives.

# SEVEN

LATER, he and Karen walked the perimeter road to Building D. The air was cool; fog had begun to form in the bowl of the community property, obscuring the stream and giving a gaseous appearance to the lights in the other buildings.

She hadn't worn a coat, and he noticed as they passed under a parking lot light that her thin shoulders were shivering. He removed his own jacket and put it over her shoulders. She gave him a fleeting smile of gratitude and pulled the collar tight around her neck.

The Merricks' home, located on the ground floor of Building D, was dark when Karen unlocked the door. She gave a slight but unmistakable gasp when she saw her daughter. Koepp saw her as well, silhouetted against a picture window. She was sitting on the window ledge facing them. For a few moments the tension in the room was palpable as the woman and girl stared at each other. But the mood passed as swiftly as it had come; Karen crossed the room to cradle the fragile child in her arms. She had the supreme good sense not to ask Erin why she was sitting alone in the darkness.

Only the foyer light burned. Koepp went into the kitchen to turn on the overhead light and a second light that illuminated the sink. When he returned to the living room, Erin was wandering about, restless and silent. She stopped finally beside the window draperies, and began to twist a drapery cord around her birdlike hands. She glanced at her mother, who was removing glass tumblers from a kitchen cupboard.

"Did you ever kill anyone?" Erin asked Koepp.

"No."

The girl seemed surprised by his answer. And disappointed.
"But you're a policeman. It's your job to kill—"

"No. It's my job to arrest people. Most policemen never
kill anyone."

Erin wrapped the cord around her wrist, then unwrapped it.
"Would you?"

"Kill someone?" Koepp found the question unsettling; he
had avoided thinking about it for years. It was galling to have
a child force him to confront it. "If I had to kill someone to
defend myself or someone else, I believe I would."

"How would you feel—afterward, I mean?"

"Pretty bad, I imagine."

Karen entered the living room. She sat on the edge of a
chair that faced her daughter. "This is a serious conversation," she said. "What brought it on?"

"Some of the kids talk."

"What do they say?" Karen asked.

"That whoever killed Dr. Issac shouldn't feel bad."

"Murder is always wrong, Erin."

"Maybe Dr. Issac wasn't murdered," the girl suggested.
"Maybe he was killed. It's okay to kill sometimes." She
looked at Koepp for confirmation. After he nodded, she padded quickly across the room and disappeared down the dark
hallway.

Over their drinks, they talked in desultory fashion about the
interaction of the debriefing session. Koepp only barely kept
up his end of the conversation because he wasn't really interested in rehashing the children's comments.

She sensed his preoccupation, and asked after an uncomfortable pause in the conversation, "Why did you accept my
invitation to come to my home?"

"Why did you ask me?"

"Because I would like us to be friends. Is that why *you*
came?"

Either a "yes" or a "no" answer seemed irrevocable. Instead of answering the question, he said, "I think it would be hard for us to be friends."

The off-center smile appeared. "Because you think I'm a murderer and you'll have to arrest me?"

"That's a complication, to be sure," he said without any humor. What kind of woman, he wondered, would make light of a charge like that? "No, it's just that society frowns on married women having men friends. People would assume—"

"That we're lovers?"

"Something like that." Although his experience with women was limited, Koepp knew they defined male friends with a wide latitude of intimacy; to some women a friend was a lifelong soulmate, to others he was the bagboy at the supermarket. He realized that any man would be at a disadvantage in this conversation.

"Didn't you have any women friends when you were a priest?" she asked.

He considered telling a lie, but decided against it. "Only one. That was one too many."

The playful smile faded away, to be replaced by an encouraging, sympathetic one. She was inviting him in an almost irresistible way to tell her about Diane. "You started out as friends with a woman and became lovers?" she suggested.

"Not exactly. We started out as lovers and finally became friends."

"While you were a priest or afterward?"

"While."

She sipped her drink for a few seconds, waiting for him to expand on his former relationship.

What could he say about Diane? She had transformed guilt from theological abstraction into personal pain. In the end, her guilt over the betrayal of her husband and her church exceeded his. She had been the one to end the affair. To underscore the finality of her decision, she had insisted that he hear her confession. Diane confessed to only one sin: adultery. She had kept score. Eleven times.

If he had possessed the strength to sever their ties, he knew he would still be a priest.

When Karen realized he wasn't going to tell her about Diane, she observed, "What you said is true, you know, about being friends last. It's easy to be someone's lover; it's much more complicated trying to be their friend. Friendship requires selflessness and it's supposed to be forever."

Because he was anxious not to get into a deeper discussion about Diane, he deflected the direction of the conversation. "Have you had any male friends since you've been married to your husband?"

Karen considered the question for the briefest of moments before she answered, "I've already told you that Roman Weber was a friend. He's an artist. I thought he had talent. I tried to encourage him."

"And Paul?"

"I don't know."

"Is Elizabeth Maklin his friend?"

"No. She's his lover." She said this in a matter-of-fact voice, as if she were making conversation about the evening news. The woman betrayed no anger, no bitterness, which struck Koepp as wholly out of character. Everything he had observed of her revealed a passionate, caring woman, yet she now seemed dead to the most intimate relationship of her life.

"We've assumed that the killer is a man," Koepp said, "but what about Elizabeth Maklin?"

"Why would she want Issac dead?" Karen asked.

"Well, she might have thought his leaving Friars' Close would spell disaster. That'll do for a start. But let's forget about motive for the moment and talk about personalities. Assuming that she had a motive, could Elizabeth Maklin have convinced your husband to kill for her?"

"I doubt that," she answered, showing a trace of a wry smile. "Paul would never let anyone have that kind of influence on him. It's not his nature."

"All right. So it's not very likely, but is it possible?"

She stared straight ahead, seeing nothing. "I suppose so. You're the detective. Why ask me?"

Koepp noted that this exchange represented the first and only time that she had been defensive since the investigation had begun. The woman was watching him warily now, as if she were afraid of his next question. Koepp perceived her apprehension, but his wits failed him utterly. He had no idea what the question was that she dreaded so much. An opaque, inscrutable expression came into her eyes, replacing the look of fear. His opportunity, if that's what it had been, had passed.

They found then that they had nothing more to say to each other. Koepp finished his drink, set the glass on the coffee table in front of him, and rose. Karen got up quickly, the inevitable way an experienced hostess encourages a guest to leave.

"Will you be here in the morning?" she asked as they paused in front of the door.

"Probably," he said as he wrapped his fingers around the doorknob. "No, *inevitably*. I'm lashed to this place like Ahab was lashed to the whale."

"Until you find a murderer, I suppose, or give up."

By her inflections she betrayed her preference; she wanted him to give up, to fail.

INSOMNIA WAS ONE of many less than dramatic maladies that plagued Koepp. Sometimes he slept well for months at a time, only to experience a three-or four-day period when he awoke without reason at about the lost hour of three o'clock. This morning he had a reason, it seemed. The picture of the children sitting in that circle at Friars' Close dominated his consciousness to such an extent when he awakened that he knew his subconscious must have been occupied with it while he slept.

He put on his robe and went to the kitchen to open a soft drink. Turning on the lights put the images in better perspective.

The children of Friars' Close hadn't liked Issac Steiner. And it wasn't just a matter of the man not "relating" to young people, as Karen had suggested; they had been afraid of him. On such matters the judgment of children was usually unerring.

## EIGHT

AT EIGHT-THIRTY the next morning, Koepp and Margaret debriefed the other detectives and uniformed officers who had been calling the residents of Friars' Close. Aside from the humorous aspects of some of their interviews, the detectives had nothing significant to relate. A report from one of the lab technicians stated that none of the rust-colored clothing picked up in the room search matched the fibers on Steiner's shirt. Youthful Mary Jo Riley, Botticelli cherub and computer whiz, stayed behind in the squad room after the others left. She clutched several sheets of computer printouts in her hands.

"What have you got, Mary Jo?" Koepp asked.

She read some biographical facts about Dr. Issac Steiner from one of the sheets.

"Any priors?" Margaret asked.

"No."

"Was he ever fired from a job? Professional reprimands? Dishonorable discharge? Civil suits? Malpractice?" Margaret sounded vexed.

"No to malpractice because he wasn't a clinician. No to the other stuff. Two divorces."

"We know about them," Koepp said. "We talked to the second Mrs. Steiner yesterday. Margaret is going to Ann Arbor this afternoon to see number one."

Mary Jo looked disappointed.

"Keep digging," Koepp told her with a smile of encouragement. Another detective, Milt Farmer, had been assigned to Koepp for the day. Koepp dropped Margaret off at the airport, then he and Farmer drove to the university to keep an appointment with Neil Erickson, the man who had called Issac

Steiner shortly before his murder. Erickson had no priors, either, according to the note DeMoss had left.

By questioning passing students frequently, the two detectives managed to find Erickson's small office on the ground floor of the sprawling new science building. The occupant noticed them outside his door and brought his conversation with a red-haired coed to a close. As she departed without looking at either Koepp or Farmer, Erickson stood up and invited them in with a wave of his hand. He didn't offer to shake hands, and resettled his lanky body into a swivel chair which had a pronounced list to one side. The cubbyhole was jammed with books and papers and smelled sulfuric like the rest of the building. Despite all the new developments in chemistry in twenty years, labs still smelled the same; Koepp remembered the odor from high school.

Farmer introduced Koepp and himself, then asked the chemistry instructor warily if he knew what had happened to Issac Steiner.

"Of course," Erickson said, looking at Farmer with disbelief. "He was a member of the faculty. People are talking about nothing else."

Koepp knew the question wasn't as stupid as it sounded; some people never watched a newscast or read a newspaper. "We're here to inquire about your phone conversation with Dr. Steiner the afternoon he was killed," Koepp said.

"There wasn't any conversation," Erickson said. "I called him, but he never called me back." The man had a squeaky, high-pitched voice which seemed incongruous in someone his size. Perhaps the Lincolnesque beard, with no mustache, was some form of compensation, Koepp thought; Lincoln reputedly also had a high-pitched voice.

"What was the purpose of your call?" Farmer asked.

"I was going to ask him if he wanted to come over to play chess Sunday night," Erickson said.

"If that's all the call was about," Koepp said, "why didn't

you leave a message? The woman who took the call said you insisted on having a message delivered, that it was urgent."

The man's large hands moved forward on the arms of his chair as if they were taking up defensive positions. He didn't respond.

Koepp felt anger beginning to simmer inside his stomach. "Mr. Erickson," he said, "we know that Dr. Steiner was running a sideline business selling cocaine to members of the faculty. He received a lot of phone calls from people here at the university. You also were a frequent visitor—"

"I don't do drugs," Erickson said.

"We're not interested in whether you use controlled substances at the moment," Koepp assured him. "We're trying to find out who Steiner's runners were, his subdistributors if you will. People who made a lot of phone calls and visits—"

Erickson's self-assurance began to fade. "Look, I don't know what you're trying to pull. I don't have anything—"

"If your phone call wasn't about a drug delivery," Koepp asked in a harsher tone, "what was it about?"

The man leaned forward on his chair, withdrew his hands from the chair arms and clasped them in his lap. Koepp hoped he was considering the potential cost of his silence.

At last he said, "I called him about a research grant."

"Go on," Farmer said.

"I had applied for a research grant from the Grayson Foundation," Erickson said. "Issac knew those people. He said he'd put in a word for me."

"Did you get the grant?" Farmer asked.

"No."

"And that's what you were calling Steiner about," Koepp said, "to tell him your application was turned down?"

"Yes."

"No doubt you were very disappointed," Koepp observed. "Did you blame Steiner?"

"He never talked to them," Erickson said. His sulky intonation revealed where he thought the blame lay.

"Steiner was a psychologist," Koepp said, "so his recommendation wouldn't have carried much weight in a science project, would it?"

"I've been working with filtration processes for machine shop coolants, which Issac didn't understand at all. But these things aren't based on scientific achievements. There's a lot of politics. Issac led me to believe he had influence. He and Merrick got big bucks from Grayson—"

Farmer asked why he had made the phone call.

"I was going to tell him what happened. Ask him to plead my case again."

Erickson insisted he hadn't seen Steiner for more than a week, and that they hadn't talked on the phone. He didn't know anybody who would want to kill him.

As they rose to leave, Koepp asked one last question. "What do you make of Friars' Close, Mr. Erickson? Do you think it's a valuable social experiment?"

"I'm not qualified to judge, but it's an interesting place. I used to teach labs there every week. They've got some motivated kids. It's nice to teach those kind."

It was hard for Koepp to imagine Erickson interacting with high school kids, motivated or otherwise. Even more puzzling was the man's reluctance to reveal the innocuous topic of his phone call to Steiner. Maybe his explanation about a grant to research the filtration of machining coolants was baloney.

When Erickson announced that he had to leave for a lab, Koepp asked for permission to use his phone. A university phone directory was lying next to it. When he reached Dr. Syrk she said she knew Neil Erickson, that he belonged to the same chess club as she and Issac Steiner.

"Do you know if they had a falling out?" Koepp asked.

"Not that I'm aware," Syrk answered. "They played chess together. Issac got him a job at Friars' Close."

"Did Neil ever talk to you about the school?"

"Not about the school. He did say he was worried about one of the students and asked me if I'd talk to the child."

"Did you?"

"I told him that as a licensed psychiatrist I couldn't do that without the parents' permission. They never approached me, so nothing happened."

"Did Mr. Erickson tell you the name of the student?"

After a pause she answered, "No."

On the way back to the Safety Building, Koepp made a short detour to stop at the condominium complex.

Charlie Tirquit and Tony Divito were washing a van in one corner of the parking lot, and looked up warily as the two detectives walked to their car.

"Good day for washing a car," Koepp observed.

"Good as any," Tirquit replied.

"Charlie," Koepp began, "do you remember that when we questioned you about finding Issac's body—"

"Sure."

"Did you go into the room?"

"No."

"Why not?"

"I was afraid to. 'Sides, it made me sick. I went for Karen."

"Where did you find her?"

"I ran down to her office, but she wasn't there so I came back to where the corridors intersect. She was at the front door, talking to Erin and Ina."

"But, you went past the intersection to get to her office. Why didn't you see her then?"

"She wasn't there. She either came into the building just then, or maybe she came down the stairs from the second floor after I ran past."

"Was she surprised when you told her what you saw?"

"Some, but she's pretty cool. Karen is like that."

"What did she tell you to do?"

"She said I should get my ice loaded and go back to work like nothing had happened. Told me not to worry, that she'd take care of calling the cops and everything."

"Why did Elizabeth slap you?" Koepp asked.

"She don't like me to talk to you," he answered. "I told her I had to. She didn't mean it."

The two detectives drove around the perimeter road to the Administration Building. Karen's office was empty, but they found her daughter in the main office. Erin turned down the volume on her Walkman. "My mom's not here," she said.

"Maybe someone else can help me," Koepp said. "I'd like to take some personnel records down to headquarters."

"Mrs. Kusava can help you. I'll find her." The girl started toward the door; the way she moved reminded Koepp of her mother's suppressed energy.

"Tell her I need these." Koepp handed her a list of names.

Ten minutes passed before Erin returned with Mrs. Kusava in tow. The woman held a manila envelope in her hand. Frowning, she handed it to Koepp. "Sorry it took so long. Charlie's records were filed out of alphabetical order."

Koepp mentally added "by Liz Maklin" to her sentence.

THEY WERE sitting in Lieutenant Tarrish's office when Mary Jo Riley stuck her curly head in the door to announce that he had a phone call from Ann Arbor.

"He'll take it in here," Tarrish said. He flipped a switch on his phone to activate the speaker. The lieutenant liked using the speaker phone; it was one of the few perquisites of his office, a power toy. They heard Margaret, slightly out of breath but obviously excited about something. Mary Jo returned, unbidden.

Koepp identified the listeners for Margaret, a courtesy he thought she might appreciate because he always hated to talk to Tarrish when he didn't know who else was listening. Then he asked, "What's happening?"

"I spent quite a while with Caroline Steiner, who was married to him for about twelve years. She still uses her married name and doesn't seem to be too hostile to him. She says she had no idea who might have killed him. She claims she's sorry he's dead, and says he was a brilliant scholar."

"Why did she divorce him then?" Tarrish asked.

"I'm getting to that," she said with a trace of irritation. "Steiner did practice psychotherapy while he lived in Ann Arbor, according to Mrs. Steiner. She said he never officially hung out his shingle, but that he did have several patients at any given time. He treated only women." Margaret paused for a moment, to give everyone a chance to weigh the implications of that. "The husband of one patient complained about sexual advances being made toward his wife. By paying the guy off, Steiner was able to prevent the man from filing a complaint. A few months later a similar incident occurred, so Mrs. Steiner filed for divorce, even though Steiner managed to pay everyone off again. That's when he came to our part of the world—about eleven or twelve years ago."

"Bringing his sexual therapy with him, no doubt," Koepp commented.

"Maybe so. However, Mary Jo said he has no priors. So nobody ever caught him at it, or he got out of it again with money. That's all hearsay, by the way. Mrs. Steiner heard from a friend at the university that he was still playing with his patients after he started Friars' Close. Nothing you could take to court, though." Margaret gave them her itinerary, then hung up.

Koepp went back to his desk and picked up Charlie Tirquit's personnel file. The folder that held it looked identical to the one he had seen in Elizabeth Maklin's hand when he surprised her in Karen's office. Was it the same one? A photograph of the applicant had been pasted to the first page of the form. He studied each entry in the biographical section and work history carefully, looking for something. But what? Some inconsistency perhaps, some fact that would give a clue why a man of Tirquit's age would suddenly decide to abandon a very conventional way of life to live in Friars' Close. Judging from the meticulous care evident from the typing, Tirquit had obtained assistance from someone, probably a woman, in filling out the application. He turned to the back page and found three personal references listed with phone numbers as well as addresses. Three separate sheets of paper had been stapled to the fourth page; each sheet gave a glowing account of Tirquit's virtues, written by one of the references.

He dialed the number of the first reference, a person named George Stengle, who lived on Seventy-first Street in the city. He got an alert signal, then a recorded voice informed him that the number he dialed was not in service. He pulled his phone book out of a desk drawer and looked up Stengle's name. A dozen Stengles, one Gregory, no Georges, no Stengle family on Seventy-first Street. He called Information to learn that there were no George Stengles. He asked the operator to spell the name *Stengel* and tell him what she found. Two Georges, junior and senior, both with Collinswood addresses. He referred to the written reference letter appended to Tirquit's application. The signature at the bottom of the page clearly read "le." It seemed logical that George knew how to spell his own last name. Koepp moved on to the second reference.

This time he consulted the phone book first. The second name was E. H. Doan, the "E" standing for Mrs. Elsie, according to the reference letter. No such person was listed at the address shown on Tirquit's application. He called Information again to check for a current listing. Negative. Then he dialed Mary Jo's extension. He read the names and addresses to her. "Call somebody down at City Hall—the tax depart-

ment, voter registration, assessor, records—and find out where
these people live," he told her.

He tried to get in touch with the third name on the list of
references. He had no more success than he had previously.
Next, he turned his attention to the section of the application
that listed the names and addresses of previous employers. He
called the most recent, a sand and gravel company on Quincy
Street, which was on the extreme south end of the city. He
didn't tell the woman who answered that he was a policemen,
but only gave his name and said he wanted to speak to someone about a former employee. He was told he would have to
talk to the general manager. Then he was put on hold.

While he waited, Mary Jo approached his desk.

"What did you find out?" he asked.

The young woman looked pleased, almost triumphant.
"Those people don't exist. What's it all about?"

"One of the suspects in the Steiner murder may have a
phony background," he told her. The general manager of the
sand and gravel company identified himself. Koepp gave him
the basic facts about when Tirquit supposedly worked there.
The manager, whose name was Morello, interrupted him impatiently.

"That guy never worked here."

"Are you sure? I mean, I've got his employment application—"

The man on the other end of the line sounded more annoyed when he said, "Look, I've hired every employee we
had in the past fifteen years. Me personally. This ain't General
Motors. Nobody by that name ever worked here."

Koepp commented that it was all very strange.

Morello didn't think so. "People lie about their work history all the time," he said. "You're smart to check references.
A lot of people don't bother anymore because they think the
old employer won't tell them the truth. But if you know what

to ask, you can still find out if a guy was a loser, whether he got fired. Me, I always check the references.''

Koepp thanked him and hung up. Mary Jo was still hanging around his desk, anxious to know the significance of somebody falsifying information on an application form. Koepp decided to fill her in. Tarrish, who was a stickler for up-to-date information about on-going investigations, insisted that each of his detectives submit daily logs of progress on their cases. It was department policy, but often was not enforced very rigorously. Although filling out the log sheets was a nuisance, it was very helpful when a new detective was assigned to a case. Koepp knew that Mary Jo read them all, so she had a reasonably good grasp of where he and Margaret stood on the Steiner case.

He handed her Tirquit's application form, which she scanned quickly. Then she looked at him, grinning. ''It's obvious his real background is more interesting than the one he put together here,'' she said.

''Maybe he's got a record.''

She shook her head emphatically. ''He doesn't have any priors. At least not as Tirquit.''

''How do you know?'' Koepp asked.

''Margaret gave me a list to check out,'' she informed him with a trace of smugness. ''His name is on the list.''

''Who else did you check?''

''The Jaroffs, that Dr. Merrick and his wife Karen, somebody named Divito.'' She paused to collect her thoughts. ''A couple of other names—women, as I recall.''

''Mrs. Kusava, Elizabeth Maklin?''

''Yeah, those names were on the list. Do you want me to get it?''

''Never mind,'' Koepp said. With her usual thoroughness, Margaret would have checked everyone for priors. ''Go back to Tirquit. What other possibility exists?''

"His name isn't Charlie Tirquit," she said. "Although that wouldn't necessarily mean—"

"No, it doesn't incriminate him," Koepp said, "but it's more than a little interesting. Run his prints through AFIS and see if you can get a make on him." AFIS stood for the state's new Automated Fingerprint Identification System. "If our computer doesn't have him, try the FBI."

ON THE FOLLOWING afternoon, Koepp received a report on the identity of the fingerprints Margaret had inked from the man who said his name was Charlie Tirquit. Koepp learned the outcome when he arrived back at his apartment and turned on his answering machine. The recorded voice belonged to Russ Kalmbach. His inflections sounded like he was reading from a script. "The prints identified as belonging to one Charles W. Tirquit are really those of Walter Omsby, 5188 West St. Claire Street. There's a fax of his car theft prior on your desk. I wish to hell everything wasn't a priority with you, Koepp. Don't you ever have any routine investigations? The only one worse is your partner."

If he waited until morning, Margaret would be available to go with him to interrogate Omsby, aka Charlie Tirquit. That was always a plus, but he decided he could save time by going to see the suspect tonight. He called him at his apartment, got no answer and tried the general number of Friars' Close. Elizabeth Maklin answered. She told him that she believed Charlie was eating dinner.

"Please tell him I'll meet him in his apartment in about half an hour," he told her. He hung up before she had a chance to protest or think up an excuse for not being able to arrange a meeting.

Charlie was waiting for him with the door of his apartment fully opened. Before Koepp could push the buzzer, the young man caught sight of his visitor and invited him in with an awkward beckoning motion. He was wearing a T-shirt and

bluejeans. When Koepp entered the living room, he was surprised to discover that Charlie wasn't alone. Elizabeth Maklin
was seated on the sofa. She was smoking a cigarette. They
greeted each other by nodding their heads jerkily. Like mar-
ionettes.

Koepp waited for her to leave, but the woman remained
seated. Finally, he said, "I have to talk to Mr. Tirquit about
the Steiner homicide. It's a private conversation."

"I want Elizabeth to stay," Charlie said. He looked anx-
iously at the woman, who rewarded him with a wintry smile
and a reassuring pat on his forearm.

"It's private," Koepp said.

When the woman spoke, her tone was cold and brittle to
the point of harshness. "I'll leave when Charlie tells me to,"
she informed him. "If you're planning some kind of third
degree, you're going to have to do it with me as a witness.
Since he doesn't have a lawyer, he asked me to sit in as a
friend. I don't see why *you* should object."

"I'm not objecting, I'm advising," Koepp said. But he decided not to argue the point.

"You have constitutional rights, Charlie," Elizabeth Maklin said. "That means you don't have to talk to him. You
don't have to tell him anything. In the morning we can get
Mr. Longworth to represent you. He can be here when Sergeant Koepp grills you."

"You're not being very constructive," Koepp said. He
looked at Charlie. "I've called the names of the people you
gave as personal references when you applied for membership
here. You made up those names. You aren't who you say you
are. Your real name is Walter Omsby.'

"Charlie, don't say anything," Maklin cried.

But the man responded despite her warning. "That's a lie.
I'm Charlie Tirquit." He sounded pathetic, like a little boy
protesting his innocence to his mother. Almost at once he
realized he had disobeyed his surrogate mother. He looked

with obvious concern at Elizabeth, who reassured him by switching on her soulless smile.

Koepp repeated the accusation and received the same response. He asked several other questions, which were treated with sullen silence. But Koepp was not disappointed entirely; he had determined to his own satisfaction that there was no innocent explanation for the identity change. At this stage he was willing to settle for that.

Koepp went to the purchasing manager's office, which was still unoccupied and unlocked. After some searching, he found a city phone book in a file cabinet. The address on Saint Claire Street, which was the one Kalmbach found in Omsby's service record, failed to show up next to either of the two Omsbys in the directory. He tried both phone numbers. His first efforts went unanswered. At the second address, an elderly woman answered the phone, but maintained she didn't know any Omsby named Walter.

It didn't matter. Knowing Charlie's real identity meant they could, in time, uncover his motivations.

WHEN KOEPP got back to his apartment and changed, he poured himself a Scotch. He ambled to the breakfast nook. The same forlorn robin was back on the birdbath, fluffing its wings from time to time and swiveling its head around as if it were looking for something it had left behind in the rainstorm Sunday morning. He poured the first drink down in a few savage gulps, and decided on a refill. I'm drinking too much, he reminded himself. He poured a second one anyway, but sipped it this time; drinking slowly was his one concession to the terrors of incipient alcoholism.

The fact that Charlie had no explanation for his name change didn't mean he was a murderer, Koepp reminded himself. But the young man might be covering for someone. That could account for the hostility of Elizabeth Maklin during the interview; she may have been worried that he would implicate another resident. That thought caused him to consider the implications that Jaroff, Merrick, and Maklin had no alibis, that they had in fact constructed bogus ones. All three had motive and means, and now, it seemed, they also had opportunity. But which of them, if any, was the killer? Maklin most probably was not because she didn't have to depend for her livelihood on Grayson Foundation money.

She did possess a killer's resolve, however.

Jaroff and Merrick were equal when judged as suspects. But as yet he had turned up nothing that would justify an arrest. They had lifted the fingerprints of Merrick and Jaroff in the computer room, but that meant nothing because both of them used the equipment frequently. No prints were discovered on the floor around Steiner's body. In the murder victim's room where the bloodstains had been found, only Steiner's fingerprints were evident. The whole situation seemed sanitized with respect to physical evidence. They had found no hair particles under Steiner's fingernails, and the fine orange fibers discovered on his shirt didn't come from any of the clothing they had taken to the lab; he had little confidence that this slender piece of evidence would lead to an arrest.

But the situation was sanitized with respect to testimony as well. He had come round to Margaret's belief that the residents of Friars' Close were withholding information. Not direct eyewitness accounts of the murder, perhaps, but some of those other seemingly innocent facts that could account for why a crime like murder happened: the gossip, the innuendos, the recalled instances of unusual or curious behavior.

That's what this investigation lacked, the human element.

He was jarred back to the present by an unusual occurrence. His doorbell was ringing. He decided his caller was the paperboy on his monthly rounds to collect his money. He peered into the security peephole, and was startled to see the foreshortened form of Karen Merrick. He felt shivers run down the tops of his forearms; it felt as if insects were scurrying across his flesh. Anticipation? Fear?

Koepp swung the door open.

She smiled warmly at him, but there was a flicker of uncertainty in her eyes. With bad grace all Koepp could think about was that her husband was out of town.

"I was in the neighborhood."

She entered the foyer and stood close to him for a moment, close enough that he was aware of her perfume and the slight chill of the night that emanated from her clothing. She was wearing a brown suit over a white blouse. He pointed to a chair in his small living room, and asked her if she wanted anything to drink. He expected her to say something like Diet Coke.

"Scotch would be nice."

No doubt she could smell it on his breath, he thought with some embarrassment. "On the rocks?"

"That's fine."

He made two, handed her one, and sat down on the couch. "Why this neighborhood?"

"Issac's memorial service. And making burial arrangements. There really wasn't anyone else. Only one of the daughters came back. Can you imagine?"

"Easily," Koepp answered. "The ex-wife in Michigan passed also. If your relatives don't like you when you're alive, they're not going to like you when you're dead." He had prayed over a lot of newly dead during his days as a priest; all too often he had been shocked by the callousness of their survivors.

"My children would come to *my* funeral," Karen said with surprisingly intensity. "I know they would. They'd mourn. Who would mourn for you, Ray? Don't you want children?"

"My sister would mourn. She'd also be a little annoyed, I suppose. If I died, it would be a big nuisance, but Ellen would come back to do right by me. She's very conventional, even though she tries to put on the blase-California mask. As for children, I'm not wild about having kids.''

"Children are great." Her impulsive enthusiasm took him by surprise; it was almost childlike.

"Having kids is not doing kids a particular favor," Koepp said, the Scotch beginning to loosen his tongue and his caution. "People have children to satisfy themselves. Having children gives us a measure of hope, but the kids have to pay for our self-indulgence."

"Thanks a lot. You've just decided I'm selfish because I wanted to have children."

He shrugged. "Most acts are selfish. Don't be too hard on yourself."

"'Alas for the rarity of Christian charity,'" she said in a gently mocking tone.

"I'm not sure charity exists—except as an ideal."

"You must have been a lousy priest."

Koepp laughed. "You've got that right, lady. What do you say we can the theology? Why don't you tell me why you really came here."

"I'm worried that you're suspicious of Charlie Tirquit, or maybe even Paul or Leon. You seem sure that someone at Friars' Close—"

"You forgot to mention Elisabeth Maklin, a very angry woman with her own agenda."

"She wouldn't do it. She might get someone else to do it for her—she has the touch of a Machiavelli—but she wouldn't do it herself."

"My partner thinks you're the Machiavelli of Friars' Close."

She laughed. "Does she! I'm not surprised. She doesn't seem to like me very well. What do *you* think?"

"I think you know a lot more about what happened last Saturday than you're telling us. You tried to make it seem in the beginning that you were cooperating, but in fact you're obstructing us. You don't want the killer caught.'' He paused, waiting for her reflex protest. She made no response.

"That was your cue for a denial,'' Koepp said, beginning to feel exasperated.

Karen watched him with her lopsided smile, saying nothing, giving nothing away.

"Do you know who killed him?'' Koepp asked.

"I've told you I don't.'' Her voice intoned just the right amount of weariness.

"Why is it that I don't believe you?''

She sipped her drink in silence. After a long time she said, "Some of your police friends have been busy. They called a lot of the residents at work.''

"Yes, and we're talking to the people who came to the art show. The names we have, anyway. We've also been waiting for lab reports, collecting background information on all of you. A police consultant is going over your books with your auditors. All of which is very boring and time-consuming. But it's necessary. And I haven't forgotten about the alibi you fabricated.''

"That was a foolish mistake—''

"Indeed it was,'' Koepp commented dryly. "But let's talk about Erickson, the chemistry teacher who taught here.''

"What do you want to know?''

"Why did he quit?''

"He didn't quit. He was fired. Leon and Paul felt he wasn't the best role model for the kids.''

"Why not?''

"They thought he was cynical, sarcastic, immature.''

"What did Dr. Steiner think?''

"He felt differently. He was the one who recommended Erickson, so he backed him. Elizabeth agreed with Paul and Leon.''

Koepp watched her warily, fascinated by her opacity. The warmth and provocative mockery in her eyes were still there, only now he realized they revealed nothing. This insight fortified him for what followed. She rose, slipped her jacket off and laid it on the chair arm, then walked to the picture window, where she paused with her back to him.

"In the end you're not going to convict anyone," she said, "because the circumstances of Issac's death are too far outside your experience. Normally that would be a miscarriage of justice. But not this time. If you were successful, you'd only perpetuate an injustice."

"Just let it die?"

"Yes."

Koepp didn't respond at first because he was shocked by the brazenness of her suggestion. He could scarcely believe she had said it. He stared down at the ice cubes in his amber drink for a moment, then he said evenly, "I can't do that."

She turned toward him again, framed in the window's rectangle of darkness. Half of her face was in shadow, half reflected the yellow glow from a floor lamp that stood near her chair. Koepp felt the silence between them was becoming oppressive. Karen began to trace the open neckline of her blouse with her fingers. The silken material formed and reformed tiny waves in the side lighting from the lamp as she moved her fingers. He silently studied the languid movement of her hand, transfixed by the notion that all he had to do was walk across the room and take her in his arms.

He tried to superimpose Diane's features on hers. Although she was neither as beautiful or sensual as Diane, she exerted a powerful attraction for him. He was convinced she had tried to entice him from the moment they met. Not in obvious ways. Instead, she revealed her vulnerability, the sophisticated woman's way of inviting intimacy.

She was becoming a dangerous preoccupation.

"What have you decided about me?" Karen asked.

Koepp started; she might have been reading his mind.

Seeing his confusion, she laughed softly with a slight treble sound in her voice. Once again her mood had changed back to playfulness. These abrupt shifts in emotion were starting to make Koepp frenetic; he suspected that she switched moods to derail his concentration.

"Decide what?" Koepp asked at length.

"Decide if I killed Issac." The promise of more laughter had evaporated. Now she seemed as intense as he had ever seen her. "You have to decide soon, Ray, one way or the other. For both our sakes."

That was the closest either of them had come to acknowledging the growing attraction between them. It encouraged him to believe he might get the truth out of her. "You know more than you've told me."

She didn't answer.

"How can you justify not cooperating?" he asked. "You're harboring a killer, someone who could kill again. The second killing comes—"

"No. Issac's killer wanted only to kill him, I'm sure."

"You're talking about yourself."

"It's not me, Ray. I wanted to kill him. I prayed to your God, in case he exists, to be able to do it, but I was too afraid. The person who killed him wasn't afraid."

She left his apartment a few moments later. Koepp insisted on walking her to her car. He watched the taillights of the station wagon until she turned the corner at the bottom of the hill. Their red glow lingered in his retinas long after the car had disappeared.

She knows, he thought. She knows who killed him.

# NINE

WHEN KOEPP returned to the squad room, he found two messagslips. He decided to deal with the easy one first. It was from Detective Farmer. He was in the canteen having coffee, according to the note. Koepp rang downstairs.

"What's up?" he asked Farmer.

"I've been looking into the Merricks' financials," the detective responded. "The good doctor and his wife had separate accounts going back quite a few years. The funny thing is that Mrs. Merrick, shortly after she came here, paid Steiner two hundred dollars a month for almost a year. Figure that out."

"You tell me," Koepp said.

"She may have been paying him for therapy. Probably the rate was so low as a professional courtesy to the doc."

The discovery that Karen had been paying money to Steiner depressed him so badly he was having trouble following the conversation. Once again it was apparent that she had withheld information from him that common sense would have told her was significant. It was also the kind of information that was bound to surface during a prolonged investigation. She would probably have an innocent explanation to offer when he confronted her, but it irritated and disappointed him that she had not taken him into her confidence. And what if the payments were for therapy? Had Steiner made love to her also? Perhaps that's why she hadn't told him about the money. His depression and irritation began to ferment into real anger. Damn her, he thought savagely. Damn Steiner.

Koepp tried again to imagine the murder from the killer's perspective. He mentally attempted to capture the feeling of shock in his arm and shoulder as he thrust the blade into Steiner again and again, the splatter of blood, the victim's gasp, the rattle of his final breath as he slumped to the floor, the smells of blood and urine and excreta. Those physical aspects he found easy to reconstruct, yet the psychological state of the killer eluded him. He couldn't feel the satisfaction of it as the murderer might have experienced it. This was unusual for Koepp; always in the past he had been able to formulate a crude sense of the crime in his imagination. Was it because he was unwilling to accept Karen Merrick as the killer?

The second message came from Detective Norris, who had promised Koepp he would check out Tirquit/Omsby's address on St. Claire. His message said they couldn't find out much about the suspect, but that Koepp should call Detective Willinski in Milwaukee. According to Norris, the suspect had gone there looking for work after he left the service.

Koepp made the call to Willinski, who could only tell him, "Your man moved around a lot. We're making inquiries. I'll get back to you."

Margaret had gone for coffee. She set Koepp's cup in front of him while he told her about Mrs. Merrick giving Steiner money. She listened with interest but said nothing. Between sips of the coffee, he recounted what the Milwaukee detective had said and also remembered to tell her about the slapping incident involving Maklin and Charlie.

"What's his motive?" Margaret asked. "We know that's the key."

"Maybe Maklin has been manipulating him for some purpose of her own," Koepp answered. "She slaps him for talking to us, she was in Mrs. Merrick's office—trying, I think, to lift Charlie's personnel file. And she was all over me when I asked him about his identity change."

"So she's protecting him," she said dubiously.

"Or the person who let him into Friars' Close."

GWEN, the office administrator, seemed surprised to see the two detectives again; she smiled uncertainly at them. When they asked for Karen, the girl told them she was with her husband in his room on the second floor. Margaret glanced at Koepp, then looked away guiltily. Her instincts had been on target, he thought ruefully; he didn't like the fact that Karen was in her husband's room.

Moments later, Karen greeted them at the apartment door, casually, as if they were expected. Merrick, dressed in a blazer and slacks, was talking on the telephone in the living room. He was giving someone, presumably Gwen, instructions about getting him a cab. Beyond him, Koepp could see the valley with the stream bisecting it, a wooden footbridge and Building D. It was a beautiful spring day, brisk but sunny, the kind Koepp relished because so much of May was winter or summer in this north central climate. Joy was largely a relative condition.

Merrick hung up. He nodded silently to acknowledge the presence of the two detectives. His dark eyes had a hooded, furtive aspect; they reminded Koepp of the eyes of an orangutan in the county zoo. He squared his shoulders and faced Koepp and his partner.

Both of them saw the rust-colored sweater underneath his blazer at the same time.

"Nice sweater, Doctor," Margaret said. "Is it new?"

He glanced down at his front the way a clumsy man looks at his tie to see how much damage he did when he spilled his chili. "No, it's old. I've had it—"

"We'd like to take it to the lab for analysis," Koepp said. "We'll trade you the brown one that we took in the room search."

Margaret, who carried the paper bag in which the brown sweater nestled, held it up for a second, then set it on the dining table.

"You must have been wearing that sweater the day we

searched your room," Koepp said, then added as an after-thought, "It's strange we didn't notice it."

"I can explain that," Margaret said. "Dr. Merrick wasn't in his room when we began our search. I had to call him at Elizabeth Maklin's apartment. Remember, Doctor, you said the door was unlocked, and we could just go in?"

"Yes, that's right," Merrick said rather absently. Impulsively he stripped off his jacket, pulled the sweater over his head, and tossed it to Margaret. She speared it with one hand, and rewarded him with an angelic smile. Koepp had to admit the man was very good-looking in a cerebral, Mediterranean way. No doubt Margaret was still impressed with his physical looks, although it was doubtful she put out of her mind very long the fact that he used phony study data to advance his career. Despite her flip manner, Margaret had a thick vein of moral rectitude that rebelled at such practices.

Watching the handsome sociologist reminded Koepp of something Mary Jo had told him the day before while she was reviewing background data about some of the more prominent residents of Friar's Close. "Dr. Merrick had a good deal of success at Michigan," she had told him. "He was very popular with the students. The head of the sociology department said that his classes were always filled and there was a waiting list. Although he was particularly popular among woman students—there's always a lot of coeds in sociology, the guy said—the university never had any complaints about him coming on to women students. He must be something," Mary Jo had declared.

Judging by Margaret's reaction to Merrick, he was very much "something."

Another facet of Merrick's character had been uncovered by the persistent Mary Jo. She had learned that Merrick had an explosive temper. It was his temper that cost him a chance at tenure and led eventually to his departure from Ann Arbor;

he had struck a research assistant because the man had challenged the accuracy of his research data.

Mary Jo hadn't been nearly as successful in finding intriguing facts about either the victim or Neil Erickson, Steiner's chess partner. Steiner's safety deposit box at a downtown bank had not yielded the cash horde they expected. And even though Erickson appeared to be a model citizen, Koepp had asked Margaret to check his financial background and his long-distance calls. He was hiding something.

Karen, who had been standing next to Koepp, went to a couch and sat down. She was wearing a plaid blazer, a sweater and blue slacks that made her look bigger than she usually did. She made no effort to play hostess in her husband's apartment by inviting the visitors to sit down.

"Which of us do you want, Sergeant?" Merrick asked. "I have to be in class in less than thirty-five minutes." He glanced at a large gold wristwatch to confirm his timing.

"Actually, we only want to talk to your wife this morning," Koepp told him. Koepp wasn't sure if Merrick knew about his wife paying money to Steiner or not. If he didn't, Koepp wasn't going to be responsible for telling him.

After Merrick's departure, Karen motioned to the other chairs invitingly. Koepp remained standing. Margaret sat down on the chair next to the sofa. She and Karen watched each other warily.

First Koepp explained about Charlie's identity change, then he asked, "How did he get in here so easily?"

She made no effort to act surprised by his revelation about Charlie Omsby, but answered crisply, "I wasn't here at the time. I was recovering from surgery, so Mrs. Kusava was in charge of the review. She'll answer your questions."

"Did he have a sponsor, a powerful friend?"

"I don't know the details—"

"Why did you pay money to Dr. Steiner?"

She slumped on the couch as if trying to ward off a physical blow. The sharp, strong chin fell on top of her forearm as it lay on the back of the couch. "I won't answer any questions about that while she's here," Karen said, nodding toward Margaret.

"Karen, if you tell me anything, it can come out later in court, so what's the difference whether Margaret hears it now or then?"

The woman made no reply. At length Margaret rose and walked out the door. She told Koepp she'd wait for him in the office.

Karen turned slowly toward Koepp, who took the chair Margaret had just vacated. It was very warm when he settled into it. The woman clasped and reclasped her small hands in her lap.

"I knew you'd find out sooner or later. But Ray, it was so long ago, what's the point of getting into that now?"

"Into what?"

"It's an unpleasant subject, Ray. I—well, something happened to me when I was a little girl, something that I've never been able to come to grips with. Issac, Dr. Steiner, thought he could help me. In the beginning he did, but after a while he began to get very familiar. I saw what was happening, or about to happen, so I discontinued the treatment. Later, he apologized. He said I had done the right thing for both of us."

"That's it?"

Her color rose slightly. "Of course that's all. What else did you expect?" Then the funny little half-smile formed in her right cheek. "I see. It's your policeman's mind at work again. You're thinking, did she enjoy it, did she encourage him, did she have sex with him—"

"I wasn't thinking that," he said lamely.

"The hell you weren't."

The passion she conveyed surprised him. "Why did you

object to Margaret being here? You had nothing to be ashamed of.''

She studied him with an amused expression, as a fond mother might observe the antics of an obstreperous offspring. ''Two reasons really. What I experienced during psychotherapy is something I won't share with anyone I don't trust completely. It was unpleasant then, it's depressing for me now.''

He nodded sympathetically. ''What's the second reason?''

''I guess I'm too proud to say some things in front of her, things of a personal nature. It's hard to talk to you when she's around. She's in love with you, you know.'' He could feel her eyes probing him then, assaying his emotions, calculating his response.

''What you see is loyalty,'' he said. ''We're partners. We have to depend on each other.'' For some reason Koepp felt it necessary to try to convince her. ''She has a boyfriend, a nice, normal guy who sells stocks and bonds. He invested some of her dad's money for her. They've been going out.''

''She won't marry him.''

''Well, maybe—''

''Not as long as you're still in circulation, which is probably a pity in a way because you wouldn't be very good for her. You're like an airplane with no engines. You're looking around for a place to crash. You're rather self-destructive.''

''As they say, it takes one to know one.''

''Yes, doesn't it?'' she replied in a small voice. ''I've been meaning to talk to you about something. Am I free to come and go as I please?''

''What do you mean?''

''Just what I said. Can I come and go as I please?''

''Sure, you're—''

''I'm planning to go to a friend's cottage up north—Granite Lake,'' she blurted out. ''Next Tuesday. I need to be by myself for a while. Is there any reason I can't go?''

This was a totally unexpected development. Koepp thought

about it for about fifteen seconds before answering, "I guess not. How long will you be gone?"

"A few days. I'm going alone."

In the space of a few seconds she had assured him twice that she would be by herself, which aroused Koepp's suspicions even more than the trip itself. What was she up to this time? Whatever it was, his instincts told him it might be important to their investigation. Without question, he and Margaret were floundering, no closer to a solution than they had been a week ago. Karen was the linchpin of the investigation. If she hadn't killed Steiner, she knew who did. And why. Considering how deliberately she acted, Koepp was sure she had a serious reason for going to Granite Lake, wherever that was; she wasn't going there to fish for bluegills. They needed luck to solve a case as old as this one was becoming, Koepp thought, and maybe this was the break they needed.

But even as he considered the possibilities, another insidious scenario began to play itself out in his mind.

# TEN

LT. TARRISH, fearful as ever of unorthodox procedure, had done his best to divert Koepp. He had argued that they should concentrate on uncovering Walter Omsby's background. Tarrish regarded him as their best suspect.

Koepp maintained that even if Omsby had killed Steiner, someone had helped him, or put him up to it. "He's the kind who only does what other people tell him," Koepp said. "Anyway, Margaret can track down Omsby's past. I'll follow Mrs. Merrick to Granite Lake and see if anyone shows up. I'll go only if it's evident that someone else involved in the case is going to meet her there."

"Exactly. And if you do go, all you do is watch the place and identify any visitors," Tarrish said. "That's all, right?"

"Right." It wasn't all; Tarrish knew it, and was creating an explanation for his superiors. In reality, Koepp planned to take some of Donnie Bruce's paraphernalia with him. Bruce was a private operator who specialized in sweeps of corporate offices to prevent industrial espionage. He was an electronic surveillance wizard. Koepp had gotten to know him several years before when their paths crossed during a stakeout of a warehouse operation that was receiving and selling stolen goods. Because he liked to stay on the right side of the police, Bruce occasionally would do a favor for a cop, like an illegal phone tap, or placing a bug. His results wouldn't be admissible in court, yet they could tip off detectives on where or how to find physical evidence legally. If Koepp did go to Granite Lake, Bruce was prepared to supply him with the necessary bugs and a receiver to eavesdrop on Karen.

Tarrish was staring at Koepp without seeing him. Something else was bothering the lieutenant, something more serious than planting illegal bugs. Koepp assumed pressure was coming from Chief Voorhees, pressure generated, as Karen had suggested, by someone at Friars' Close. Jaroff, maybe? If the powers at the university were the cause of Tarrish's preoccupation, he probably was worrying about the fact that Karen was married to a prominent faculty member.

He seemed to confirm Koepp's speculation by saying, "She's not taking her kids, huh?"

"No, she's not. She's up to something, George." Everything about her, her shifting moods, her perceptivity, her little verbal probes followed by cool searching analysis, had convinced him that she not only had a plan to derail their investigation, but that she was continually adjusting it as circumstances changed. He hoped the curious trip to the north woods meant she was getting desperate.

Whatever she was up to probably involved Walter Omsby, alias Charlie Tirquit, so his whereabouts would have to be monitored. Koepp also wanted Roman Weber watched. The junkie was not only a likely suspect, but Karen had called him a friend, and Weber had been at Friars' Close the day of the murder.

Tarrish apparently had worked out the details of his cover explanation because he told Koepp he could follow Karen Merrick to Granite Lake.

Koepp explained the need for surveillance of both Tirquit and Weber.

Tarrish made notes on one of his ubiquitous lined yellow tablets. "What about tailing *her*?"

"On Tuesday we'll follow her to make sure she's going to Granite Lake. Until then there's no need," Koepp said. "It would be just about impossible anyway, considering the layout of those condos. If she goes to Weber's place, then the cop watching it will report." He handed his superior a picture

of Karen which Margaret had obtained from the Department
of Motor Vehicles.

The lieutenant studied the photograph with interest. "Get
word to me if you go," Tarrish said. "I'll tell the Granite
County sheriff you'll be in the area."

The sheriff's name was Bergan.

AT MIDMORNING Tuesday a cab came to Friars' Close to collect Karen Merrick. At least Koepp assumed that it was for
Karen. He was waiting in his car near the main access road.
When the cab returned fifteen minutes later, he caught a
glimpse of her in the backseat. He told Margaret what was
happening on the radio and watched in his rearview mirror as
her car swung in and out of the traffic and took his position.
Her job was to maintain surveillance on Charlie Tirquit. He
followed Karen to a rental car parking lot, waited across the
street, then followed a green Ford to the Interstate. He stayed
close enough so that she would spot him. He wanted her to
see him following and to see him turn off at the county line.

Next, he called the surveillance car on Henson Street to ask
for an update on Weber. He was told that Weber had not left
his apartment. Detective Mulrooney, who was in the surveillance car, told him that a blond model had gone into the building at nine o'clock. Mulrooney thought that Weber was painting her in the nude. He insisted on telling Koepp a joke, an
artist joke. "This guy is a portrait painter for rich people, see.
And this gorgeous socialite says to him, 'I want you to paint
me in the nude.' And he says, 'Sorry, lady, I don't do that
kind of thing.' And she says, 'I'll double your normal fee, I'll
pay you five thousand dollars.' He says, 'No.' She says,
'Okay, I'll pay you ten thousand dollars to paint me in the
nude.' So finally the artist agrees, but he says, 'I'll do it on
one condition, lady—you let me keep my socks on. I have to
have someplace to put my brushes.'" Margaret, who had been

monitoring Mulrooney's banter, thought it was very funny; she laughed aloud, which was unusual for her.

The next day at about ten Mulrooney called in to report that Weber's car was out of the garage in the next block and parked in the street in front of his apartment. Half an hour later he called in again and asked for Koepp. Koepp went to the dispatcher's room; he picked up a mike so he could talk to Mulrooney. "Where are you?"

The patrol car responded at once. "On Orchard heading east, about two blocks from the Interstate." Detective Mulrooney gave him the license number and a description of the vehicle.

"Tell me if he goes north on the Interstate."

Moments later Mulrooney reported that the Volvo was indeed headed north.

"Follow him to the county line, then pack it in. Thanks."

"Car sixteen, that's a ten-four. Out."

It was happening. Koepp's hunch had begun falling into place as if he had written the script; his players, Karen Merrick and Roman Weber, were enacting their roles flawlessly. It crossed his mind, as he was replacing the microphone in its cradle, that perhaps Karen was writing the script. He tried to dismiss that unsettling idea from his mind.

WITH DONNIE BRUCE'S chest of eavesdropping devices, a sleeping bag, and some outdoor clothes, Koepp flew in a small chartered Cessna to the Forest Junction airport, where he secured a rental car. An hour or more before Weber arrived in Granite Lake, Koepp was parked on a side street waiting for him.

Shortly after four o'clock he spotted the blue Volvo. He pulled onto the county road, taking up position about ten car lengths behind it, and followed the vehicle down the main street of Granite Lake. They rounded a bend just after passing through the village. A large lake, glinting orange and foamy white in the late-afternoon sun, came into view on their right. They passed a park, then a boat dealership with an "Evinrude" sign supported in not quite level fashion between two rusty metal poles. Several lakeside homes, which looked more like sheds than residences, appeared on either side of the road. As they plunged into forest, side roads branched off to the right every two hundred yards or so. At each of them Weber slowed down so he could read the signposts; Koepp was forced to do the same to maintain his distance, all the while hoping that the search would preoccupy Weber enough to prevent his detecting that he had a tail. About three miles from the village Weber turned off into a stand of birches.

Koepp stopped on the roadway two hundred yards from the access road. Weber had only one way out, so Koepp didn't have to be in constant visual contact.

He forced himself to wait fifteen minutes before easing the rental car into the entry lane. As he made the ninety-degree turn he noticed that one of the weatherbeaten slats on the wooden signposts read Pine Grove Resort. Once he had passed through the grove of birches, a marsh came into view on either side of the road. He crossed a rickety single-lane bridge and headed into another area of thick woods. Suddenly, he saw the outbuildings of what he assumed was the resort. He parked his car and proceeded on foot.

He had advanced only about twenty yards when he saw a figure through a break in a stand of ash trees. Beyond the trees a rustic lodge came partially into view and a second grove of trees—the pines that presumably had inspired the name of the place. The tall figure was hunched over, shoving at the prow of an aluminum fishing boat. Moments later the cranking sound of a starter cord being pulled on a two-cycle engine disrupted the quiet of the lake. The motor, a black one, started on the second pull. The bow of the boat disappeared behind the screen of vegetation. Koepp moved closer to the shoreline to get a better view of the lake.

It was crescent-shaped. Toward the end where Koepp stood, several small islands were located about five hundred yards offshore. On one of them he could make out the horizontal lines of a man-made structure; Weber's boat was heading directly toward the building.

Her cottage was on a goddamned island!

KOEPP ran back to his car and ripped open his luggage. After rummaging through his clothes for a few seconds, he found his binoculars. He went back to his vantage point to study the island, which was covered with trees and ringed with orange boulders. In a break in the rocks he could make out a spit of sand and a wooden dock. Behind the dock on higher ground was a small outbuilding, an outhouse maybe, or a woodshed.

He adjusted the focus on the right eyepiece. Standing on the dock in a pair of jeans and a white blouse, with her arms folded over her chest, was Karen Merrick. Watching her from a distance like this, unseen by her, made him uncomfortable, but he kept the binoculars trained on her until Weber tilted up the outboard motor and climbed onto the dock. The man secured the boat rather clumsily to a set of cleats. Koepp switched his attention once more to Karen, until she went to Weber and was swallowed in his embrace. Arm in arm, the two figures disappeared into the trees.

Koepp went back to his car in a black mood. Nothing he had seen surprised him, but he felt jealous just the same.

During the plane ride to Forest Junction and while he was waiting in the village, he had tried to construct a scenario that included the lanky artist. He hadn't been successful then, and he could make no sense of it now. How could a woman like Karen have become involved with a junkie like Weber?

He glanced at his wristwatch. Almost four-thirty. The stores would close at five, which meant he had to act quickly if he was going to buy something that would deal with the complication presented by the island. He had eliminated from consideration both swimming, because he knew the water would still be too cold, and the use of a metal boat, because it would be too noisy. Then he remembered the discount store he had passed at a small shopping mall on the way into town. He climbed back in the car, managed to turn it around on the narrow road and sped back to the village.

He made it into the store with ten minutes to spare, and looked for the sporting goods section. With considerable relief he saw a gray inflatable boat with red trim suspended from two cables above racks of fishing lures. After a short search, he found a box with a picture on its side showing the boat floating through a foaming rapids. The price, including a tiny electric motor, was $139.99. Instructions on the box said he would need to buy a twelve-volt, deep-cycle battery to operate the motor. They said nothing about oars. No, he couldn't risk depending on a cheap motor; he'd need a set of oars anyway and an air pump.

He found a pump for $32.00 and PVC oars for $17.99. An identical set of oars was mounted in the suspended inflatable's oarlocks, so he knew the pair he held in his hands would fit. He also bought a hacksaw.

He paid for everything with a credit card. The checkout clerk, a fat girl who chewed bubble gum with noisy insouciance, grinned stupidly each time she picked up one of his curious purchases and read the price tag.

He stopped for hamburgers and fries at a drive-in, then bought meager provisions for the next day. When he reached the city park, he turned to the right, following the road that seemed to service the cottages on the side of the lake opposite the Pine Grove Resort. Based on his earlier reconaissance, he knew this eastern shore was more sparsely settled. What he needed was a piece of underdeveloped property somewhere near the southeast end where he could park his car and launch his boat without being seen. He tried four different access roads without finding one suitable. When he entered the fifth one he came to a chain barrier just out of sight of the highway. He attacked the padlock with his hacksaw. After ten minutes of sawing and cursing, he severed the hasp. He twisted the chain free of the hasp, dropped the barrier to the ground and drove the car across it. He reconnected the chain, and eased the car in another hundred feet or so to get it out of sight of the chain barrier. The island cottage was visible through the trees. He walked the remaining fifty feet to the shore.

Now the island was north of him, considerably farther from shore than it had been from the Pine Grove Resort. Still, this vantage would suffice. Only one cottage was in view, situated to his left across a small inlet. He sat in the car to eat his sandwiches and French fries. Then he made two trips to the water, lugging the boat, pump, oars, and Donnie Bruce's kit of "do-it-yourself" bugs. He connected the pump to the intake nozzle in the inflatable, and began to raise and lower the handle vigorously. The boat unfolded and took shape in jerky spurts like an old man getting out of bed in the morning. Before long he had an insubstantial but for his purposes serviceable craft for getting to the island. He went back to the rental car, climbed inside, rolled up the windows to ward off the mosquitoes and tried to doze.

He couldn't sleep, though. Karen wouldn't let him. He forced himself to concentrate on other things, but she kept coming back to reclaim his consciousness. He hated what was happening to him because he knew one of the most unprofessional acts a policeman could commit was to develop a relationship with a suspect. As usual, he was thinking of himself in the third person, of her effect on Koepp, Koepp the ex-priest, the failed cop, the romantic juvenile. He never thought of himself in this frame of mind as Ray, as other men might have thought of themselves as John or Tom; he was always Koepp.

"Koepp better find a new line of work," he said aloud.

From off toward the little inlet he heard the unearthly

mocking cry of loons, and now and then the splash of fish jumping or a small mammal diving into the water. Out on the island, which he could see through the trees, a flickering orange light came on. He assumed that the place had no electricity, and that its occupants were lighting Coleman lanterns. The scene inside the cabin forced its way into his consciousness. By now they were eating dinner on a small table next to the window, from where they could see the last strands of ocher trailing the sunset. Perhaps a pair of candles flickered on the table between them, accentuating the curve of her throat, the sharp planes of her face, her firm, defiant chin. They would be drinking wine to break down whatever inhibitions they might still have. Across from her, the craggy face of the artist would be contorted with growing impatience and lust. His eyes would be riveted on the gentle swelling of her breasts, anticipating the pleasures to come. Koepp felt the reassuring weight and hardness of his Detective Special against his clammy skin. The primitive image, unbidden, of shooting Weber in the crotch formed in his brain.

About ten-thirty the lights on the island flickered out, as if unable to resist any longer the overweening blackness of the night. Koepp settled down in his seat, spared for the moment any further vigilance, determined to get some sleep before two o'clock in the morning, the time he had decided gave him the best chance of making it to the island undetected. He didn't fall asleep at first because his mind remained fixed on Karen Merrick. Tomorrow night he would have to monitor the breathlessness of their lovemaking while he waited for one or the other of them to give him the identity of the murderer.

On that unhappy notion he drifted off to sleep. He awoke about half past two—late, but refreshed. He wasn't even very stiff from sitting in the car. Koepp hurried to the place where he had hidden the bugging equipment; he set the chest in the boat compartment normally reserved for the twelve-volt battery. Because he had no battery, he didn't need the electric motor, which remained in the trunk of the car. He put the cheap oars into the boat's locks and shoved off.

The boat proved difficult to maneuver at first, tending to turn end-for-end with little provocation. However, in a short time he became more expert with the oars, and began to make unspectacular but steady progress toward the opaque, pyramidal shape of the southernmost island. He seemed not to be closing the distance at all when suddenly the branches of the island's biggest pines reached out from shore and engulfed him. The bow of the boat bounced against some large boulders. Gingerly, Koepp crawled ashore and tied the craft to an exposed tree root. His eyes were well adjusted to the darkness; he could see the outdoor privy roof and the cottage in its entirety.

Koepp opened the box of the electronic gear, removed a pair of rubber gloves and yanked them on over his cold fingers. Bruce had cleaned the equipment thoroughly to remove any latent prints. He had also obliterated the serial numbers on the equipment with some chemical process that he maintained left no residual impressions. Koepp judged that there was a slim chance that his bug would be spotted, so he had insisted that nothing be traceable.

Everything from now on was illegal. He pulled a small penlight from his jacket and directed its beam into the box. First he withdrew his bug, a thousand-ohm, super-sensitive microphone embedded in a suction cup; a thin cable connected it to a small transmitter. For this part of the operation this was all he needed. After shutting off the light, he crept up the hill past the outhouse toward the dark, horizontal shape of the main cabin. When he reached the building, he found himself just below a porch that thrust out from one side. He painstakingly worked his way up a small incline until he was level with a window. He peeked in, but could make out none of the details of the room. However, there was a faint, solitary light in the distance, probably from one of the cabins opposite

the window he was looking through. This meant that the cabin
was just one room, or more likely that a doorway was located
directly between two windows. Either situation would serve
his purposes, given the sensitivity of the mike. As long as the
door was open, he would probably be able to hear conversa-
tions anywhere in the main cabin. Anything said on the porch
would not be audible.

This window would do well enough, provided he could find
a way to camouflage the mike. A low branch of an ash tree
was almost brushing the windowpane, and a drapery covered
the edges of the window. If he placed the suction cup near
where the tip of the branch projected toward the window, the
mike might not be noticeable unless one of the cabin occupants looked for it. It gave him some perverse pleasure to
push the suction cup against the windowpane; they'd have too
much on their minds to notice a bug.

That was all there was to it. He could activate the transmitter from shore.

He slipped back down to the dinghy and gingerly pushed
himself away from the rocks. The boat constricted under his
weight, feeling tippy and unsubstantial, then sprang away
from the shore. He slowly spun the little craft around and
rowed toward his outpost ashore. From this vantage it was
impossible for him to determine exactly where he had come
from; everything looked the same. He picked out a dim outline of a high tree and rowed toward it, reasoning that if he
failed to reach the correct landfall, he would work his way
along the shore until he arrived at the inlet and cottage he had
observed earlier. As it turned out, he came close by pure luck,
reaching land just to the left of the inlet.

In a matter of minutes he had hidden the boat ashore and
was back in his car. He set up the receiver/recorder on the
backseat of the car and activated the transmitter. A red light
came on, indicating that the receiver was picking up the electronic signal from the island. He put on a headset and listened.

At first he could hear only a jumble of sounds, muffled and unfamiliar, but then he was thrilled to identify the unmistakable squeak of bedsprings as someone changed sleeping positions. He thought for a moment that he could discern snoring; he dismissed the thought, refusing to believe his gadget could be that sensitive. Like most people who were not mechanically inclined, Koepp trusted machines only when he had personal experience with their reliability. In his hands things were malevolent.

After half an hour of futile eavesdropping, he turned down the volume and settled back in the car seat.

When he woke some hours later, the sun was up; light washed the treetops with iridescent green and filtered tentatively through the vegetation near his car. Something had awakened him; he experienced a moment of irrationality and confusion because he couldn't identify what it was.

"Are you awake?"

Koepp, startled by the intimacy of her voice, by its apparent closeness, sat upright in several stiff, jerky shifts of his body. Something about her voice compelled him to respond. "You bet I am, sweetheart," he said aloud; it came out half strangled by a yawn. He sounded pitiable.

More sounds of bed springs. A woman's laugh, gentle, teasing. A male grunt, muffled, thick with sleep. He heard the faint rustle of bedclothes, of someone moving. He imagined the actions that had created the sound: a man reaching out to bring the warm, yielding female body under the crook of his arm. More rustling. Weber's face emerged with startling clarity from the recesses of his memory, but Karen's countenance eluded him.

Both of Koepp's hands gripped the car's steering wheel; he noticed with detachment that the fingers were white, drained of blood by their desperate grip. A thin trickle of perspiration began under his arm and ran down his side. The sweat felt cold. Or maybe the sweat was warm and his skin was cold.

Curious that he couldn't even identify his own bodily sensations accurately. He turned the volume down to where he thought he would hear conversation and nothing else. He had too little experience with the system to know when that was. He had to guess.

After a long time, perhaps ten or fifteen minutes, he heard a muffled male voice. He turned the volume back up, in time to hear Karen's reply, "Yes, it was good, like before. It's always been good between us."

This time he could hear Weber clearly. "What time is it?"

A pause. "Six-thirty," she said. "Did you bring up some water last night? I want to take a bath."

The moan groaned. "Damn, I forgot. This place doesn't even have running water."

The woman laughed. "I'll heat some water for you if you like when I'm finished. You can take a sponge bath. That's what I do."

"That's not the same as a shower," he complained. "I'll wait until it gets warmer, then take a swim. I can enjoy your smell on me until after breakfast."

"Please!"

"Oh, sorry, your scent."

"That's better." Bedclothes rustled again.

"Where you going?" Weber asked, his voice edged with irritation.

"To make breakfast. We have to eat."

"You take your sponge bath," he told her. "I'll make breakfast." Suddenly, he seemed wide awake. "What have you got to eat?"

"Bacon and eggs," she answered proudly, as if that were a special accomplishment.

"All that cholesterol!"

"Bacon and eggs won't kill you. We're in the great north woods. We're not going to eat wheat germ this morning. Get with it."

After that the conversation ceased for thirty or forty minutes, to be replaced by the sounds of dishes being moved, metal pans being extracted from cupboards, water being poured from one container to another. These sounds of domesticity came through clearly from the powerful transmitter on the island, but distorted, so that Koepp was reminded what it was like to hear noise underwater. He also found it next to impossible to tell which sound sources were close to the sensitive microphone, which were far away. His concentration on the acoustics at this stage of his vigil presaged a long, boring day. Despite what he thought had been careful preparation, he had not even brought a book to read. He munched on crackers and corned beef.

The pair said little at breakfast, and nothing that might bear even indirectly on the Steiner case. What conversation he did hear seemed awkward and restrained, not the intimate verbal shorthand that lovers usually employed when they were alone. This cheered Koepp somewhat. He noticed also that Karen's phraseology and inflections betrayed either nervousness or outright anxiety. He couldn't judge much from the timbre of her voice—the electronics filtered out too much of the humanity—but he knew she sounded different now than when she talked with him. Although she bantered with Weber, the warmth was absent. This realization also comforted him emotionally. But events had tainted his solace; she was a tramp and a liar for certain, and she had revealed a penchant for manipulation and scheming that few women, at least those of Koepp's acquaintance, could rival.

Was she also a murderer? Her guilt or innocence alone mattered to Koepp. In time the other things, the deceit, even the promiscuity, could be rationalized if he found irrefutable evidence that she had no part in Steiner's death. He clung to his conviction that she was incapable of such an act, buoyed by the knowledge of how she had earned the respect of the other residents of Friars' Close. Could a woman who cared

about other people as she did stick a butcher knife in a man?
Was it possible that so much good and evil occupied the same
brain?

Koepp felt certain he knew the answers to those questions.
Now all he had to do was prove it—for her sake, but equally
for himself.

Following a leisurely breakfast, the couple in the cottage
unaccountably began the intimate sort of teasing that served
as a prelude to lovemaking. For several irrational moments he
couldn't believe they would do that to him again. He was
wrong. He heard sexual innuendos, whispered endearments.
His instruments were diabolical; they fed him every nuance
of developing lust, every sigh, each gasp from intimate physical contact, the breathiness of arousal. At some point Weber
had swept her into his arms because the footfalls of a single
person resonated in his earphones. Inexorably they grew
louder; he was carrying her back to the bedroom. It was as if
some invisible, malicious theatrical manager were directing
the action to center stage for Koepp's benefit, so he wouldn't
miss any of it.

But Koepp rebelled at enduring another coupling. He removed the earphones and turned down the volume.

He had no reason to turn it on again for some time. Shortly
after nine o'clock, both inhabitants of the island appeared,
fully clothed, on a thin ribbon of beach that faced Koepp's
vantage point. They filled several pails of water, carried them
into the cottage, and reemerged moments later. They pulled a
canoe from behind the privy and dragged it down the hill out
of Koepp's sight. The appearance of the canoe explained how
Karen had managed to get back to the island after leaving the
rowboat ashore for Weber.

When he could see them again, they were paddling the
canoe toward the north, parallel to the long axis of the mirror-
smooth lake, with Karen in the forward seat and Weber near
the stern. Koepp watched the graceful craft slowly shrink in

size, fantasizing that it was hurrying to a well-deserved rendezvous with infinity.

About two hours later they paddled back to the lonely island, only to depart once more by motorboat for the landing at the resort. A few moments after they debarked, Koepp caught sight of the Volvo driving along the access road back to the highway. Apparently they were going to the village, perhaps to buy supplies. Koepp lay down on the backseat to get some sleep, confident that the sound of the boat's outboard motor would wake him when they returned. He slept fitfully.

About two-thirty they came back to the cottage. Koepp was again in the front seat with the earphones to his head before they reached the island. They went inside only long enough to change into swimming suits, then reappeared on the beach. Karen dove into the lake, after making some teasing gestures about jumping in to her companion. Weber stepped down on the narrow beach near the boulders, touched the water experimentally with his foot and decided against going any further. Instead, he went back to the cottage for a deck chair, which he lugged to the shore. He settled down to read, ignoring the swimmer and her cries that he join her.

They stayed at the lakefront, well out of the range of Koepp's equipment, until a little after four o'clock. When they went inside, they spoke little to each other and then only about the most mundane subjects. Karen had brought some steaks. Weber would cook them on the grill. Yes, red wine was fine. Was there a radio in the cabin somewhere? Some music would be nice.

It wasn't until almost six o'clock, just as Weber was getting ready to take the steaks out to the grill, that they started to discuss the knife.

# ELEVEN

AT FIRST Koepp didn't know what they were talking about,
so innocuous was Karen's question. "Did you bring it?"

"Huh? Oh, sure," Weber said. "I told you I would. Don't
worry about it."

"How could I possibly not worry about it? Give it to me,
Roman."

"Hey, don't sweat it, baby, I'll get it for you when we get
ready to leave. That's my insurance policy, that's what I have
to keep in my possession so you don't run out on me. We
can't have—"

"You know I won't do that," Karen said with some impatience. "Whatever else I've done, I keep my promises.
Show it to me. I want to see it."

"I told you not to worry." Weber's voice had taken on an
edge. "I've kept it safe so far. You can trust me to make sure
it doesn't get into the wrong hands. Remember, baby, I could
have just turned it over to the cops. I could have been a pub-
lic-spirited citizen." He laughed in a way that was not pleasant to listen to through earphones; Koepp thought it probably
didn't sound much better to Karen. Koepp couldn't help it,
he was starting to enjoy their conflict. Weber continued, "It's
a good thing I was around to fish it out of the creek." He
pronounced it "crick."

That's when Koepp first became certain they were discussing the murder weapon. He had tried to believe they were
talking about something else. A miasma of depression enveloped him.

Webber, the bastard, was talking again. "Where would you

be if I had turned it over to that pig friend of yours—what's his name?

Karen didn't respond to that.

The conversation ended as suddenly as it had begun. Weber grilled the steaks. They ate dinner in almost total silence, then washed the dishes, also in silence. Even tied to them by so slight a strand as his bugging equipment, Koepp could still feel the tension inside the cottage.

A strange little exchange followed the dish washing. It had to do with Webber wanting a mirror and Karen objecting to his looking for one. For a few minutes Koepp was nonplussed, until he remembered that cocaine users often employed a mirror to lay out lines of coke.

The realization that the artist was going to get high accelerated Koepp's alarm; the tension inside the cabin was high enough without adding drugs.

Weber, apparently managed to get set up without Karen's help. He invited her three different times to join him, but each time she declined, quietly but firmly.

Darkness crept out of the heavily wooded shoreline, spread across the burnished surface of the lake and enveloped the cottage. Koepp, edgy with strain from his long vigil, removed the earphones and began to nibble on his soggy potato chips. He climbed out of the car to stretch. He kept thinking about the knife. Obviously, Weber had seen her drop it from the bridge. He had probably been manning a booth during the art show in the vicinity of the footbridge and walkway. Koepp could check that out later at Friars' Close. Why she wanted it back was equally obvious: so long as Weber possessed physical evidence, he was a potential witness against her in a murder trial. Without the knife, she probably reasoned, it would simply be a matter of her word against his. Koepp wondered if she really appreciated how precarious her situation was. Cocaine users frequently developed symptoms not unlike those experienced by psychotics; two homicides Koepp had investigated in the past eighteen months resulted from the delusions of heavy coke users. Believing themselves to be persecuted, they often carried firearms.

Koepp listened to the sounds from the cottage with growing apprehension. However, after a while Weber began to sound agreeable, even happy. He embarked on an egotistical soliloquy about his latest sculpture, which he claimed was going exceedingly well and in which a Chicago gallery had expressed an interest. Karen encouraged him to talk about his art.

"The subject is two amorphous, childlike forms, connected by sharing the same horizontal plane, but isolated from each other. It's existential, subjective, their minds are undergoing an exosmotic transformation—no, not their minds, dear lady, their spirits. It's personal, uniquely personal, yet it's shared, shared experience, until ultimately symbiosis emerges. For the person who mixes his life force with the metal, it's symbiotic."

Karen made the careful observation that it sounded very challenging.

The artist continued in the same vein for more than half an hour. Then, with a startling change of character, he began making amorous advances. Karen tried to discourage him, even pulled away from him physically, judging by the sounds of movement Koepp picked up. Webber's passion seemed to dissipate as rapidly as it had developed, much to Koepp's relief. After a short time, snoring—heavy, male snoring—became the dominant sound coming from the cottage. Later still, Koepp heard music. Probably a radio on the porch from the faint sound of it, he decided. He wondered what Karen was doing.

Satisfied that nothing would happen until morning, Koepp took off the earphones. He left the receiver/recorder on with the volume turned up. That way, if anything really noisy occurred, he might still be able to hear it through the earphones.

He decided to get some sleep, still sitting in the front seat, but with his head propped against the car window. He arranged a sweater to insulate his head from the chilly glass.

But sleep eluded him. With his eyes shut, the sounds of the night—the insignificant noises of unseen insects mostly—became discordant and irritating. His body wanted sleep, but his mind was hyperactive. His mind won.

Despite what he had overheard about the knife, he still had some reservations about Karen's guilt. She had disposed of the knife. To protect herself? Or to protect someone else? He knew he probably wasn't going to get the answer to that question by eavesdropping, but he had a more compelling reason to stay here. He had to protect her.

WHEN THE harsh sounds from his electronic umbilical awakened him, he was fully alert. His subconscious mind had probably been monitoring the sounds from the cottage, so he knew at least that the chaos inside had been going on for some time.

Both of them were now in the main room, not in the bedroom; Weber was doing most of the talking. His voice had a slurred, malevolent quality to it that had been absent earlier. By now the euphoria of the coke had probably been replaced by the inevitable depression. Depending on how long he had been on the stuff, Weber might be subject to hallucinations, which would make him exceedingly dangerous. Koepp felt inside his jacket for the .38, secured in a belt holster against his left hip. He took out the weapon to check it again; it was loaded. He put it back in its leather cradle.

"You were going through my stuff, you bitch!" Weber shouted at her. "Get the hell away from that bag." Karen didn't respond. But Koepp heard a faint shuffle, as if she had tripped over something. "You'll get the knife when I'm through with you."

Karen spoke then, her voice incredibly calm and determined. "I'll stay with you as long as you want, only give me the knife, Roman. You promised you'd bring it, but I don't even know if you did. At least show it to me."

He didn't answer her. Again Koepp heard the sound of movement, indecipherable, ominous because of its quickness. What the hell was going on? Then he heard the unmistakable sound of slapping, of flesh smashing against flesh, a sound that somehow overcame the inherent insensitivity to nuance of his sound system. He heard her cry out with pain. Her voice was choked with emotion or fear. "Get away from me, you bastard." If Weber had not struck her again, Koepp might have been able to restrain himself. The distant cottage exploded with the sounds of violence, with cries of pain, swearing, desperate movements all mixed together. Koepp was out of the car and stumbling through the darkness toward the shore. He tripped over a tree root and fell heavily on his left side; a quick stab of pain shot up his arm. He got up and continued toward the lake, only this time he proceeded more cautiously, his panic in check for the moment. As he moved, he couldn't help thinking about the absurdity of his position; he was going to have to go to the island, to a place where a murder might be in progress, and all he had to depend on was a toy boat!

It was right where he had left it, his oars tucked inside. In moments he was afloat, rowing with sure, powerful strokes across the still lake. He had trouble making out the contours of the island now for some reason; its shape seemed to blend in completely with the opposite shoreline. The silence, the calm through which his little inflatable passed, struck him as disorienting, wildly improbable, almost incomprehensible, after listening to the sounds of their conflict through the bug.

An eternity passed before the island suddenly gathered itself together out of the blackness. As he touched shore and scrambled out, the sounds of violence erupted once more from the little building on the cap of the island. Or at least he began to hear them again. His earlier visit to the island proved valuable now because he knew where the door was. He veered to the right, reached the corner of the cottage and stopped long enough to pull out his .38. It felt heavy, awkward.

Keeping low to the ground, he moved toward the door. He caught sight of a quick beam of light, which cut through the interior of the cottage like a glint from a giant scythe. A flashlight. A moment later Koepp saw a flashlight beam cross the room like a Fourth of July pinwheel. He heard a crash of breaking glass and the cabin returned to total darkness. The flashlight wasn't going to be a problem. Koepp's training began to reassert itself: don't go through a door without backup unless you know what's on the other side.

He transferred his .38 to his left hand and turned the cold doorknob with his right. He rushed quickly through the doorway. "Police, freeze," he said with a softness that sounded terribly inappropriate.

His instincts had been sure. All movement stopped within the main room of the cabin. The two figures off to his right, which were connected in some kind of savage embrace, stopped struggling immediately. He heard a distinct gasp from a female throat; the other sound was Weber's labored breathing. If he has a gun, I'm gone, Koepp thought with a strange, fearless detachment. Cautiously, he moved two paces to his left, getting away from the door and trying to confuse the other man. Enough light filtered in from outside for him to make out Weber's shape. Karen was right behind him, slightly less visible even though she seemed to be wearing some sort of white nightdress. Then Koepp realized that Weber stood out more because he was nude, or nearly so. His skin had a luminosity that separated him from the background colors. Koepp had to split the pair in case he needed to use his weapon.

"Get away from her," he told the man. "Right now. Get away."

The shape dropped something—Karen's arm?—and moved off a little to Koepp's left.

"Further. Keep moving." After a slight pause, the figure moved again. "It's Koepp, Karen, come over here." There was no hesitation from her; in moments she was standing at his side.

"Ray, thank God—"

He wasn't ready yet to have her talk to him. And he let her know it. "Shut up. Get some light in this place, Karen."

She moved around behind him, fumbled in the darkness for a few moments, then began to pump up a Coleman lantern. He could tell by the sound what it was. It was a remembered sound, a sound that he had been introduced to by his father on deer-hunting trips. A long time ago. But the boy in him remembered. Karen struck a match. More fumbling. A faint yellow-orange glow suffused the cabin interior, etching dark shadows from the backs of chairs, an empty vase.

Koepp felt a surge of relief because now he could make out his adversary clearly enough to be accurate if he had to shoot. Weber, attired only in a pair of Jockey shorts, stood next to a wooden table on which his duffel bag rested. He looked at Koepp with passive, sullen hatred.

"That's fine, Karen," Koepp said in what he hoped was a reassuring tone. "You—don't move until I tell you."

Karen found another lantern and lit it. She placed it on the mantel of the stone fireplace. Because it was higher, it bathed the room in light, enabling Koepp to see her clearly. She had several ugly red welts on the side of her face. Blood trickled from the corner of her mouth, from where it dripped down on her white chemise. The garment, insubstantial under any circumstances, had been torn so violently that it no longer covered her slight frame. She had abandoned any hope of covering herself from the waist up, so that she stood with her breasts exposed, and held what was left of the nightdress at her navel. He should have been enraged by her appearance, or moved to pity, or shocked, yet Koepp felt none of these emotions as he stared at her. All he could see was her wantonness. If she read condemnation in his eyes she was not intimidated by it; she met his gaze with dignity, and with something more. Defiance? Contempt?

With an effort, he managed to stop staring at her. "You'd better get some clothes on, Karen. And you're bleeding. Put some ice on your face if you've got any in this damned place."

"I know I'm bleeding, Ray," she answered. She decided to take care of the blood first, and went to the sink in what passed for a kitchen. She poured cold water from a pitcher into a metal bowl, then dabbed at her face.

Koepp noticed that Weber had never taken his eyes off the gun in his hand. He seemed fascinated by it, as if he had never seen one before. Perhaps staring into the barrel of a .38 focused one's attention.

Karen went to the bedroom to change.

Until now Weber had said nothing. "You got a warrant?" he wanted to know.

"I don't need one. Not when a felony's in progress."

"Felony!"

"Yeah, that's what aggravated assault is called. You're also a drug user. Consider yourself under arrest. I'm now advising you that anything you say can be used against you in a court of law. You have the right to remain silent. You have the right to engage an attorney. If you do not have the financial resources to hire an attorney, the court will appoint one for you."

"You can forget that shit. I heard it all on *Law & Order*.

"Good for you," Koepp said.

Weber looked very frightened. Which made him even more dangerous. "What are you going to do?"

"I don't have to tell you," Koepp said. "That's an advantage I have because I've got the gun." In fact, Koepp had been asking himself the same question. The best thing would probably be to search Weber's luggage first, make sure he didn't have any weapon, then get him dressed. After that they could wait for daylight, go to the resort by motorboat and call the local sheriff. It would mean a long and tedious wait, but Koepp had no intention of getting into a boat with Weber while it was still dark.

"At least let me put some clothes on," Weber said in a whining voice. "I'm freezing my balls off."

"I certainly hope so," Koepp said. "Stay right where you are for now."

Karen returned a few minutes later wearing a sweater and bluejeans. The bleeding seemed to have stopped. She stood next to the mantelshelf, exactly where she had been standing before, as if she were following the blocking instructions of some theatrical director. He wanted to go to her and put his arms around her, but the impulse passed in an instant; Weber was far too dangerous in his drugged condition.

"You can change in the bedroom now," Koepp said.

The man immediately turned as if he were going to the duffel bag on the table.

"Stop," Koepp commanded. "Stay away from that bag."

"My clothes—"

"Where are the clothes you took off when you went to bed?

"In there." He pointed toward the bedroom.

"Wear them. Move slow. I'm right behind you."

Koepp stood in the doorway while the man dressed. Weber took his time, suddenly loquacious. "I knew they'd find a way to drag me into this," he said. "As soon as I heard about Steiner, I knew they'd try to involve me. All of them were against me. You know, Jaroff, Karen, her old man, even Steiner."

"What are you talking about?"

"Friars' Close—all the damned people in it—they were all

scheming against me all the time. They were reporting me to the cops all the time, trying to get me on something." He slapped at his body as if he were tying to kill a mosquito. "Damned bugs, all over me. Bugs, bedbugs."

Koepp couldn't see any bugs on Weber or anywhere else in the room; it was too cold for bugs.

"Got to get my watch," Weber said. He held two bare wrists up for Koepp's inspection, just as Omsby/Tirquit had done a few days before.

"Where is it?"

Weber pointed at a shelf of paperback books behind the headboard. Koepp saw the watch and tilted his head slightly, signifying that the man could get it. Weber sidled around the foot of the bed, keeping as much distance between himself and the gun barrel as possible, then moved along the edge of the bed with his back to Koepp.

Karen had come up behind Koepp. He could feel her presence even though he couldn't see her.

"Ray—"

Her voice carried some urgency, distracting him for an instant, but he heard nothing after his name. His attention fixed on Weber, who was reaching across the head of the bed with his left hand to collect his watch. But the man had turned his body so that his right hand was not visible for a second.

Weber was reaching for something under the pillow.

"*Stop!*" Koepp cried.

"Only take a sec—it's right here." Weber tried to use the words to mislead Koepp, to put him off guard.

Koepp had let control slip from his grasp. He didn't know how to grab it back.

Weber turned slowly, holding up the watch in his left fist. Then his right hand came up as if it had been actuated by a giant spring. But Koepp had time to see the blue metal of the .45 automatic. He had time to feel the man's rage.

Then, because it was part of the macabre script, Koepp pumped two .38-caliber slugs into Roman Weber's vulnerable chest.

# TWELVE

THE BODY—already that was all that remained of Weber—pitched back against the wall, twisted onto the bed, and flopped onto the floor. It collapsed in a nearly horizontal position, except for its head, which propped itself against a pine closet door. Koepp studied his horrible handiwork. The corpse gave the impression of listening to noises from inside the tiny closet.

Karen was still standing behind him. Because he was leaning against the doorjamb, she could see Weber's body past his shoulder and arm. He blocked the doorway with his arm in case she had any idea of entering the room.

That was the furthest thing from her mind. She backed away from the bedroom, her face pinched with terror and revulsion.

Koepp's legs threatened to collapse. He staggered to the closest chair and dropped heavily into it. Karen had crossed the larger room to the kitchenette counter and sink. She put cold water on a paper towel and rubbed it on her forehead and the back of her neck.

For once Koepp could watch her with no emotional involvement at all; killing Weber had reordered his priorities.

In time he got control of his legs again. He walked to the sink, found a glass in the cupboard and filled it with water from an aluminum jug. He could still smell fear on her. They stood side by side for a few moments, staring out a double window into the darkness and the trees. Koepp glanced down at her at length and saw that her eyes had filled with tears. Her face had been drained of color by the ordeal. Instinctively, Koepp reached out with his left hand to grasp her shoulder.

He tried to turn her toward him, only she stiffened under his touch. Her rejection of his clumsy attempt to comfort her gave him an odd relief. Koepp the priest had failed again, but Koepp the cop had a lot of tidying up to do, and not much time to do it.

He turned to move away.

Then, unexpectedly, she was in his arms, clutching him around his waist. He encircled her shoulders with his arms, holding her gently, surprised by how fragile she was. Karen was sobbing now, her head tilted downward against his chest so that he could not see her face. Each sob sent a convulsion down her whole body.

He had no idea how long they stood together, locked in their shared misery, but he did know that he needed her now in his arms. She offered him human compassion, as he offered it to her. He needed somebody's acceptance: he had just killed another human being.

When she released him minutes later and stepped back, he said softly, "Those gunshots will wake everyone on the lake. Someone will be coming to investigate. I have to do some things before they get here. Do you understand what I'm saying, Karen?"

She nodded. Then she raised her face so she could look into his eyes. Her critical intelligence was at work once more, studying him.

There was a lot to do. In his mind Koepp had been arranging his priorities. He wanted to check on Weber's pistol first, to find out if it was loaded. He also had a lot of problems to contend with in removing all traces of his illegally employed bugging equipment. He had decided to drop everything in the lake; the trouble was that the microphone and transmitter were here on the island, while the receiver/recorder and earphones were ashore in his car.

He went to the bedroom and knelt beside Weber's body, which he explored for a pulse, even though there was no

possibility of finding one. He wanted to be able to swear under oath that he had made an effort to determine if Weber
was dead. The .45 pistol had fallen from Weber's hand onto
the bed. After donning gloves, Koepp picked it up and
punched a button on the side of the weapon. An ammunition
magazine popped out of the bottom of the gun butt into his
palm. The round nose of a .45-caliber cartridge was evident.
Next, he pulled the pistol's slide mechanism to the rear, expecting a bullet to be ejected; he was surprised when none
was. Weber knew pathetically little about guns, Koepp concluded, because the dead man had tried to shoot him without
a round in the chamber of the pistol. He would have had to
pull the slide back and return it to put a round in the chamber
and cock the firing pin. Weber's attempt to kill had been even
more foolhardy than it first appeared.

When Koepp emerged from the tiny bedroom moments
later, he saw that Karen had moved to within a few feet of
Weber's duffel bag. He was sure she hadn't dared to search
it yet; she would be waiting for a better opportunity, after he
went outdoors. Did she comprehend that he had been bugging
the cabin, that it was the only way to account for his timely
arrival? he wondered. He would try to mislead her if he could;
in the charged atmosphere in which she now found herself,
perhaps she could be duped.

"I came just in the nick of time," he said as he walked to
the duffel bag. He could see the bitter disappointment in her
eyes when she realized he was going to rummage through it.

"Yes, that was lucky. How did you—"

"I followed you here. I've been watching this place to see
who comes and goes. When I saw the flashlight beam moving
around, I thought something might be wrong. I came a little
closer just in case, then I heard him going after you. I thought
I better break it up."

She was watching him intently, giving no sign that she
believed or disbelieved his story. Her face registered relief

when he failed to discover the knife in Weber's belongings; that would mean she felt she could get back to Weber's place, find the knife herself and dispose of it. Koepp saw that a sardonic smile had formed on her mouth, off to the side, as she realized Weber had not brought the knife with him. She had surrendered herself to him repeatedly for something that he had no intention of giving her. Because neither of them had spoken of the knife, Koepp decided on a simple experiment to see if she really believed his story about arriving on the scene by good luck.

"Why, Karen? Why did you come up here with him?"

If she knew he had been bugging the place, then she also knew that Koepp had heard her beseeching Weber for the murder weapon. She took a long time to answer. "We used to be friends, actually something less than friends—if you recall our conversation about friends the other day. I wanted to convince him it was over."

"Convince him while you were wearing a negligee?"

"I know how it looks. But I needed time with him, to make him understand that I wasn't in love with him. And yes, I allowed him to make love to me again."

That was artfully done, the unpleasant truth unhappily revealed so that the rest of the lies will be more believable. Koepp knew now that she wasn't going to tell him about dropping the knife off the footbridge, or about Weber having it in his possession, or about anything else. He could still find explanations for her actions. She was, for instance, protecting someone else—Charlie Tirquit, maybe—when she dropped the knife in the creek. Yet everything she did made it more and more difficult to believe in her. He decided to shock the sense back in her head.

"Come with me, Karen," he said, taking hold of her left elbow. "I want you to come outside and see something."

She followed reluctantly, her face drawn tightly together as if she were prepared to ward off a physical blow. He dropped his hand from her elbow to her wrist, steering her to the window of the bedroom by dragging her behind him.

Koepp reached up with his free hand to the suction cup and pulled it off the window. She said nothing. He yanked the transmitter out from under the floorboards and held it in front of her. Still she said nothing. Her face was devoid of expression, of emotion.

"Stay here, Karen," he said. "I have things to do that better be done fast."

When he took off from the dock in Weber's boat the small outboard motor sounded like thunder to him. He hoped the lake residents had not come across his car yet and that the motor would not lead them directly to it.

He wondered if anyone had figured out where the gunshots came from.

With the outboard providing the power, the trip back to his car took only about one and a half minutes. Once ashore, he loaded the receiver in Donnie Bruce's metal box, conducted a careful inspection of the car and environs for incriminating residue and reboarded the boat. He wound the transmitter and microphone together with the wire that connected them, dropped the bundle in the chest, and shoved the chest overboard about one hundred yards from shore. He wondered, as the box filled with water before plunging out of sight, how much money this would cost him.

He put the outboard in forward gear and eased the bow around to point at the island again. Only then did he notice that the cottages around the lake were ablaze with lights. Fortunately, it was still too dark for anyone to have seen him "deep six" the electronic gear. Everyone heard his outboard, but he could claim a fisherman was out on the lake early. It was flimsy—but hard to disprove.

When Koepp reentered the cabin, Karen didn't look at him or speak to him. He didn't blame her.

They sat apart, Karen in a rocking chair in front of the north

window, Koepp next to the table. Neither of them spoke for
a long time, until dawn's gray light began to slither into the
cabin.

"Why did you show me—that thing?" she asked at last.
"I'm so stupid I would have gone on thinking you arrived
when you did by good luck."

Why had he done it? He knew what Diane would have said:
"You did it to punish her for not being your ideal woman."
Which was close to the truth. Why else did he do it, if not to
get revenge? She had done what no woman could do with
impunity; she had disappointed him in virtue.

He gave her no response.

She seemed not really to expect one.

They waited in silence for someone to come. At last they
heard the drone of outboard motors out on the lake. Koepp
walked to where he could stand behind Karen's chair and look
out at the lake over her shoulder; both of them watched two
small boats skimming toward their island. The boats spread
their wakes like great, sparkling wings behind them. Inside
the craft, as yet indistinguishable, sat several forms—lawmen,
emergency men, men charged like himself with setting right
whatever had unbalanced the pristine peace.

Society had sent them to censure and to tidy up. And perhaps to punish.

THERE WERE four men in all, three of them in uniform. Two
of the uniformed men expertly tied up the first boat. The
patches on their arms identified them as members of the Granite County rescue team. They looked expectantly at Koepp.

"You won't need any gear. There's a dead body in the
house."

A sandy-haired man, who appeared to be in his early
thirties, nodded and moved past Koepp without saying anything. He headed for the house, followed by his Hispanic

companion. The second man carried a first-aid kit and an oxygen tank. He also said nothing.

A second boat pulled along the dock on the side opposite the first boat. The younger man, the one in the uniform of a deputy sheriff, tossed Koepp a line from the bow, then scrambled to the stern to jump onto the dock as the boat skipper backed down. He fastened his line to a cleat on the dock just as Koepp had done. The boat driver was tall and gaunt, a man in his late fifties or early sixties. He wore the shirt and trousers issued by the county under a handsome brown leather jacket. A western-style hat completed his carefully fashioned ensemble; the man looked the way a sheriff was supposed to look.

"You Sergeant Koepp?" the sheriff asked. He pronounced it "Keep."

Koepp nodded. "You Sheriff Bergan?" he asked.

The other man nodded and shut off the outboard motor. The two of them stood for a moment in silence, two lawmen measuring each other. Bergan was as tall as Koepp. His face looked as leathery as his jacket, but more weather-beaten and furrowed, like driftwood. His eyes were as dark as obsidian and sunken deep in his skull like those one saw in the peripheral characters in El Greco paintings.

His young companion appeared to have been selected for deputy on the basis of his contrast to his boss. He was short, plump, and smiled constantly.

They went up to the cabin. The two paramedics, their faces white and strained, reported that Weber was dead and told the sheriff how he had died. Bergan asked them to go back to the mainland and to call the district attorney right away. "Tell him I'll need a scene-of-the-crime unit from the state crime lab," Bergan said laconically. "Find the coroner and tell him and the DA what's going on."

The pair returned to the boat. Koepp and the two lawmen went inside. They stopped to look at Karen, who had remained in the rocking chair. Koepp realized that she wore no makeup and looked uncharacteristically disheveled; her face reminded Koepp of travelers in an airport after a long wait. Now she appeared surprisingly homely; perhaps she was one of those women whose beauty emerged from her animation.

Bergan didn't spend much time with the body. He removed his hat, introduced himself and his deputy to Karen and invited Karen and Koepp to join him at the main table. Once upright, Karen seemed to rouse herself from her stupor. "I'll make some coffee," she said. She didn't wait for the sheriff's permission. Bergan watched her for a while with frank curiosity but with no apparent moral judgement. Koepp found himself starting to like the man.

Sheriff Bergan asked Koepp who the dead man was and listened patiently to his explanation. In repose, the lawman's leathery features reminded Koepp of a bassett hound's, intelligent but sad.

"I'd like to get statements," Bergan said.

"We understand, Sheriff," Koepp said. "It was self-defense. I have no objection to giving you a statement."

The sheriff glanced up at Karen, who numbly nodded her assent. He didn't look too happy about their decision; Koepp guessed that the man felt his life would be much easier if both of them refused to talk to him. He bent over to make some laborious notes with arthritic fingers at the top of a notepad.

"Your lieutenant called about you," Sheriff Bergan said. "He told me you were going to be on a stakeout. I didn't figure it'd turn out like this." He looked at Koepp with a grave expression. "Guess you didn't, either." He chuckled; it came out dry and mirthless, the sound of a man trying to laugh who was sadly out of practice.

Gently, he asked Karen to tell him everything that happened the day before. She proceeded to do so in a dispirited monotone, as if she were repeating some other person's experiences rather than her own. Koepp had to admit she told it pretty much the way it happened. She didn't mention Koepp's bugging device.

"How is it you came when you did, Koepp, like John Wayne, just in the nick of time?" the sheriff asked.

"I heard a lot of noise. He sounded violent."

"You heard the noise from shore—the east shore?"

"No, I was about a hundred feet offshore. I was sitting in an inflatable." Lie number one. He probably would have to tell it again at the inquest. Under oath. Thou shalt not take the name of the Lord, thy God, in vain.

"Describe the shooting again," the sheriff requested of Karen.

As she related it, her recollection of the shooting was identical to his. Her self-possession, given the traumatic circumstances, was remarkable. "If Sergeant Koepp hadn't come in, well, he was beating me, Sheriff," she added.

"Yes, that's plain enough," Bergan said. He glanced at the welts on her face briefly, then shifted his attention back to the stenographer's pad balanced on his knee. "Why did he try to kill Sergeant Koepp, Mrs. Merrick?"

"I don't know. The drugs, I suppose. He used cocaine. He snorted some earlier in the evening. First he was high, upbeat. Later, he became mean and abusive. That was his pattern."

"Why did you come here with him if that's the case?"

"I planned to end our—affair. I was going to tell him."

"Why? Why break off the relationship? Why come here with him to do it."

"The relationship? I'm a married woman. I was ashamed of what I was doing. I came here with him so no one would be around to witness a scene. I knew he'd be upset. I hoped to get him through it here—isolated." She stopped to gain her composure; she looked thoroughly despondent. "Also, I didn't want to tell him at home because he had made threats against my children if I—"

"What kind of threats?"

"He said he'd teach my son the joys of cocaine. He knew I hated his drugs. I would do anything to protect my children."

Koepp wondered with interest whether the drug threat had any truth to it, or whether it was another extemporaneous lie. Thou shalt not bear false witness against thy neighbor.

Their interrogator seemed loath to press her further. He turned his attention back to Koepp. "I'm curious why your department sent you up here to do a simple stakeout. Why didn't you have us do it? Would have saved a lot of money."

But it wouldn't have gotten an illegal bug planted, Koepp thought. He wondered how much Bergan suspected. Probably all of it; the man was no fool.

"We weren't sure who would show," Koepp said. "We wanted somebody here who knew the potential visitors by sight." Lie number two.

The sheriff nodded thoughtfully. "You folks better get your traveling clothes together. This place will be off limits to civilians for a few days. And Bud Wagner, the DA, will want to see you down at the county seat. That's in Forest Junction. Anyway, I got to stay here till the coroner and the crime lab boys get through." He sounded apologetic that he wouldn't be available to act as their host.

They went ashore in the aluminum boat that had borne Roman Weber to the tiny island. The ever-smiling deputy, who said his name was Robert Haskell, accompanied them. Once ashore, they were confronted with the kind of prosaic complication that inevitably takes on comic proportions in times of high drama: what to do about all the cars? Haskell thought they all should ride to Forest Junction in a county vehicle. But they had to go to Koepp's car on the other side of the lake so he could get his clothes. Maybe Koepp should drive his own car. But then, what about Mrs. Merrick's car? If they all rode together, then people would have to come back for both cars. That seemed pretty stupid.

Eventually the deputy decided that Mrs. Merrick should follow him to Koepp's car, then all three would drive to the county seat. Haskell would maintain a loose custody of sorts by driving last in the formation.

They stopped for breakfast in a small diner which smelled of cigar smoke and bacon grease. The place was filled with avuncular men of indeterminate age, most of whom were attired in mackinaws and bluejeans. Except for a skinny waitress, there were no women in the place. The restaurant announced through its smells, the deer trophy on the wall, and the knotty pine that this was one of the last bastions of male dominance in small-town America. The other customers studiously avoided noticing Karen, the interloper.

Because it was too early for Margaret to be at work, he called her at home. She answered almost immediately, although it sounded like she hadn't been up long. Koepp knew from experience that she would be fully functional; good cops could wake from a sound sleep and be clearheaded. He told her that he had killed Roman Weber in self-defense and that he was going to see the Granite County DA. ''Get to Weber's apartment with a lab unit and find that damned knife. But tell them to give it the works. We might turn up some fibers to match those on the stiff.''

''Why do you think the knife is there?''

''That's a long story,'' Koepp said.

''Is—was Weber the one who killed Steiner?''

''Probably not. But he has the knife.''

''Okay. What else?''

''Tell Tarrish what's going on. Internal affairs will want to send somebody. Tell them to make it a lawyer.''

''Are you—''

''I'm all right, I think. Karen was a witness. She confirmed it was self-defense. I'd feel better with a lawyer around is all.''

''We found out where Omsby was living before he went

to Friars' Close," Margaret said. "I'll start checking out his neighbors."

"No, I'll do it when I get back."

"Ray, who *do* you think killed Steiner?" she asked in a voice soft with concern.

He paused a long time before he answered. The phone line buzzed loudly, as if it, too, were impatient to hear his answer. He knew what he was going to say, only he couldn't get the words to come out. It was as if verbalizing his suspicions would confirm them. "Maybe it was Karen."

An even longer pause occurred. Finally, she said, "Ray, I'm sorry."

"About Karen?"

"No, I'm sorry you had to kill a man."

After breakfast Karen made a phone call also, presumably to her lawyer, although she didn't tell them anything. Then Haskell called Bud Wagner, the DA, and had a long discussion with him; the deputy appeared to be very nervous when he got back to the booth. "DA says to stay here for about fifteen minutes. He'll stop by on his way to the courthouse. Wants to talk to youse both."

So they waited, toying with cups of coffee, listening to Haskell prattle on about how much violence there was, how dangerous it was to be a cop, how everyone, even kids, had guns, how the damned NRA seemed to want to get every peace officer in the country shot. "Half of the men in this place got a handgun stuck away somewhere," he said, waving his hand in an arc for emphasis. "That ain't bad enough, now they're all drugged up. I'm telling you, it's getting real dangerous to be a cop."

Koepp assumed he was saying all of this to impress Karen with his bravery. Just sitting silently, looking beat and rather homely, she could excite a man. Karen was a complex, dangerous woman.

"Good thing you was ready for him. He'd akilled you, sure

as I'm sitting here. Especially with that .45. Nasty weapon. Saw some bodies once—wife and two kids—can you believe it, kids—that their old man shot with a .45. Never saw anything like it. Nasty weapon, a .45.''

Koepp had stopped paying attention when the deputy talked about how Weber would have killed him. That was something he hadn't let himself think about until now. Would Weber have tried to shoot him? Or was he only looking for a chance to control the situation until he could get away? Did he have to be killed? Could he have been stopped with a warning? What if Koepp hadn't made the mistake of letting him reach under the pillow? Did part of him suspect that Weber would go for a gun—that part of him that might have wanted to kill a rival? No answers came back to him from the recesses of his consciousness. Was it because the chemistry of his emotions somehow snuffed out the answers, or because no answers existed?

The promised fifteen minutes turned to thirty, then to forty-five. And suddenly he was there. His presence filled the room. You didn't have to see him; he was one of those men whose aura preceded him, announced his coming, served notice that he was Emil ''Bud'' Wagner, the duly elected man primarily charged with keeping order in the sprawling piece of geography known as Granite County.

In this place he was the law, by God.

# THIRTEEN

THE IMMENSITY OF the man startled Koepp. He stood at least six feet four. And he was wide. His shoulders looked as if they had come off a large bovine; his chest and stomach strained against his tweed sports jacket. He wore a western-style string tie; it almost got lost visually, so massive was the expanse of blue shirt behind it. His head was shaved to gleaming incandescence; it reminded Koepp of pink marble. But the focal point was a luxuriant red handlebar mustache, a really fine specimen which curled up at both ends in near perfect symmetry. Koepp was sorry about the color of the mustache. He held a prejudice against redheads, ever since an unfortunate experience with a bully during his freshman year at the seminary.

Just standing in the doorway, Wagner had made his presence felt throughout the restaurant, a condition he now amplified by moving his huge bulk between the tables of diners. Even though no one had to get out of his way, other men seemed to recede as he approached; he diminished everything around him. He caught the waitress's eye, which took no effort at all, and pointed a huge finger at a table in the corner which had been vacated recently. The pointing finger looked like a banana to Koepp. She hurried to clean the table, sweeping the crumbs from its surface to the floor with abandon. The lawyer looked at Haskell, who immediately nodded.

"DA wants us to sit at that table," the deputy informed them. The request made sense; there was certainly no way Wagner could insert his bulky frame into the booth. The three of them sat on the sides nearest the wall, leaving the outside edge of the table entirely to the attorney. No one attempted to make introductions.

As it turned out, they weren't necessary. "Have Mrs. Merrick and Sergeant Koepp given statements to the sheriff?"

"Yes," Haskell said.

"You hear them do it?"

"Sure did, Mr. Wagner."

"Fine," the attorney said. "Wait for me outside."

As soon as the officer was out of earshot, Wagner said, "When you leave here, go to the Camelot Resort—it's on the main highway on the south edge of town. They'll take you in even though the sign outside says they're closed. Don't leave the place unless I tell you to. The owner, Holly, will fix something for you to eat, so there's no reason to go out. The press will be coming around pretty soon. You'll have nothing to say to them. This will make it easier for you."

Karen started to say something, but Wagner held up a hand, demanding silence. "I'll talk now. You talk later. I'm going to ask the circuit court judge to schedule an inquest on this shooting ASAP. That may be as early as tomorrow afternoon, depending on how much time the crime lab boys need to work over the cabin. The body will be moved to the county hospital, where a pathologist from the university will do the autopsy. At the inquest you can have counsel, but your lawyer can't say anything. A jury of six will decide one thing, whether or not the shooting was justifiable. If they say it was, that'll be the end of it. If they say it wasn't, then we'll have a full investigation. I'll ask for a closed inquest, so there won't be any spectators. Any questions, problems, whatever, call me at this number. If I'm not there, somebody will find me." He gave each of them one of his business cards. Koepp looked at his. At the top of the card, above the address and phone information, was an artist's drawing of a handlebar mustache.

"If you haven't got a lawyer, get one. And don't do it by looking in the Yellow Pages."

"We've both got lawyers coming," Koepp said. His voice sounded defensive to him.

Wagner didn't seem to notice. "From what little I know about this incident, my guess is it's going to turn into a media circus. Now, I can keep them out of the inquest and off your backs until then, but I can't break their cameras." He looked at Karen with a fierce expression. "You're going to get crucified, Mrs. Merrick. That would happen anytime after something like this, but on top of the Steiner killing…" He paused. "That's the price you have to pay for living in a country that thinks free speech is a good idea."

"I know," she mumbled. It surprised Koepp that she seemed to be afraid of him. Often, men who frightened other men didn't frighten women at all. Wagner was different: he scared everybody.

"When your lawyers show up, have them get in touch with me ASAP," he said. "Any questions?"

They had none. Wagner departed as he had come, his nimbus diminishing people and physical objects as he passed.

Despair began to suffocate Koepp; he had been hoping, expecting, to tell his yarn to a country bumpkin.

KOEPP'S ROOM was located at the corner of the lodge on the second floor, overlooking a lake that reflected the gunmetal color of the lowering sky. Large sliding-glass doors led to a small concrete veranda from where the view of the lake was especially dreary. Koepp had showered and dressed earlier and now sat on a lawn chair on the veranda. The day was humid, threatening rain, although the temperature was mild enough that he could sit outdoors comfortably. He had been listening to the sounds of water running from the next room, her room, but now the lodge was quiet as a church on a summer afternoon. He assumed she had gone to bed, which is what he had planned to do; only he knew he couldn't sleep with all the turmoil in his mind. He wondered if he would ever be able to sleep again.

To keep the terror at bay—the sharp images of Roman Weber's shocked body pitching over the bed and jackknifing into the closet door—he went over in his mind what he planned to do to bring this cursed case to a conclusion. That is, what he would do if he remained assigned to it after this. The internal affairs department surely would take a dim view of what he did. Killing a man in self-defense was one thing. With Karen, the only witness, corroborating his story, he had little to fear on that score. But how could he explain that he rowed out to the cabin when all he was supposed to be doing was conducting a stakeout? He didn't want them to take him off the case even though it was eating his soul; he had to finish it himself.

He heard a rap at his door, and went to answer it. He had expected to meet the proprietress; instead he found Karen standing in the long hallway, wearing a bathrobe and slippers with tiny tassels on their topsides. Her hair shone brightly even in the dimness of the corridor.

"I'd like to talk to you," she said. "He didn't say we couldn't talk to each other."

Koepp felt himself grin a little. "That's right. He didn't." Koepp opened the door and stepped back to let her pass. She sat down on the end of the bed, leaving the only comfortable chair in the place vacant for him. But Koepp sat down on a straight-back chair from the writing desk so they could be closer together.

"God, I wish I had a cigarette," she said.

"I didn't know you smoked."

"I did, for years. I quit four years ago, but I really miss the damned things at times like this."

"Do you have many times like this?"

She looked startled by that. Then she smiled. "Good point," she said. Some color had returned to her face. She studied Koepp carefully for a few moments, just as she had so often before. "It will be all right, Ray," she said. "A jury will see it just like I did. It wasn't intentional. You had no choice. They'll rule it was self-defense."

"Probably." His voice carried no optimism, a deficiency that she noticed.

She sought to reassure him. "You didn't set out to kill him, Ray."

"Didn't I?"

Her face registered genuine shock. "My God, what are you saying?"

"Maybe I was looking for an excuse to get rid of him, to get revenge." He blurted it out, trying to drive some of his guilt into her. Make her feel some of what he was feeling.

Karen looked at him with a guileless expression. When it suited her, she could disguise totally what she was thinking. For some reason he found himself contrasting her inscrutability with Margaret's openness. Women, he decided, differed more at their extremes than men did.

Her diffidence annoyed him. "I had the place wired, Karen. I heard it all. I heard you making love to him. I thought about how much pleasure I would get blowing away his private parts. Then a little while later, I did kill him. That's something the jury won't know about."

"Did you intend to kill him when you came into the cabin?" Her voice was devoid of emotion.

"I hope not."

She had not acknowledged in any way that he had made a kind of revelation of his feelings for her. She didn't now. Instead, she changed the subject to what she had probably wanted to talk about in the first place. "You heard us arguing about the knife, of course."

He nodded dumbly.

"He saw me drop it in the creek during the art fair. His booth was the closest one to the footbridge. I thought no one was watching." She studied him very carefully now. "He fished it out. That's why your officers didn't find it when they used the metal detector. He called me later to tell me what he had done."

Koepp didn't say anything.

"I tried to get him to give it back to me," she continued. "He wouldn't, of course. He made me bargain for it. I was never in love with him, Ray. I ended the relationship months ago. But I had no choice about coming here. I had to get the knife."

"It's probably in his apartment. They're looking for it now."

"When they find it, are you going to arrest me?"

He wasn't sure then if she really didn't understand the situation or was simply being disingenuous. In either case it didn't matter if he told her the truth; her lawyer would explain it soon enough anyway. "You don't have much to fear from the knife, now that I've conveniently eliminated Weber from the scene."

"What do you mean?"

"He can't testify that he saw you drop it in the creek."

"But you heard us arguing about it. I've just admitted it."

"I found out what you did with an illegal bugging job. That's inadmissible evidence."

She paused to think about that. Maybe she was experiencing the lag in comprehension common among private citizens when they were involved in a criminal proceeding for the first time: factual reality and courtroom admissibility were often vastly different.

"But I wouldn't get overconfident," he continued. "You're still a prime suspect in Steiner's murder. *I* know about the knife, which narrows the field of suspects. If you didn't do it, then you're protecting somebody who did. Maybe Charlie Tirquit, maybe your husband. You deserve special attention yourself because of that money you paid Steiner for almost a year—the two hundred dollars per month.''

"I've already explained to you that the money was for therapy," she said, staring out the window toward the sullen lake.

"Want to tell me about it?''

"No.''

"That's a bad idea, Karen," Koepp said. "It's just plain stupid. You better play it straight with me. You haven't got anybody else.''

She sighed and flicked at the corner of her eye with a small white handkerchief which appeared mysteriously from somewhere. "My father died when I was eight yours old. A year or so later my mother remarried. My stepfather was no good. He didn't work regularly, he drank too much and he beat up on my mother.'' She paused for a little while to stare out the window, giving herself time to decide what to say. Finally, she looked at Koepp once more. Her eyes were dry now. "Red—that was his name—sexually abused me, almost from the day she brought him into our house.'' Another long pause ensued. "Do you want to know specifically what he did to me, or is it sufficient if I tell you that he fondled and kissed me, raped me before I was eleven and sodomized me. He did other things, too, and made me do things to him, but that gives you the high points," she said in an unnaturally high voice. "This was not an isolated experience. He came into my room whenever he was drunk, which was pretty often. It became almost normal eventually.''

"What about your mother? Didn't she—''

"At first she pretended it wasn't happening, then she told me that it wouldn't hurt—what Red was doing—and that he'd quit soon. In time the cops solved the problem for her—God knows, she couldn't deal with it—and picked him up for fencing stolen television sets. He'd been arrested before and was on parole, so they hauled him back to prison. By the time he came back I was in college. I didn't go home again.''

"And the reason you went to Steiner is because you were trying to get therapy to deal with the problems of your stepfather?"

"Yes. It seems grotesque now, because of what Steiner turned out to be, but that was my intent at the time, to get cured."

Koepp knew what was coming next and hated to put her through it. Still, he had no choice. And maybe now, committed as she was, she had to tell the whole sordid story.

"Steiner was helpful in the beginning, kind, considerate, and very wise," Karen said. "He really did help me at first. Later, of course, he proved to be very little different than my stepfather. The only difference was Red was violent and Issac wasn't. But they were both sexual deviates."

Koepp tried to encourage her. "Tell me about Steiner."

"He was a voyeur. But I didn't know anything about him at first. You have to trust your therapist if you have any hope of recovery. That trust gave him enormous power over me because I told him everything. He encouraged me to. Anyway, I wanted to tell someone. I'd felt dirty, guilty, debased for years. I had to find some way to deal with it and start to lead a normal life. I was a married woman with two children who was still only nine years old in terms of sexual development. Issac said it was important for me to act out whatever it was that was holding me back from reaching maturity."

Her throat rippled as she swallowed hard. Tears filled her eyes once more; she turned away from Koepp so that he could only see her in profile. "It must have been awful," Koepp said. He didn't want to hear any more; it was like listening to confessions again.

"Issac never touched me that I can recall," she said. "His form of rape was more subtle, more permanent." She raised a hand languidly to stop him from saying anything; it was more like a warning. "He convinced me that I could put things right if I would act out certain fantasies. He said that

I used sex as a means of punishing my mother when I was little, that I wasn't entirely the victim. Red actually preferred me to my mom. I can remember lying in the dark waiting, then hearing him bumping into things in the kitchen. I'd pray that my mom would let him come to bed with her, that she wouldn't lock him out of the bedroom because he was drunk. Sometimes she didn't. I can remember crying with relief, knowing that he wasn't going to come for me. But Steiner said I also felt rejected on those occasions, that a part of me really wanted to seduce him from my mother's influence.''

"How did Steiner treat you?" Koepp asked, not knowing what else to do.

"How did I treat him, you mean?" She laughed bitterly. "I'm the one who did the therapy. Oh, I put on quite a show." She began to rush her words, anxious to get it over with. "He planned each session for me. Sometimes he even wrote out a script for me to follow, but mostly he depended on me to be creative. He said my own creativity was the best way to expunge my guilt. He made me pretend—re-create—the things I had to do with Red. I could never be sure but I think he recorded everything I said. Sometimes he told me to act and talk like a prostitute, you know, say obvious and provocative things, debase myself. That was the substance of what he wanted, to see me debase myself totally."

Koepp was unable to say anything.

"You can't understand the power he had over me," Karen said. "Nobody can unless they've been through it. You believe in him because you know you may not get another chance."

Even though Koepp tried not to let the image of that scene form in his mind, he could see her cowering in front of the malevolent eyes of Issac Steiner. The last traces of sympathy which he had experienced while looking at the crumpled corpse in the computer room ebbed away.

She turned away from him and lay down on the bed. For

a long time she didn't say anything else. She was slipping away from him; having made some subtle plea for understanding to which he was powerless to respond, she would simply drift beyond the reach of his stunted empathy.

A part of Koepp, the part that had once been a priest, wished he could intervene; he knew that only through physical comforting of some kind could he forestall what he saw happening to her. Yet he was frozen in his chair, unable to offer solace. He could not go to her. The distance between them was too great, both because of what she had shared with him in her pathetic confession and because of what she had inadvertently revealed about herself. She could have killed Steiner after all; indeed, it was almost inevitable that she would kill him. Debasement and degradation were motives every bit as credible as avarice or revenge.

The room was closing in on him. To get some air, he went out on the concrete porch, where he stood watching the roiling clouds. He didn't hear her leave.

TWO PEOPLE came to the lodge that afternoon about one-thirty. One of them was a police lieutenant from internal affairs, the other a lawyer from the district attorney's office in Koepp's home county. Her name was Kate Munyos, his Ben Levine. He met them in the dining room for a late lunch served by the ubiquitous proprietress of the Camelot herself.

Koepp went over his story several times for the pair. The attorney, a woman in her mid-to-late forties, asked him how it was that he arrived in time to stop the beating. She listened to his explanation that he was just sitting offshore in his toy boat and heard some noise. It displeased her. She looked at Levine to see how he was taking it. The lieutenant wore a pained expression as well. Ms. Munyos didn't press the matter, though, probably because she could see it was as good an explanation as she was likely to get. At least it couldn't be disproved with physical evidence. Later in the afternoon they went to the third floor of the county courthouse to give District Attorney Wagner a statement. While Koepp was waiting for a stenographer to transcribe what he said, he saw Karen pass by the door of the meeting room in which he waited with Munyos and Levine. A tall, distinguished man bearing a large alligator briefcase accompanied her. He assumed that she was about to give her statement to the DA as well.

Toward late afternoon Koepp received a phone call from Margaret. A clerk suggested that he might like to take it in Wagner's office, a place that turned out to resemble a warehouse more than someone's work station. Koepp concluded that either Wagner didn't spend much time there or he had insufficient staff to do any filing; file folders and law books were stacked everywhere, including the floor, and at first he had trouble even finding the telephone. He discovered it setting, inexplicably, on the district attorney's oversize swivel chair.

Margaret reported that a lab team had searched Weber's apartment. They had found the knife, which Tom Sturmer said matched the wounds in Steiner's corpse perfectly. The knife had been wiped clean; no fingerprints. Margaret had not bothered to look for fibers in Weber's clothing to match those found on Steiner's shirt because, she explained, the fibers in question came from the second sweater they had taken from Paul Merrick.

Koepp brought the phone conversation to an abrupt halt in order to answer a summons to a meeting in one of the unused courtrooms. The DA wanted everyone assembled who was involved in Weber's killing.

Wagner was waiting for them, his huge bulk deposited precariously on top of a wooden railing that separated the audience seats from the witness box and judge's podium. Karen and Koepp sat in the first row of the spectators' seats, with their lawyers one row behind them. Wagner held up the statements the two of them had signed earlier.

"These two documents support one another," he said. "That means either (a) they are *ipso facto* true statements or (b) you've rehearsed your story to perfection."

"Mrs. Merrick's statement is true, sir," the distinguished lawyer from the prestigious law firm said.

Wagner stared at the man with a distaste that bordered on contempt. "Let me tell you another version which I think makes as much sense as the one in these statements. Koepp here and Mrs. Merrick are lovers. This guy Weber, her soon-to-be ex-lover, objects to being displaced and keeps causing trouble. These two decide to get rid of him. So Mrs. Merrick lures him to the cottage. She plants a .45 automatic which Koepp has given her—for a cop to have extra handguns around isn't unusual. At a prearranged time Koepp goes to the island, pumps a couple of rounds into Mr. Weber and the two of them settle down to wait for Sheriff Bergan."

"Pure conjecture." The distinguished lawyer snorted. Wagner's contemptuous manner evidently still rankled.

Wagner grinned; it was not a pleasant sight. "Okay, try this one. Things happened like Koepp and Mrs. Merrick said except that the sergeant wasn't just floating around in his bathtub boat like he claimed. That statement is silly. So how did he ride to the rescue with such timeliness? Easy. He had an illegal bug on the place. When he heard things getting nasty, he jumped into his boat and paddled out to rescue the lady in distress. How does that one sound?"

This time lawyer Munyos felt compelled to object. "To quote my learned colleague: 'Pure conjecture,'" she said. "Where is the evidence?"

"At the bottom of Granite Lake, Counselor, if that's the right scenario." He withdrew a small notebook from the inside pocket of his sport jacket; with a pronounced squint he consulted it. Then he said, "Unless I tell you otherwise, be here by two o'clock tomorrow. Inquest starts around two-thirty. Judge Phillip J. Gregory will preside. Don't talk to anybody, especially the press. Any questions?''

Nobody had any.

Wagner directed his attention to Koepp and Karen. ''I wanted you to know I see various scenarios here. You might think about that before the inquest tomorrow. In case you've not been informed by your learned counsel, you should know that a coroner's inquest is advisory. The jury may decide the shooting was self-defense. Maybe I won't like it if that happens. Then I might just charge you—Sergeant—with homicide and the little lady with conspiracy.''

# FOURTEEN

"YOU DO SOLEMNLY SWEAR that you will diligently inquire and determine on behalf of this state when, and in what manner and by what means, the person known as Roman Weber, who is now dead, came to his death and you will return a true verdict thereon according to your knowledge, according to the evidence presented and according to the instructions given to you by this court," Judge Gregory said.

The sixth and last juror to be selected, a stocky, middle-aged salesman with a florid complexion, answered yes and withdrew his hand hastily from the bible on which it had rested. He looked around for instructions. The district attorney told him to take his seat in the jury box. Because there were only a half dozen of them, the jurors had left vacant chairs between themselves.

Two potential jurors had been dismissed, one by the judge based on his own examination, one at the request of the district attorney.

The judge, a slight man with thinning hair and a pronounced paunch, instructed them on their duties. They were to determine the probable cause of death and were to return a unanimous verdict based upon the evidence presented. He explained the phrase "probable cause" to them. Several jurors nodded that they understood. Their verdict should indicate whether the deceased came to his death by criminal means and, if so, the specific crimes committed and the name of the person or persons who committed the crimes, or whether the deceased came to his death by natural causes, accident, suicide, or an act privileged by law. When he saw the puzzled expressions on their faces, he said, "Self-defense is an act privileged by law. In other words, a man can legally kill another man if he does so only to keep the other man from killing him.''

Wagner called his first witness, a pathologist from the state university. He was a younger man with black hair and a swarthy complexion. In his neat dark-gray suit he looked distinctly out of place. The judge administered the oath.

After a few questions regarding his name, address, place of occupation, and qualifications, Wagner asked if he had conducted an autopsy on the body of Roman Weber.

"Yes, sir," the doctor answered.

"What was the cause of death?"

"Death was instantaneous and was caused by gunshot wounds—one shot passed through the left ventricle of the heart, one passed through the aorta.''

"When did the death occur?"

"Between three and four A.M. on June 3."

"Are there any other facts which you discovered in your autopsy which might have a bearing on this inquiry?"

The pathologist shifted position in the witness chair. "Yes. I found high cocaine concentrations in the blood of the deceased. Also, his nasal passages were ulcerated.''

"Indicating what?"

"It's a condition characteristic of a long-term habit of inhaling cocaine.''

Wagner looked at the judge, who glanced at the witness, then surveyed the impassive jurors. "You're dismissed, Doctor," he told the pathologist.

Sheriff Bergan took the witness stand next. After a few starter questions from Wagner, he told the jury in a conversational tone what had happened on the island from the time of his arrival until the crime lab team from the state capital joined him.

Wagner walked to a table that stood next to the court stenographer along the wooden railing that separated the judge from the spectators. He picked up Koepp's gun and showed it to the sheriff. "Do you recognize this weapon, Sheriff?" he asked.

"That's a .38. I took it from Sergeant Koepp when I arrived at the scene of the shooting. It has my tag on it." He pointed to a buff-colored tag wired to the barrel. The same sequence occurred again, only this time the weapon was the .45 which Weber had taken from beneath the pillow. The sheriff explained where he had found it.

A technician from the crime lab, the next witness, also identified the .38; he stated that an examination of the slugs found in the body of the deceased showed they were fired from the first gun the sheriff had identified. The young man pointed out that he had initialed Sheriff Bergan's tag. He also confirmed that the gun had been in his possession or under lock and key ever since the sheriff had given it to him.

Then it was Koepp's turn. The jurors stirred slightly, more interested now.

Because this was an inquest and not a trial, Wagner let Koepp tell them what had happened with few interruptions. Koepp identified the .38 as his. He also admitted that he had shot a man he believed to be Roman Weber with it in the early-morning hours of the previous day. He identified the .45 automatic as well. "He was turning on me with that weapon," Koepp said, "so I had to shoot him in self-defense."

"Why didn't you shoot him in the arm or in the leg?" Wagner asked. "In other words, try to maim him rather than kill him?"

Koepp waited a long time to answer, weighing carefully in his mind what he was going to say. He could see the jurors leaning forward as one, fascinated to hear his reply. "Because I was trained in those circumstances to aim at the center of the target," Koepp said. "Even if I were a good enough marksman to hit him in the arm or leg, he still might have killed me. Wounded suspects kill policemen every day."

Out of the corner of his eye Koepp could see the jurors settle back. They were satisfied.

"You were conducting a surveillance of the cottage because Mrs. Merrick was there, is that correct?"

"Yes."

"Because she was a suspect in a murder investigation—the murder of Dr. Issac Steiner?"

"Not necessarily a suspect. A material witness."

"Thank you for explaining that distinction, Sergeant," Wagner said. For the first time his tone was skewed toward sarcasm. "If your purpose was surveillance, why did you go to the island?"

"I heard a lot of noise in the middle of the night. It sounded like there might be violence. I was afraid for Mrs. Merrick's safety."

The district attorney took out a handkerchief and blew his nose, giving the jurors extra time to absorb Koepp's last comment.

"How could you hear the noise when you were on the east shore? That must be more than two hundred yards away."

"I was just a few yards offshore, rowing a small inflatable boat. It sounded like Weber was threatening Mrs. Merrick, so I went to the island and directly to the cabin."

"And you held Weber at gunpoint?"

"Yes. He was very agitated. I thought he might be dangerous. I told Mrs. Merrick to get dressed—her nightdress had been torn—then I told Weber to put some clothes on."

"And that's when he turned on you with the gun?"

"Yes."

Koepp waited with dread for the next series of questions, which he thought would be designed to plant the idea that he had put an illegal bug on the cabin. But Wagner didn't ask them. Instead, he inquired softly, "Did you go to the cabin because you had a prearranged signal with Mrs. Merrick?"

"No. She didn't know I was watching her cabin."

"Or a prearranged time?"

"No."

Moments later Karen was answering "no" to the same questions. She had previously explained why she was at the cabin, why she had invited Weber there, how the shooting had occurred. Koepp watched with a mixture of admiration and fear as she calmly stitched truths and falsehoods into one seamless fabric. It was impossible to tell for sure how much of the collective credulity of the jury she had exploited, but Koepp sensed that they believed her on the points that mattered. Had he not known the real facts, he himself would have been convinced. Part of her success derived from her unashamed candor about her affair with Weber. Perhaps the jurors were thinking that a woman who would admit to adultery so openly would tell the truth about other events, other motivations.

Suddenly, it was over. The judge gave each of the jurors a set of written instructions, told them again what he had said at the beginning of the inquest, then turned them over to a somber old man who was identified as the bailiff. The jury retired to a room nearby to consider its findings. The witnesses had departed. The judge and the district attorney also left. Only Karen, Koepp, and their legal counsels remained. They had no idea how long the jury would deliberate, but they had no place to go.

One other dark spectator kept their vigil. Karen's husband, not so estranged after all, sat next to her. He had arrived at the lodge late the previous afternoon. Koepp had heard him come in, heard their muffled conversation before and after dinner. Knowing Paul Merrick was here, Koepp had skipped dinner entirely; having to share a meal with the two of them appalled him. At first he assumed that her lawyer had summoned Merrick for no other reason than to make a good impression on the inquest jurors. But Koepp's carefully nurtured delusion fell apart later in the evening; Merrick spent the night in her room. Koepp heard their voices through the thin walls well past midnight.

He had slept badly once more because of this new, unexpected development. Sleeping with her husband again struck him as even more obscene than her rendezvous with Weber. It was as if she were flaunting her promiscuity, rubbing Koepp's nose in the fact that she had misled him totally about her character. Koepp wondered now to what extent the two of them had conspired to rid Friars' Close of Issac Steiner. Was Karen an accessory before or after the fact? Was she in fact the killer? It even occurred to him that Karen might have lured Weber to the cottage in the expectation that Koepp would follow her, and that something would happen that would enable her to get rid of her lover. If so, it had worked to perfection. But was anyone that Machiavellian? It was absurd. Absurd or not, the thought would not go away. He reconstructed her phone call to her husband. "Darling, it worked. I didn't have to stage an accident. The stupid cop shot him instead. Isn't it marvelous?"

Ruefully, he remembered how often Margaret had tried to warn him about Karen. Now he was no closer to solving the case than when he started. He didn't have enough to charge either one of the Merricks, let alone convict. He had almost two hours to ponder his dilemma before the jurors filed back into the courtroom. None of them betrayed their decision by their expressions; Koepp once again was impressed with the discipline that enabled jurors not to give the game away at the moment of high drama.

District Attorney Wagner walked to the foreman, who handed him a slip of paper with the verdict on it. Without looking at it, Wagner passed it to Judge Gregory. The foreman, an elderly farmer who leaned on a cane, remained standing.

"Have you reached a finding?" the judge asked him.

"Yes," the old man replied. "We find the shooting a lawful case of self-defense."

The judge rephrased the juror's statement in more legalistic terms for the benefit of the court stenographer, then excused the six men and women. "This inquest is concluded," he informed one and all.

The district attorney took over immediately. "The press is all over the courtyard by the front door," he said. "They also got some whistle-blowers in back. However, there is a loading dock at the basement level on the Mason Street side of the building." He jerked a thumb in the general direction of the street. "I can have my van brought around to the loading dock. The Merricks and Sergeant Koepp can leave with me in the van. The rest of you can preen for the television cameras. How does that idea strike you?"

A melee of arguments, discussion, and counterproposals ensued. It ended after three or four minutes with everyone not only in agreement with Wagner's plan, but grateful to him for suggesting it. Koepp's two protectors from the city appeared very relieved; evidently they were familiar with their client's reputation for making injudicious comments to the media.

Wagner barked orders at an underling. Then the four of them, stimulated by conspiratorial giddiness, rushed to the basement. Moments later they boarded the van undetected. Wagner, who hunched over the steering wheel like some outsize Quasimodo, chortled gleefully when he looked in his rearview mirror and saw nobody in pursuit. He wheeled the van gently around a corner; a two-story office building screened the courthouse from sight. Then he jammed down the accelerator. Koepp, in the front seat, felt his head snap back.

"I hope everyone likes fish," Wagner yelled, trying to be heard above the roar of the straining engine.

Koepp glanced over his shoulder at the seat behind him. The Merricks' expressions reflected his own puzzlement.

Karen, not surprisingly, comprehended the lawyer's intent first; her little off-center smile reappeared. "I think we're being abducted for dinner."

Wagner neither confirmed nor denied her suspicions. However, Koepp could see that he was grinning broadly. The vehicle careened down some side streets, then turned onto the state highway, which was the town's principal artery. About five minutes from town, Wagner took a turn into a forest-shrouded lane. They soon came upon another lake and a two-story house sided with weathered gray shingles, which reminded Koepp of homes he had seen on Nantucket Island. Wagner's house even had white trim and a red door. It was nearly dark. A light on the garage illuminated the driveway and a side door where a slender Asian woman awaited them.

Wagner introduced her by name—Anna Seng—but not by function or relationship. Whether she was a wife, mistress, children's governess, or housekeeper, he did not say. She was the hostess for the evening quite clearly because she invited them into the house in a soft, cultured British voice.

They entered the living room, which connected directly with the dining room. Both rooms boasted dark hardwood floors covered by sisal carpets. In the first room two wicker chairs with quilted chintz upholstery flanked a wooden fireplace. Above the mantel was a Wyeth print of a New England farm. It was a friendly house, a house for somebody who enjoyed life.

Anna Seng took their drink orders and prepared them at a portable bar which had been set up in a corner of the room. Their arrival had been anticipated. Wagner's abduction had not been an impulsive act, as he had first made it seem, but a calculated one. The huge attorney's outrageous self-confidence and walrus-like sangfroid captured Koepp's envy and admiration; he even found himself looking forward with some relish to whatever surprise Wagner had planned for them.

The lawyer had disappeared. Once the drinks were served, the woman invited Karen to see the rest of the house and gardens. Karen readily agreed to the suggestion, leaving Koepp and her husband to deal with their shared uneasiness.

When the women were out of earshot, Merrick said, "I guess I owe you my thanks for helping Karen. That guy might have killed her."

"Possibly," Koepp answered. "Would it have made any difference to you if Weber had killed her? Would you have cared?"

Merrick lifted both dark eyebrows in surprise. "Don't be ridiculous. Karen and I are devoted to each other, but our relationship doesn't preclude an occasional dalliance. I'm no prude. Neither is she. We've both strayed." He chuckled, sipped his martini and chuckled again. "For a while I thought you were up here with her. I mean—"

"I know what you mean," Koepp said. He wished their host would return.

"I'm sorry it was Weber instead. Cokeheads are dangerous. It wasn't like Karen to get involved with someone like him. She's always been more discriminating in the past." He delivered this indictment of his wife's fidelity in a tone of casual indulgence; he might have been discussing her penchant for squeezing the toothpaste tube from the wrong end. Hearing Karen denigrated by her husband this way infuriated Koepp, which is undoubtedly why Merrick did it; the amused expression in his eyes betrayed him.

Koepp knew that some of what Merrick said was pure invention; for one thing, Karen didn't view her husband's relationship with Elizabeth Maklin as a mere "dalliance." Still, the Merricks were trying to effect a reconciliation, in appearance if not in fact. Why? Was it a last-ditch attempt to make their family whole again? Or were they closing ranks temporarily to defeat Koepp's investigation? This much was clear: one of them had killed Steiner, or induced Tirquit/

Omsby to do it. One way or the other, he'd pay a heavy emotional price for thinking of Karen as anything but a suspect.

Never, ever, get involved with a suspect. That was the rule. Break the rules, you get punished.

His most likely suspect had pulled out a meerschaum pipe, which he was carefully filling with tobacco. The rituals connected with pipe smoking had always amused Koepp, a nonsmoker. His father had smoked for thirty years with all the compulsive concentration characteristic of true pipe aficionados; as his father performed the rites, smoking had been more like an occupation than a recreation. Koepp's mother, in a rare moment of real bitterness, complained that his father fiddled with a pipe to mask his sense of failure. It gave Koepp some bleak satisfaction to speculate that Merrick smoked a pipe for the same reason.

Soon the women returned, to be joined a few moments later by Wagner, who was now attired in a fresh pair of trousers and a doeskin sport jacket. Anna Seng poured a tumbler of Scotch for him. Karen began to quiz him about his background. Stimulated by her barrage of questions, he said he was from the East Coast, that he had been a craftsman of several major leveraged buyouts for an investment banking company, that he had made a lot of money. To his credit, he revealed none of this in a boastful or self-serving manner; he sounded somewhat apologetic, Koepp thought.

"How is it you came here?" Koepp asked.

"I like to hunt and fish," he said, grinning slightly and rearranging the ice cubes in his drink with his banana finger. His admission appeared to embarrass him.

Karen, becoming intrigued, asked, "Why a job like district attorney? Wouldn't private practice give you more time for fishing?"

"It would," Wagner said. "But criminal law has always interested me. The first lawyers were probably people who spoke on behalf of their friends to the elders during the Stone Age. And in a place like Forest Junction you can still smell justice sometimes.''

"And you couldn't in New York?" Karen asked.

"The kind of law I was doing had nothing to do with justice," Wagner answered. "We were cutting megabuck deals, issuing junk bonds to finance takeovers, laying a mountain of debt on the companies—we made a pile. But a lot of the companies went down the tubes. People lost their jobs." He studied Karen in silence for a few moments, but it was obvious he wasn't seeing her. Koepp wondered if he was seeing the faces of those displaced workers. In a lighter tone Wagner added, "Aside from the morality of what I was doing, I would have left. New York is uninhabitable."

"From a sociological point of view, that's certainly true," Merrick said. "I lived there for five years. Or survived for five years."

Wagner abruptly redirected the conversation. "Tell me the circumstances of the Steiner case, Koepp. Murder is always a fascinating topic." He glanced at Paul Merrick, as if looking for support, but the sociologist studied his clasped hands in silence.

Koepp recited the facts of the case much the way he had outlined them to Styles, the assistant district attorney. The only difference was that this time he could include the suspicious circumstances of Charlie Tirquit's change of identity. When he had finished, Wagner commented, "So your prime suspect is this Charlie character?"

"Suspicion points that way," Koepp said. "But we've got other suspects. Charlie doesn't have a motive, so maybe his identity switch has no connection with the murder. We don't have any evidence to tie him—"

"Maybe he's somebody's dupe," the lawyer suggested, showing his familiar evil grin. "Maybe somebody with a motive hired him to cut up Steiner." Wagner let a long pause develop before he asked in a musing tone, "Anyone trying to cover up for him?"

"A woman named Maklin," Koepp said. He watched both Merricks and was disappointed when he saw no reaction.

At this point Anna Seng invited them to the dining room. Once they were seated, the Chinese woman disappeared into the kitchen, then reappeared moments later with a bottle of white wine. While she served the wine, Wagner, obviously enjoying his role as host, dispensed a tossed salad in generous portions to his guests.

"It's customary to say grace in some households, but I don't know your religious convictions, so I don't know what's appropriate," Wagner said. "Give me some guidance."

Karen laughed softly, then said, "I'm an atheist, Paul is an agnostic." She looked at Koepp with a faint smile. "Ray would favor grace. Perhaps he should offer it. He used to do it professionally."

"I'm retired," Koepp said.

"We're a mixed group," Wagner said. "Let's try a compromise." With that he proceeded to advise them of their Miranda rights. He did so in a slow and deliberate fashion, giving them a chance to get over their shock. When he had finished, an embarrassed silence settled around them; they could not have been more surprised if he had stood up, opened his fly and urinated into his salad bowl.

Eventually, because someone had to say something, Paul Merrick told him he had an unusual sense of humor.

"You'll find, if you get to know me, Doctor, that I have no sense of humor whatever. But at my table are one or more of the murderers or conspirators in the death of one Dr. Steiner, as well as the peace officer pursuing said murderer. Said officer may also be a murderer. As I am an officer of the court, duly sworn to uphold the laws of this commonwealth, it seems like a wise precaution." Unaccountably, he looked at Koepp. "What do *you* think of my sense of humor, Sergeant?"

"I'll pass on that," Koepp said, grinning in spite of himself, "but I applaud your sense of caution."

The cook and Anna served the meal, which proved to be a culinary delight. The main course consisted of fresh walleyes—Wagner boasted that he had caught them himself that morning—stuffed with crabmeat. Koepp could taste minced shallots, mushrooms and parsley in the sauce that accompanied the fish. It was gourmet fare, beautifully presented. Lemon pie, a selection of liqueurs and coffee followed the entree.

Conversation during dinner had been sporadic at best and limited to mundane topics. Wagner didn't return to the subject of Steiner's murder until the coffee had been served. He procured a box of cigars from the fireplace mantel, offered one to Koepp and Merrick, both of whom declined, and took his seat at the head of the table.

"Tell me how Mr. Weber came to be the first shooting victim in my jurisdiction in more than three years," he said, looking pointedly at Koepp.

Before Koepp could frame a response, Merrick interrupted. "We've enjoyed the hospitality, Mr. Wagner, but I've just decided that my wife and I desire legal counsel."

"In that case I have no choice but to begin an investigation into a possible homicide here in Granite County," the attorney said evenly. He drew heavily on his cigar and exhaled a cloud of ominous blue smoke.

"A jury just decided—"

"An inquest is advisory, Doctor. I told you that. I can still charge the sergeant here with murder and your wife with being an accessory. It would be better for everyone if you'd humor me."

Koepp was tempted to ask what he planned to use for evidence. He didn't, however, because this conversation held out intriguing possibilities.

Karen evidently didn't agree with her husband's assessment that she wanted to confer with her attorney. "What do you want to know?" she asked. "You've already decided we're guilty of murder or conspiracy."

"Convince me I'm wrong," Wagner said. It was a command, not an invitation. "Start with how that guy Weber got his ticket punched by Wyatt Earp here."

"I've told you—several times."

Wagner turned his attention back to Koepp. "You probably wondered during the inquest why I didn't go after you for that dippy yarn about paddling your dinghy offshore? That's pure bull. I know you weren't just conducting a visual surveillance because you were on the wrong shore for that. You can't see the dock from the east side of the lake where you were, so how the hell could you tell who came and went? You went to the east shore because you needed seclusion for your illegal bugging equipment. Finally, and this is so obvious it makes me laugh still, you bought a rubber boat. You didn't buy it to get close to the island, you bought it so you could go out and plant a listening device in the cabin. You knew things were getting rough inside because you could hear everything that was going on."

Koepp remained silent.

"What I want to know, Sergeant, is what you heard that has a bearing on the Steiner murder." He puffed on the cigar some more. "Don't worry, I'm not going to charge you with an illegal bugging offense. Cops do that all the time. I'd do it myself if I thought it would get a legitimate conviction."

"I have nothing to tell you," Koepp said.

"If you're worried about Mrs. Merrick, be discreet. I'm not interested—" He realized too late how indelicate he sounded.

Karen colored visibly. So did Paul Merrick.

"Nothing material to the Steiner case took place," Koepp

told him. He was getting good at lying. A bad sign. He was aware that Karen's gaze was welded to the side of his face.

"Your DA, that guy Styles, is not going to be pleased to hear that. I talked to him for a long time this morning. He's making a cross, so he's all ready for you when you get back. That is, if I don't drag that bugging equipment out of the lake and send you to the state pen for a couple of years. And I still might if you don't start to cooperate."

"That sounds like extortion," Paul Merrick said.

"Styles is only an assistant DA," Koepp added.

"That's comforting," Wagner growled. "How could a lawyer with a lisp get a conviction?"

"I think I'd like to go back to the hotel now," Karen said. "It's been a long day."

"That it has," Wagner said without any real sympathy in his voice. "I'll take you back soon, only we haven't explored the Steiner murder completely. Where do you stand on that one, Koepp?"

"We haven't made an arrest," Koepp said.

"I know that. Styles filled me in. Did the murder weapon surface yet?"

Koepp decided that telling him the truth would just cause him to ask more questions. So he shook his head. Then he added that other evidence had been uncovered. "Some fibers taken from Steiner's body are a match for a sweater which Dr. Merrick owns," Koepp said casually. All eyes focused on Karen's husband.

After a long pause, Merrick said, "That's easily explained, although the explanation is very embarrassing for me. Issac and I had, well, a small physical encounter, I'm afraid."

"Where and when?" Koepp asked.

"At the Planners' meeting. That's when he told Elizabeth and me and Leon about discontinuing his research project. He said he was going to leave the community. All of us were upset. We tried to reason with him, to no avail. Then he started to leave. He was like that. He wouldn't discuss things, or listen to another side. That's when I got out of control for a few moments. I grabbed him by the arm as he was opening the door. He tried to get free, so I wrapped my arms around him. It was stupid. It made him violent and we grappled. As soon as I let him go, he calmed down. Leon and Elizabeth were there. They'll confirm what I've just said.''

For Wagner's benefit Koepp explained who the two witnesses were. He couldn't help adding, ''Early in the investigation both Jaroff and Maklin lied in an effort to set up an alibi.''

''Not very reliable witnesses,'' Wagner observed. He watched Karen intently when he spoke.

''Dr. Merrick was an accomplice in the lie, by the way,'' Koepp said.

Wagner grunted. He puffed at the cigar for a while, studying Karen with a puzzled expression. Anna Seng offered to pour more coffee. All of them declined. Finally, Wagner looked toward Koepp. ''What else do you have?'' he asked.

Before Koepp could reply, Merrick turned to the Chinese woman. ''Please call me a cab,'' he said, ''if they have such a thing in this godforsaken place!''

Anna acted as if no one had spoken to her.

''There are no cabs,'' Wagner informed him with obvious relish. He made it sound like there not only were no cabs in Forest Junction, but none in the rest of the world as well. Koepp was enjoying himself.

''What else, Sergeant?'' the district attorney asked in a voice that boomed around the room.

Caught up in the spirit of their inquisition, Koepp got reckless. ''Mrs. Merrick paid money to Dr. Steiner. She says it was for therapy.''

The first thing Koepp noticed was Karen's hand. It moved to the edge of her chair and gripped hard, then just as suddenly relaxed. But the effect of his words on her husband didn't dissipate so quickly; the color ran out of his face as if someone had pulled a drain plug. He sat at rigid attention and stared uncomprehendingly across the table at his wife.

Under his heavy eyelids, Wagner's eyes slid back and forth in their slits, surveying first one of the Merricks, then the other. Koepp was astonished by Merrick's reaction to his revelation about the money. Although he had not intended to tell him about it, he didn't regret it.

Seeing Merrick's surprise confirmed what he had suspected; the two of them kept a lot of secrets from each other. With sudden insight he realized he might be able to use that situation to his advantage. If every conventional technique of detection failed, maybe he could play them off against each other.

# FIFTEEN

DISTRICT ATTORNEY WAGNER decided to abide by the inquest jury's conclusion that Roman Weber had been shot in self-defense. The matter was closed. Koepp found out from Ben Levine of internal affairs the morning after he returned to the city. "It was a clean kill," he said. For all the passion he conveyed he might have been describing how Koepp had bagged a luckless mallard.

Then Levine told Koepp the bad news. Lieutenant Tarrish had been suspended from duty and Chief of Detectives Voorhees wanted to see him immediately.

The chief was in his office on the fourth floor when Koepp arrived and invited him to enter by a curt nod of his head. It was curious that the more power a man accumulated the more economical became his efforts to have his commands carried out; being the big cheese meant you never had to yell or wave your arms.

Koepp was angry and he assumed he was about to be suspended himself, so he was in no mood to be deferential. He demanded to know why Tarrish had been suspended before the other man could say anything.

J. T. Voorhees had the reputation of being a man who never lost his temper. This gave him an enormous advantage over other people.

He demonstrated the validity of his reputation by ignoring Koepp's impertinence entirely and answering his question in a voice devoid of passion. "I told George to take you off the Steiner case. He didn't do it. Instead, he let you go up north to silence the state's prime suspect with gunfire. What would you have done in my place?

Koepp ignored the question; the chief's logic was unassailable. "I assume I'm also under suspension."

Voorhees, an angular, craggy man whose gray hair had begun to recede, studied him thoughtfully for a moment. At length he said, "If it were up to me I'd have you shot, Sergeant. You're not a team player, you're a cowboy, and cowboys are dangerous. However, you're not suspended."

He waited for a few seconds, allowing his message to sink in. When Koepp said nothing, he continued. "The media are captivated by your derring-do, so it would be awkward to get rid of you right now. But you'll screw up the case, I'm sure, and when you do I won't suspend you, I'll transfer you to the most demeaning job I can find."

Time was on Voorhees's side and he knew it.

Abruptly, the chief switched to the Steiner case. It was apparent that he had been keeping up on it. "What about the murder weapon?" Voorhees asked. "Your partner found it in Weber's apartment—buried in a potted cactus. Can you tie that to this kid Omsby or someone else?"

"Not yet." If Charlie was the killer, what was Karen doing with the knife? Why did she try to hide it?

"How did you know the murder weapon was stashed in Weber's place, by the way?"

"You don't want to know."

After studying him again briefly, Voorhees nodded. "How do you know Weber wasn't the killer?"

"The same way I knew where the knife was."

MARGARET was working on another case, but she had left the information he had requested from the Milwaukee PD. She had tracked Tirquit/Omsby further and found the address where he lived before he went to Friars' Close.

Milt Farmer accompanied him to the address on Quincy Street, Omsby's last known residence. It was a dilapidated, three-story frame building directly across the street from a

Laundromat. A service station was located on one side of it, a vacated office building on the other. On the side of the brick office building the faded letters "Southside Printing Co." still showed. Directly behind the Laundromat the ground sloped steeply into a shallow valley filled with gleaming railroad tracks, boxcars, and thick blue smoke.

They parked in front of the apartment building. Farmer, armed with a copy of Omsby's photograph, crossed the street to talk to the patrons of the Laundromat, while Koepp entered the apartment house. The building superintendent was at work in the railroad yard, according to his wife, but she was sure the man in the photograph had never been a renter during their tenure of four months. Omsby had been gone for at least two years, Koepp calculated, so he moved on to the other apartments. He found occupants in two of them, but again they hadn't been there long enough to have known Omsby.

When Koepp got back out on the street, Farmer was waiting for him. They looked at each other and shrugged. "Too early for the bars," Farmer said.

"Any diners around here?"

Farmer jerked a thumb over his shoulder. "There's a greasy spoon down the block."

They walked to the place, called Evelyn's, and showed their shields to the waitress behind the counter. She was a large woman with skin that looked like bread dough. She had a mole next to her mouth.

Farmer showed her the picture. She recognized it right away. "He used to come in here a long time ago. I ain't seen him in a two or three years, though. He was a nice boy. His name was Wally, I think." She didn't know anything else.

"We'll show this to the customers," Farmer said.

It didn't take long. Only two customers were eating breakfast; neither of them had laid eyes on the man in the picture. In their peremptory dismissal of the photograph the diners managed to convey their disdain for the police.

Koepp mumbled his thanks as they departed. He felt acute frustration. Unraveling the mystery of Omsby's name change might or might not lead them to Steiner's killer, but the whole exercise was so unnecessary. He and Farmer should have been interrogating the late Roman Weber. From him they could have learned enough to grind the truth out of Karen Merrick. Killing Weber was the worst mistake he had ever made as a cop.

After leaving the diner, the detectives went in opposite directions along the rotting carcass of Quincy Street, knocking on doors indiscriminately and stopping to show the photo to the few pedestrians they encountered. When they met an hour later by their car Farmer said he had talked to a woman whose friend ran a bar Omsby had frequented. "Said she used to see Omsby," Farmer reported, "although she didn't know his name. Her friend runs a place on Ninety-eighth street—The Right Spot. Her friend lives in the apartment across the street. She knew our man."

"Let's go," Koepp said.

The owner of The Right Spot was a wiry woman with bleached blond hair, angular features, and a mouth that dipped down at both ends in perpetual disapproval. She recognized the picture at once. "Wally Omsby! I haven't seen him in years. What'd he do?"

"Not anything as far as we know," Farmer said. "But he may know somebody who did. We just want to ask him some questions." Farmer was lying about the fact that Omsby was a suspect in case this woman was a friend of his.

The woman, a Mrs. Suchek, was not fooled. "Don't hand me that shit. You're probably here about that thing with his sister, ain't ya?"

Koepp's instincts went on full alert. "Among other things," he said. "Why don't we start with the sister?"

"The suicide, huh?"

"That's right," Koepp said. "Tell us about the suicide first."

"Well, I don't know much myself. I mean, I wasn't told nothing directly by Wally. It's just scuttlebutt I heard in the bar. You know, there was a lot of talk about it. In those days everybody in the old neighborhood knew everybody else. So there was a lot of talk about the sister. Betty, I think her name was. Maybe that wasn't her name. She never came in the bar much. Her old man sometimes, but not her. Had some young kids, I understand, so she couldn't get out much."

"Tell us what the scuttlebutt was," Farmer prodded.

"Sure, I'm getting to that," Mrs. Suchek said. "This Betty went into the garage, shut the doors and turned on her car. By the time the paramedics got there she was long gone. Wally, her brother, kept telling people that she was murdered. Can you believe it, *murdered?* Hell, everyone knew she took the carbon monoxide herself. Her ex-husband never said much about it. In fact they said he tried to shut Wally up." The woman shrugged. "After a while things blew over. I never saw Wally much after it happened. Finally, I never saw him at all. He just disappeared. Nobody knew what happened to him. He was a likeable guy. Lots of people missed him."

Farmer asked, "That it?"

She shrugged again. "What can I tell ya? That's all I know about it. Woody Richardson—he was a cop then—he might remember something. Seems like he investigated it or something. He used to come in the old place on Quincy Street after work sometimes. He wasn't a bad guy. He was a cop and all, but he wasn't a bad— Oh, sorry."

"That's okay," Koepp said. "You know if Woody is still around?"

"Sure, he used to come into The Right Spot all the time after he retired. That is, until he got sick." She lowered her voice out of respect for Woody's illness. "He's got the Big C. They said he ain't gonna be around long. But he lives three or four blocks from here. I can get his phone number if you want.''

''That would be very helpful,'' Koepp said. ''Maybe we can use your phone?''

She looked up the number and read it off slowly while Koepp dialed. The woman who answered identified herself as Richardson's daughter. After quizzing Koepp about his business, she agreed to fetch her father. ''It'll take a while for him to get to the phone,'' she said. When the man finally came on the line, he confirmed that he had been one of the investigators on the Betty Hutchison suicide. He remembered it, he explained, because it happened just before he retired. Yes, he recalled that the victim's brother was upset because he said some doctor had driven her to do it. Some psychiatrist.

''Do you remember the name of the psychiatrist?'' Koepp asked. His breath was coming in short, nervous bursts.

''I wouldn't have remembered him because it was so long ago. But the other day, I saw an article in the paper about that murder in Hillside. That's the same doctor.''

''You mean Issac Steiner?''

''Yeah, that's the one. Hey, it never occurred to me that there was any connection. That thing—the suicide—that happened a long time ago. Hey, there couldn't be any connection, could there?''

KOEPP CALLED his office and was patched through to Sergeant DeMoss, the acting watch commander. He explained the significance of what they had learned from Mrs. Suchek and Woody Richardson. ''I'm bringing Omsby in for questioning.''

''We don't have anybody for backup,'' DeMoss growled with impatience. ''But Margaret will be back in a few minutes. I'll get somebody else or go myself. While you're coming in, Mary Jo is going to check Richardson's story.''

By the time they arrived back at headquarters Margaret was

there. They gathered in Tarrish's office to hear Mary Jo's briefing. Four years before, Omsby's sister had committed suicide by suffocation, resulting from carbon monoxide poisoning. She had been divorced a year earlier, and friends said she was depressed and uncommunicative. She had been undergoing therapy from a psychiatrist named Issac Steiner. Ten days before she took her life she admitted to a neighbor that Steiner had abused her sexually several times during "therapy" sessions. A neighbor said Omsby had sworn to kill Steiner if the authorities didn't convict him.

A medical review board exonerated Steiner. The DA's office, for lack of evidence, decided not to bring charges. That was all the police records of the incident revealed.

When Koepp called Friars' Close he reached the woman named Elaine. She found the date when Tirquit/Omsby had applied for a rental apartment; it was less than two months after Betty Omsby took her own life. At that time Karen Merrick, who usually conducted the research on a new prospect, was recovering from surgery—a hysterectomy—at Ross Lutheran Hospital. Because she was not able to qualify Charlie, Helen Kusava had handled the task instead. Helen liked Charlie right away, Elaine remembered. She managed to convince the rest of the selection committee to make it a unanimous choice. Karen, upon her return, had no reason to question the committee's decision.

Omsby's pathetically transparent identity and cover story went unchallenged.

As a reward for her efficiency, Mary Jo was dispatched in the second car with Milt Farmer to assist Koepp and Margaret in case Tirquit/Omsby offered resistance.

The setting sun drew long, deep shadows from the trunks of ashes and maples that ringed the community compound. The smells of water and fecund, newly turned earth assailed Koepp's nostrils as he climbed out of the car.

Movement in a second-story window arrested Koepp's attention. He caught a clear glimpse of Elizabeth Maklin, paint roller in hand, before she turned and disappeared.

The backup car with detectives Farmer and Mary Jo Riley inside pulled to a stop on the roadway that connected the various residences. An east wind, promising rain again later in the evening, brought the smells of the kitchen to mix with the aroma of the soil. In the shadow of Building B Koepp and Margaret checked their weapons, then entered the well-lighted interior. They found themselves in a small vestibule; a dogleg corridor off to the left led to the central hallway, which ran east and west. An elevator and an open stairwell connected the vestibule to the floor above. They quietly climbed the stairs. As they emerged from the stairwell into the second-floor corridor, Margaret stopped suddenly and pointed ahead. Omsby's apartment door was wide open. Koepp drew his .38 Detective Special; Margaret also had her automatic in a ready position. He ducked into the apartment, took up a firing position and called out to his partner. In a second she was beside him, breathless and excited. In the next thirty or forty seconds they methodically searched the apartment.

No one was there. That fool Elizabeth Maklin had warned him.

"There he goes," Margaret cried. She was standing at the double window looking out toward the dining hall. She shoved the automatic back in her handbag and looked away before Mary Jo Riley rushed into view below them. But Koepp had not turned. He saw the woman approach Charlie alone, wondered where Farmer was, then watched in growing dread as their young suspect ignored Mary Jo's demands that he stop and lie face down. Koepp could hear the woman officer's commands clearly from the second floor, well enough to know they carried no command presence at all. The gun that she pointed at his chest didn't matter; her voice said she wouldn't use it.

Charlie heard the same voice, the same lack of decisiveness.

He rushed Mary Jo, grabbed her gun arm and wrested the weapon out of her grip. Then, holding on to her arm, he bent down and picked up the automatic. Koepp and Margaret collided on the way out of the room. Koepp swore. Margaret wrapped her arms around her ribs and grimaced at him in silent pain. They ran down the stairs, then split up by some intuitive means of communication, with Koepp exiting by the parking lot door and Margaret rushing out the opposite side of the building. Koepp found Farmer at the corner of the building, peering around at Mary Jo and Omsby. Koepp took up a position off his right shoulder.

In a thick, raspy voice of fear Farmer tried to explain what had happened. "I saw him come out the other side of the building and said 'that's him,' and the next thing I know she pulls out her gun, jumps outta the car and takes off after him. I told her to stop. She kept going. Jesus, Ray, I tried to stop her."

Omsby had begun to move in a half-circle around the two detectives as if he intended to go to the roadway where Farmer's car was parked. He held Mary Jo in front of him with his arm around her neck. He had the muzzle of her .32 pointed toward her side. He glanced back at the front of the building. Koepp guessed he was watching Margaret. Probably she was leaning against the corner of the building on the other side. In his peripheral vision Koepp caught sight of two figures emerging from the rear of Building A directly to the east of them. He swore under his breath; bystanders posed the greatest complication in a hostage situation. One of the figures, a small, familiar one, separated herself from the other person and began to run toward them on the roadway. He shifted his attention to the newcomer. As he suspected, it was Karen. When she was about twenty yards away, she stopped

running and began walking purposefully toward the empty
police car.

"Get back!" Koepp cried. "He's got a gun." She ignored
his warning. When she reached the point where Omsby turned
his attention on her, she stopped. For a moment everyone
froze in a soundless tableau. Finally, Omsby began moving
again with his human shield, while shifting his attention between the three points of danger. Karen moved toward him.
Koepp's heart was beating wildly now. Irrational plans flashed
through his mind. Somehow he had to reach Karen before she
got to the car. He thought Omsby might kill her if she got in
his way. But the moment he moved, their quarry stopped and
screamed at him, "Get back, get back. Don't move or I'll kill
her." Mary Jo was close enough now that Koepp could see
the terror in her eyes. She gasped piteously for breath either
because of her fear or because of the tight grip her captor had
on her throat. The situation was beyond Koepp's control. He
realized with rising panic that he was going to be a bystander
while something horrible happened. He waited in anguish for
the soft pop of the automatic.

A few yards separated Karen and Omsby now, the two of
them polarized in a deadly minuet. The policemen had become absurdly inconsequential. The only reality was Karen's
soothing, mellifluous voice, reaching out to Omsby. "Charlie,
there's nothing to be afraid of. There's no reason to run
away."

The man's bulging, glazed eyes blinked several times. He
stopped and fixed an uncomprehending stare on Karen Merrick. He also tightened his grip on his hostage.

When she saw that she had made no impression, Karen
altered her appeal. "It's over and he's gone. Let them take
you, Charlie, don't hurt anyone. Your sister Betty's at peace.
Don't ruin her memory by hurting someone else. Betty
wouldn't want that. It's over, Charlie. Let her go."

Koepp waited to hear the gunshot, waited for the sickening

spray of blood, waited for the bungled mess to explode all over them. But the sound of the gunshot never came. Instead, the gun in Charlie's right hand began to dip slowly. He released his grip on Mary Jo and pushed her violently aside, as if she disgusted him. Karen took the gun from his hand and laid it gingerly on the lawn. Then she put her arms around his waist and held him tightly as he leaned forward and dropped his head on her left shoulder. His body shook in rhythm with his muffled, childish sobs. Long arms wrapped themselves around her thin shoulders.

All Koepp could think of was: how the hell did Karen know about Charlie's sister?

Mary Jo Riley was leaning against the county's squad car, vomiting on the right front tire.

THEY WAITED until morning to interrogate Omsby because of his agitated condition. Besides Koepp, Margaret and the suspect, a stenographer and an attorney hired by Friars' Close were present. Margaret had Mirandized Omsby before they put him in their car at Friars' Close. Now she read him his rights again with his lawyer present. Then she asked, "Did you kill Steiner?"

"Yes."

"Why?"

"Because of what he did to my sister." He sounded out of character, almost triumphant.

"What was your sister's name?"

"Betty."

"What did he do to her?"

"He raped her!"

"Where? When?"

"In his office. When she was being—getting therapy."

"Did you come to Friars' Close to kill him?

"Yes."

Margaret leaned back in her chair and said softly, "Tell us how you killed him."

Omsby was calmer and more confident than Koepp had ever seen him, almost as if he were enjoying his predicament. Probably he had never gotten this much attention in his life; being a murder suspect was important.

Some other motivation might be at work as well, something neither Koepp nor Margaret understood. That possibility depressed him more with each question, and each proud and defiant reply.

"I saw him go along to the computer room, and noticed that he hadn't locked the door. It was open a crack. So I went to the kitchen as if I was getting more ice. I took a knife from the rack, and went back and walked into the room and killed him. I told him, 'This is for Betty.' After that I went back to the kitchen and got the ice."

No you didn't, Koepp thought. He said, "And you left the door open wide this time?"

Omsby tensed at the question, suspicious of it because he saw it as an attempt to lead him. After thinking about it, he replied, "No, I shut the door. If I had left it open, someone woulda seen what I had done right away."

Koepp remembered their first interview and how Margaret had explained to him why shutting the door was so important; he had recalled his lessons well.

"The bloody knife was a problem, though, wasn't it?" Margaret suggested in a casual tone of voice.

"Yes, I had to clean off the knife," Omsby said confidently.

Koepp admired the deft, sure way his partner was setting up the witness. It was pathetically familiar. He had seen dozens, maybe hundreds of self-confident, compulsive people trying to confess to crimes they had not committed. No matter how many times they were unmasked they remained optimistic that *this* time they would be believed. It was so easy after all; the police desperately wanted to arrest the criminal, and they were giving the police what they wanted, a confession. What they never seemed to learn was that it's difficult to claim responsibility for a crime one hadn't committed because the police knew more of the facts of the case than they did.

Margaret sprang the trap. "So you went down to the basement to the sink in the utility room?"

This time he was ready for the leading question trick. "No," he said, "I washed it off in the kitchen in one of the sinks there."

Margaret glanced up at Koepp, who had been leaning against the wall throughout the short interview, with a glimmer of triumph in her eyes. It took no imagination to know approximately what she was thinking. *Did you hear that, Sergeant Koepp? He says he washed it in the kitchen, yet we know it was washed off in Steiner's bathroom. He's lying. He's not our killer. Karen Merrick is the killer.*

By mutual consent they went into the adjoining corridor to talk. Detective Farmer, who was extracting a soft-drink can from the dispenser, saw them and called out, "Tarrish is back." He grinned like a school kid.

"That's good news," Margaret said. "I missed the old crock." Then she shifted her attention back to the matter at hand. "We can book him for assault with a deadly weapon, or resisting arrest, but he's not our man—I mean murderer."

"Agreed. I'll tell Tarrish. He can tell the DA."

But they were not to be so lucky. Assistant District Attorney Tom Styles was sitting in the lieutenant's office when they arrived. It's pitiful how calm he looks, Koepp thought, and how unhappy he's going to be in a minute.

Both men looked at him expectantly. "You got a confession, I assume?" Styles lisped with unusual politeness.

Koepp nodded. "But it's worthless," he said. "The man is lying. The physical evidence contradicts his version of where the knife was cleaned."

The attorney lifted his eyes toward the cracked ceiling. "Then why the hell would he confess?"

"Usually they do it to make somebody pay attention to them," Koepp said. He suspected Karen might have a more precise explanation; he resolved to ask her for one.

"Sweet Jesus!" Koepp noticed for the first time that Styles didn't lisp when he swore. "You have a confession from a guy who just got finished taking a police officer hostage at gunpoint—while he was trying to escape arrest—and you don't think he's the killer. If you can't book him on that, you better get in some other line of work."

"He didn't do it, Counselor," Margaret said in measured cadence. "He probably wishes he had, but someone else did it for him. My candidate is Lady Macbeth."

"What's she talking about?" Styles said, looking at Tarrish in exasperation.

The lieutenant shrugged.

"She's talking about Mrs. Merrick, the business agent at the co-housing project," Koepp said. "It was Mrs. Merrick who got Omsby to turn Officer Riley loose and give up without shooting someone."

Margaret muttered something under her breath. Koepp couldn't make out what she had said, but felt a perverse sense of satisfaction anyway.

"So, how come you haven't arrested this Mrs. Merrick?" Styles wanted to know. The words rolled out on a cushion of sarcasm. His lisp was more pronounced than ever.

"Evidence," Koepp said. "Or the lack of it."

"The lieutenant and I are getting a lot of heat on this one, my friend," Styles said. "The sheriff is on his ass and the DA is on mine. You better wrap this thing up damned quick." The lawyer shifted his attention to Margaret. "Why do you think this Merrick woman is the killer?"

"Because Steiner abused her sexually when she went to him for treatment." Margaret glanced at Koepp, giving him a chance to dispute her conjecture. When he didn't, she went on. "Mrs. Merrick controls the place. Like yesterday. That pathetic creature downstairs was ready to shoot us if we made a move on him. But Mrs. Merrick just walked up to him and took the gun away, the way you'd take a toy away from a little kid. She can make people do or believe anything she says." She looked at Koepp with a meaningful, sad expression.

"What do you think, Koepp?" Styles asked. "Could she be your killer?" He gave the appearance then of thinking out loud. "She hated him for putting his hands up her dress and because he was going to pull the plug on her precious co-housing experiment. She had two reasons."

Koepp had mulled over both motives for a long time himself. If she had wanted to kill Steiner for his sexual misconduct, she probably would have done it before now. But could she kill to save Friars' Close? She had said it could keep going without the benevolence of the Grayson Foundation; he was inclined to believe her. But perhaps she knew it couldn't stand alone. Then she had a very strong motive because she was deeply committed to it psychologically and emotionally. She was the one who described the corrosive effects of modern isolation and talked of the community as an antidote.

"Maybe she does have two valid motives," Koepp answered. "But no evidence has surfaced so far."

"What about the murder weapon, Koepp?" Styles growled. "It turned up in the apartment of that junkie you killed. Maybe he murdered Steiner."

"No, Koepp said, "he had the knife, but we're not sure yet how he got it." It was just like they said, Koepp thought. Once you started lying, there was no end to it. "Weber was getting his fixes from Steiner, so he needed Steiner alive, not dead."

To Koepp's surprise the assistant DA didn't press him. Instead, he seized on the match of the fibers from the body and Dr. Merrick's sweater.

"Merrick has an explanation, which is supported by two witnesses," Koepp told him. "Merrick and Steiner had an altercation when Steiner said he was leaving the project."

"Sweet Jesus," Styles said in mock despair. "Get me something. Channel Six did an editorial last night on the ineptitude of the DA's office. Get me *something*." He picked up a bulging briefcase, stared at it with distaste and departed.

After the attorney had gone, Tarrish visibly relaxed and asked Margaret for the list she had made of people in the Administration Building at the approximate time of the murder. He started to read: "Gwen Culver."

"The office girl," Margaret said. "She was selling crafts from the local handicapped school. No motive."

Tarrish grunted. "Mrs. Jaroff and Erin Merrick."

"Mrs. Jaroff is the wife of one of the Planners," Margaret told him a little impatiently. "She doesn't seem the type who'd do anything for herself, much less murder anyone. She's rather silly. The girl, Erin, is only thirteen. Neither of them has a motive, either."

"Mrs. Kusava's on the list," Koepp said. "Competent. She manages the kitchen. Doesn't have a strong motive, but she was supposed to check out new applicants while Mrs. Merrick was recovering from surgery. We need to find out how come she let Omsby get in posing as Charlie Tirquit."

"When you gonna talk to her?" Tarrish asked.

"Today."

Another grunt. "And then we have the Planners." Tarrish muttered.

"All have the same motive—a fear that Steiner's departure would put the experiment out of business," Koepp said. "Dr. Merrick has an additional one. Steiner evidently knew about his falsified research and was holding it over him."

"What else?" Tarrish asked.

"Maklin tried to protect Omsby," Koepp said. "I caught her taking his personnel file. She also hit him in the face and insisted on interfering when I tried to question him. She's the one who got him the lawyer. My guess is she had something to do with Omsby getting into the place. If so, she'd got a lot of explaining to do."

Tarrish stood up and stretched. He reminded Koepp of a cat. Margaret began to fidget.

"And finally the last name—Karen Merrick," she said, unable apparently to wait out the stretching routine.

"We discussed her already," Tarrish reminded her.

"I'd like to know what happened at Granite Lake."

"I had to kill a man," Koepp said, annoyed.

"What else?" she demanded with surprising belligerence. "Which one told you where the knife was? Weber or Lady Macbeth?"

"That's not material—"

"The hell it isn't." She looked at Tarrish for support.

Fortunately for Koepp, Tarrish had been briefed by the chief about what happened at Granite Lake; he didn't want to know any more than he had already been told. He tried to calm her down. "Hey, lighten up, Margaret," he said, grinning. "Have a fight with your boyfriend or what?"

Koepp knew that was the wrong thing to say.

"I'll thank you to keep your sexist comments about my personal life to yourself," she cried, abruptly rising from her chair.

For a moment she appeared to be leaving. But she turned toward Koepp and, back in control, said, "Oh, by the way, while you were up north *fishing,* I checked the phone company records of that teacher who was fired. It turns out Neil Erickson called the Grayson Foundation a lot recently."

"Who'd he call?" Koepp asked, surprised.

"Couldn't tell," Margaret said, "because the calls went to a general number. A woman in the grants department told me

Erickson's application had been turned down five months ago. She hasn't heard from him since.''

Margaret had remembered that Erickson said he called Steiner to get his grant application back on track. She hadn't been present when he and Farmer interviewed the teacher; that meant she had read it in his daily log sheet. Thorough, like the lab boys said.

Margaret's disciplined methods had turned over another academic rock and another lie had slithered out. If he finally blew this case, and Vorhees exiled him to community relations forever, he could blame professional courtesy—university faculty lying to save each other's reputations.

What in the hell was Erickson up to?

## SIXTEEN

HE HAD A message to call Karen. He dialed the number of Friars' Close and felt his stomach tighten when Ina Jaroff came on the line. They exchanged a few pleasantries about the fair weather they were enjoying before the woman went in search of the business manager.

As soon as Koepp heard Karen's voice, his anger reignited. "You knew about Charlie's motive—why he came here. Why didn't you tell us?"

"Do you think that's my function, to point my finger at my friends?" When he didn't respond to that, she must have concluded that she had won the argument. "What's going to happen to Charlie?" she asked.

"He's going to be charged with assault. The attorney Maklin hired thinks the court will want a full psychiatric evaluation before they do anything."

"He's not legally insane, of course," she said, "but he's not a criminal, either. There are a lot of people like that. Society doesn't have any limbo for the disturbed."

"That was a brave thing you did, making Omsby give up the gun," he said. "You may have saved Mary Jo's life."

"Is that her name—Mary Jo? She didn't seem the type who should be running around with a gun."

For some reason he was disappointed that she didn't acknowledge his compliment. "When you got him calmed down, it sounded like you thought he killed Steiner—getting revenge for his sister."

Her voice immediately took on a texture of concern. "I told Margaret right away that I didn't mean Charlie had killed him. Didn't she tell you what I meant?"

"Yes, but—"

"Oh, he wanted to at one time. He told me he came here so he'd have a chance to kill Leon. But he wasn't capable of it. In the state he was in yesterday I thought the only way to reach him was to remind him of Betty's gentleness. That was about the only thing I could think of. But I wasn't suggesting he did it. I convinced him long ago to look instead for evidence that Issac had caused his sister's death."

"That was a dangerous game to play. Suppose he had changed his mind again? Gone after Steiner?"

"I knew he wouldn't."

"You take a lot on yourself," he told her.

"You have to believe in people," she answered.

"Why did Charlie confess?"

She paused, appearing surprised by his question. "I thought you understood people better than that, Ray."

Koepp felt the stir of annoyance. "Enlighten me."

"His honor required that he avenge his sister. When he failed to kill Dr. Steiner, he tried to claim credit for the murder to expiate his guilt."

The explanation sounded like a case study from Psychology 101. Her glibness was starting to get on his nerves.

"We'll be coming by to see you again," he told her.

"You know where I am."

By midmorning Koepp was once again at Friars' Close. His purpose was to interview the manager of food service, Mrs. Kusava. He had called ahead and made an appointment to conduct the interrogation in her apartment. As he approached Building C, he noticed a group of about a dozen teenagers sitting on the grass under a large oak tree. A middle-aged man in baggy pants was drawing equations on an easel. Young Phil Merrick, one of the students, saw him and spoke briefly to the instructor. Then he came hurriedly toward Koepp. He was carrying a clipboard, which had a pencil attached to it with a cord.

"Can I talk to you?" the boy asked. He looked worried.

Koepp stopped. "Sure," he said.

"Actually me and—my sister and I both wanted to talk to you. I sorta promised her—"

"Then we had better include her in this conversation," Koepp said, smiling.

The boy's expression brightened a little. "She's in the garden," he said. "I can get her quick." He turned as if to run off, but Koepp put his hand lightly on the boy's shoulder.

"Why don't we just walk over there together? It'll be more private."

The boy rewarded him with a fleeting expression of gratitude. He also visibly relaxed, which Koepp noted with some satisfaction. The boy probably hadn't been sure Koepp would wait for him even though he said he would. Adults often didn't think lying to children really counted as lying; Koepp had promised himself when he was about Phil's age that he wouldn't be like that when he grew up.

They walked in silence for a short distance, then Koepp decided to use this opportunity to find out what he could about Neil Erickson and his brief teaching career at the university-sponsored school in Friars' Close.

Phil said that Erickson had taught him chemistry for about six months.

"How did you get on with him?" Koepp asked.

"Okay," the boy said. "He yelled at all of us sometimes, but he was a good teacher. He was fair. I mean, he didn't play favorites."

"What did the other students think of him?"

"Mostly, they thought he was okay."

"Does he come back here at all?" Koepp asked. "Have you seen him since he left?"

Phil looked down at his shuffling athletic shoes for a few paces before he answered, "Yeah, I saw him here a couple of weeks ago. "Before—you know—"

"Did you talk to him?"

"Just for a few seconds. He was at John Jaroff's home when John and I came back from baseball practice. They asked me if I had a tape recorder for playing those little micro audio tapes. I said I did."

"And you got it for them to use?"

"Sure."

"Do you know what they listened to?" Koepp asked.

The boy shook his head. "As soon as they had the tape recorder, Leon and Neil got into Neil's car and went somewhere in a hurry. I don't know where they went."

They turned the corner of the building and found themselves about twenty yards from the vegetable gardens. A small, lone figure was vigorously hoeing weeds in a row of radishes. She wore jeans and a white T-shirt, which seemed to be her uniform. As they approached her, Koepp could hear her talking to herself. The boy heard her, too; his face registered acute embarrassment. He yelled her name to get her attention, and to silence her.

The girl studied Koepp with dark, impassive eyes; once again he was struck by how much she resembled her mother.

"Erin, the sergeant said he'd talk to us," the boy told his sister. The two youngsters watched each other, transmitting an emotional empathy peculiar to some siblings.

Phil was the designated interrogator. "The news on TV Six said my mom was a suspect. The police think she—"

"They shouldn't have said that. It was stupid."

"That man Weber tried to hurt mom. They said you stopped him."

"Yes."

"Is she?" he asked.

"Pardon me."

"Is Mom a suspect?"

Koepp wished the boy hadn't asked. Still, true to his childhood promise to himself, he answered as honestly as the evidence permitted, "She is one of several 'suspects.'" He decided that not lying to children was a burden.

"What about Dad?"

"He's a suspect, too."

For the first time the girl spoke. "They were going to get a divorce," she informed him in a flat, dispirited voice. "But now they aren't." Her tone didn't change while relating this supposedly happy news. She made Koepp uneasy. Children who displayed no emotion seemed deformed to him, deprived of their essence, like birds that couldn't fly or flowers that didn't bloom.

"My parents wouldn't kill anyone," Phil said. "Issac was their friend."

"Did they tell you that?" When Koepp got no response, he continued, "Sometimes people just pretend to like another person—to get along with that person."

"I know that," the boy cried impatiently. "I'm not stupid." Koepp remembered the day that Phil's friend John Jaroff had teased him about being slow. "My parents wouldn't kill anyone," the boy said stubbornly. His eyes moistened. The girl's eyes, in disquieting counterpoint to her brother's, were dry.

"If you're right, then you shouldn't be worried about them," Koepp told the boy. "We don't arrest people if they haven't committed a crime."

"Please, please don't arrest them," the boy begged. Suddenly he was crying. He slumped into a crumpled sitting position in the dirt between the rows of vegetables.

Erin never took her eyes off Koepp, but she did move behind her brother and put one hand on the back of his head. Although junior to him by three years, she seemed much older. Maybe she's older than both of us, Koepp thought dismally. Never before in his police career had he been forced to deal directly with the offspring of the accused. The experience angered him because of its unfairness; arresting killers was emotionally crippling enough without having to justify one's actions to their children.

*"Erin, Phil."* Surprised, Koepp turned to see Karen Merrick approaching rapidly from one of the co-housing pool cars which was parked haphazardly on the roadway. She advanced purposefully toward Koepp. Some people could convey anger just by the way they walked; Karen was such a person.

"Phil, you should be in class," she said. "Erin, I want you to wash yourself, put away the hoe and come to my office with your schoolbooks." When the children failed to react quickly enough to suit her, she snapped, *"Now!"* Her actions were completely out of character.

They moved off together toward Buildings C and D. Even before they were out of earshot, the woman said in a shaking voice, "So now you're grilling my children."

*"They* asked to speak to *me."*

"You should have had the decency to refuse. How dare you talk to them without my permission?" Her voice was full of anger.

Koepp ignored the question. He was tempted to tell her that nothing he said would be as bad as what they heard on Channel 6, but decided against it. He was determined not to let her gall him to anger.

"Why was my son crying?" she demanded. "What did you say to him?"

"He's afraid I might arrest his parents. And I'm afraid at least half of his fear is justified."

"What do you mean?" Finally, her voice betrayed real fear.

"I mean we're close to having enough to charge your husband Paul with Steiner's murder."

For once she didn't automatically protest. Koepp took that as an encouraging sign; she might be susceptible to psychological pressure after all. But he had to be careful. Several things had happened in the past two days that made her suddenly less vulnerable. The fact that she had shared her bedroom with her husband again at the hotel in Forest Junction indicated a reconciliation was in process between the Merricks. Their daughter, in her strange, detached way, had just confirmed that by saying the planned divorce had been called off. And Paul Merrick's shock in learning that Karen had undergone therapy from Steiner suggested a degree of concern that had not been evident before. Karen cared about her husband, just as Merrick still cared about her.

He tried to exploit her weakness. "The case is mostly circumstantial," he told her, "but it's compelling just the same. Weber saw you drop the knife in the creek, which means either you or Paul killed Steiner. Paul had ample motive. Steiner was holding something over his head, something to do with falsifying research data. He also was afraid that Steiner's departure from Friars' Close would break up the project. That would have been catastrophic for both of you, and for your children as well, I would judge."

She watched him with an expression he had not seen previously. Despite her studied control, he imagined he saw fear and hatred. Was this the real Karen at last?

She turned wordlessly away from him and started back toward the Administration Building. Koepp watched her go, feeling the ache of irretrievable loss.

MRS. KUSAVA, attired again in the loose-fitting dress she had worn during their first conversation, offered him a cup of coffee. He accepted, then watched as she poured from a pot that stood on the stove in her tiny kitchenette. Her living room and connecting dinette were filled with antiques and bric-a-brac of all kinds. It was strange, he thought, how single people sometimes dispensed with their conventional idea of order in a household. Objects rested on chairs that she didn't sit in, furniture was arranged in the odd, eccentric geometry favored by people who were always alone, and living space took on an aspect of warehouseing. His mother's house had looked the same before she died.

"How can I help you, Sheriff?" the woman asked as she removed a wooden clock from a wing chair. She put it on the floor next to her and sat down. The clock, Koepp suspected, would remain in its new position indefinitely.

"It's about Charlie," he said. "And I'm not the sheriff. I'm a sergeant of detectives."

"Oh, yes, I must remember that. Karen told me." She nodded knowingly, sympathetic that his career was stunted.

"About Charlie. You were in charge of processing his application, is that right?"

"Yes. Karen normally would do that. She has great skill in sizing up people."

Ruefully, Koepp had to admit the truth of that assessment. "Would you tell me how you investigated Charlie's background?"

She shifted uncomfortably in the unfamiliar chair. In view of what had happened to Charlie, she would naturally feel defensive about admitting him to Friars' Close.

"He came to the office one day, making inquiries. I talked to him for some time. He seemed like a nice young man, very quiet and polite—you know, shy. I gave him one of our application forms to fill out. He said he would prefer to take it with him and bring it back later. I think he couldn't read or write as well as he thought he should, so I assumed he planned to have someone help him with the ap. He didn't want me to know, well, how he couldn't fill out the form by himself.

"But I wanted someone else to talk to him. Paul—Dr. Merrick—had just come back from the hospital. I asked him to talk to Charlie, which he agreed to do."

"Did Dr. Merrick think favorably of the new candidate?"

At first she looked at him uncomprehendingly, then she said, "Oh, yes, he said he thought the young man would be an asset because he was very mechanically inclined. People like that have a lot to contribute to a place like this. Things are always breaking down, you know. He was really quite clever even though he couldn't read and write well.''

"Did he bring the application back?"

"Oh, yes, a few days later. All neatly typed, which meant he had someone else fill it out for him."

"Did he list references?"

"Of course," Mrs. Kusava said. "We always request personal references."

"And you checked them?"

"Always."

"What about Charlie's? Did you personally check them?"

"Well, no," Mrs. Kusava admitted. "I'm not used to that. I don't know what questions to ask. I gave the application to Paul and asked him to call them."

"Paul Merrick?"

"Oh, yes. He called them all. Everyone he talked to said good things about Charlie, how he was very reliable, how he got along well with people."

Koepp nodded absently. For the first time the bizarre episode of Walter Omsby, alias Charlie Tirquit, fit inside the framework of Friars' Close. When Merrick discovered that young Omsby had vowed to kill Steiner, he saw it as an opportunity to rid himself of a blackmailer. So he helped Omsby get accepted into the project by not reporting his identity switch. Elizabeth Maklin apparently knew about the deception, which was why she tried to steal Omsby's application form. She was protecting her lover.

"Anyone else call Charlie's references?" Koepp asked.

The woman blinked several times, trying to comprehend the reason for the question. She sensed that he was going to imply that she had somehow been derelict. "I didn't see any need for anyone else bothering those people. Paul—"

"Those references would not have been bothered."

"I beg your pardon. I don't under—"

"None of Charlie's references is a real person."

"But—"

"Several days ago I tried to call those people," he told her. "They don't exist. And Charlie Tirquit doesn't exist, either. His name is Omsby. Everything on the application form is untrue. But you are telling me Paul Merrick said he talked to all the references?"

"Yes, definitely. But why would Paul have said that?"

"Why, indeed?"


KOEPP explained to Margaret and Lieutenant Tarrish how Paul Merrick had covered up Charlie Tirquit/Omsby's real identity. Margaret was excited. Tarrish was not. "It's interesting and pretty suspicious," he said, "but it isn't enough for an arrest, much less a conviction. It's just not enough." He settled back in his chair with his arms folded, a sign of intransigence.

"Ray knows that, Lieutenant," Margaret said. "I think he has something else in mind." She had met Koepp in the squad room a few minutes before this meeting. And although Koepp invited her to join in a "skull" session with Tarrish, he had not had time to brief her on his scheme. Nevertheless, she knew him well enough to sense when he smelled a breakthrough.

"I don't think Merrick killed Steiner," Koepp said. "I think his wife did. But we've got more on him than on her. I want to use that to break her."

"I don't like the sound of that."

"We don't seem to have any choice."

Tarrish started to protest, but Koepp raised his hand to stop him. "Lieutenant, hear me out. Pretend you're Karen Merrick, not a jury, while I make my case."

"Okay, but don't take all night. My wife's got some friends over for bridge tonight." He glanced at his watch to underscore his admonition.

"Here goes. Remember, you're Karen Merrick now. First point. Merrick lied about being at the Planners' meeting continuously. The meeting broke up for a while, more than long enough for Merrick to stick a knife in Steiner.

"Point two. Merrick had a fight with Steiner. The fibers from his sweater match those on Steiner's clothes. Also, Merrick admitted he had the fight."

"Merrick explained about the fibers by saying he made physical contact with Steiner—pushing, shoving," Tarrish reminded him.

"Yes, it may have happened that way. So it's inconclusive if we accept the fight as really happening."

"He's got two witnesses," Margaret pointed out.

"You're thinking like a DA," Koepp said. "Point three. Merrick had the motive of killing a man who knew about his falsification of test data and who no doubt possessed hard evidence of it.

"Point four. Merrick falsified his report on Omsby's references. However quixotic that was, it can be construed as an effort to help a potential killer gain daily access to his intended victim." Koepp paused. "What do you think?"

Margaret was sure of her answer. "I think I jumped to the wrong conclusion a little bit ago. You can make a fairly good case against Merrick."

Koepp was grateful for Margaret's support; her opinion weighed heavily with their watch commander. "You can make a lot of the fact that Merrick invited Charlie to join the project," Margaret said. She had begun to smile faintly. "I can't wait to hear the rest."

"Well, suppose we add—" Koepp hesitated.

Tarrish glanced at his watch and frowned.

"Point five," Margaret disclosed confidently.

"Point five," Koepp repeated. "We find one of Merrick's fingerprints on the knife."

The lieutenant looked irritable. "We checked the knife. No prints. *No prints,* Ray."

"Karen Merrick doesn't know that," Koepp said.

Margaret looked at Koepp with sudden interest. Her tentative smile turned into a grin. "She'll know we're running a frame if her husband didn't do it," she said. "On the other hand, if he did it, she wouldn't be certain she wiped off all his prints."

"Assume *she* did it. She'll know it's a frame, of course. I'm betting she won't let us lock up an innocent man with phony evidence. Either way, we pressure her. Maybe enough to get a voluntary confession."

Their supervisor had been adding up the hazards while he listened. "Sooner or later, Koepp, you're gonna cost me my pension. Let's see, entrapment, tampering with evidence—but what the hell, how would you play it?"

"I don't think she'll buy it if we just *tell* her we're going to tie Paul into it with fingerprints on the knife," Koepp said.

Margaret nodded. "I agree. You have to 'package' the fingerprint sting in a way that makes it credible. She's smart."

Koepp said, "I think I have a way." He was aware that Margaret was looking at him with an expression that suggested concern, maybe even pity.

KOEPP WAS WAITING for Russ Kalmbach outside of his lab in the basement of the Safety Building the next morning. He anticipated difficulty in getting Kalmbach's collusion, so he was there in person; experience had taught him that it was more difficult for a person to turn down a request for a favor if it was made face-to-face. Kalmbach watched him warily as he unlocked the door to the lab. He knew as well as Koepp how the game was played. Once they were inside the laboratory, Koepp told him what he had in mind.

"Absolutely not," Kalmbach said. "I wouldn't falsify evidence for my mother. My job is to put people in prison, not

go there myself." After ten minutes of pleading from Koepp,
he was saying that it wasn't fair to ask him to do such a thing.
Within twenty minutes Kalmbach conceded that he would
make up a bogus report for Koepp if the assistant district
attorney on the case authorized it. In Kalmbach's view, this
amounted to outright rejection because Styles had the reputation of being a stickler for due process and the integrity of
evidence gathering, not to mention his childlike faith in the
rights of the accused.

Koepp had no choice but to try Styles. Miraculously, the
assistant district attorney was in the first time Koepp phoned
him. The detective explained what he wanted to do, and that
Kalmbach would only cooperate if Styles told him he could.

"You're a couple of bricks short of a full load, Koepp,"
the prosecutor told him. "I'm not going to authorize anything
like that. Sweet Jesus!" He hung up.

Considering Styles's normal disposition and how angry he
was at Koepp anyway, the attorney's rejection had not been
as apocalyptic as Koepp had feared. He felt encouraged
enough to call District Attorney Wagner in Granite County.
Wagner was out but returned Koepp's call an hour later. If
he was surprised by Koepp's unusual appeal, he gave no indication of it. Probably he was flattered that Koepp would
think he could intervene successfully with Styles; the surest
way to get a man to do something was to appeal to his vanity.

"Okay, Sergeant, I'll give it a try," Wagner said. "If you
get your stage prop, do you think you can pressure her into
a confession?"

"I don't know. It's about the only chance I have left. I can
never get either one of them convicted if I have to rely on
physical evidence."

"You know," Wagner said, "if she stuck the knife into
Steiner, she'll know the fingerprints are phony. All she'll have
to do is play it cool. She'll know you won't dare use it in

court for fear of having her defense attorney expose your lab guy when he perjures himself. Then what?''

''She can't be sure that we won't commit perjury in order to get a conviction. It wouldn't be the first time a lab guy did that. At any rate, it won't get that far. She'll crack before then. She's on the edge right now.''

''She has to believe you're a big enough bastard to send an innocent man to prison. Will she?''

Koepp didn't know for sure. He thought she might. He also wondered if she could let her husband go to prison, knowing he was innocent. The two of them were going to find out a lot about each other in the next several days. Finally, Koepp said he didn't know what Karen would think.

''I thought it was him—Merrick,'' Wagner said. ''Putting a creature like Mrs. Merrick in prison amounts to sacrilege. God, she's a sexy woman.''

Asking the eccentric district attorney to intervene with Styles was a long shot, but his powers of persuasion proved to be as formidable as Koepp had hoped.

Styles, once he was convinced by Wagner to give Koepp's plan a try, didn't tell Koepp about his change of heart directly. He told Kalmbach, who called Koepp. ''The ADA says it's okay for me to dummy up that print report. You can probably have it by late tomorrow afternoon. Call me before you come down.''

''Okay, thanks, Russ. I owe you one.''

''*One!*'' Kalmbach began to laugh. ''One?'' Still laughing, the lab technician hung up.

This case was tearing Koepp apart. But now he saw the end of it. When he made an arrest, he could finally begin to get her out of his head, out of his soul.

# SEVENTEEN

LATE THE FOLLOWING afternoon Koepp picked up the print report from Kalmbach. It looked like any other lab report. Notations explained where the prints had been located; a photo reproduction of Merrick's right index finger, taken from his personnel file at the university, appeared next to a reproduction of a print allegedly taken from the murder weapon found in Weber's apartment. Even to a casual observer it was obvious that both prints were made by the same finger.

Koepp inserted the report into an envelope addressed in Lieutenant Tarrish's scrawling hand to "Sgt. Ray Koepp." In the upper left-hand corner the name "P. Merrick" had been printed in pencil in Margaret's neat penmanship. He went upstairs again and sat down on a chair next to Mary Jo Riley's desk. The young woman watched him expectantly.

"Let's go over it all one more time, to be sure."

She nodded. "You're going to the project, to Friars' Close now. You'll be there for no more than an hour. I park the squad car by that service station down the road and wait for you to pass. As soon as you do, I go directly to the office at Friars' Close and ask for you. They'll tell me you're interrogating some of the residents, but they won't know for sure where you're supposed to be. I'll ask if you're coming back. They'll say you're expected back. Tell me again, why will they think that?"

"Because I'll tell the person on duty that I'm going to come back to the purchasing agent's room," Koepp said.

"Then I'm to act kind of unsure of what to do. And then I'll ask the woman in the office to make sure you get the envelope because it's very important. I leave the envelope with her.''

''What if she won't keep it?''

''I'm to try to get her to let me leave it in the purchasing agent's office. That's it. I split.''

It was little enough, what he was asking her to do, and somehow it seemed silly now, even absurd. Nothing in the detective's manual suggested that psychological warfare like this had a place in a murder investigation. It wouldn't work, Koepp was now convinced, because it was too unorthodox, too bizarre, too likely to be upset by the unexpected. Karen was too smart to be taken in by his ruse. All she had to do to frustrate him again was do nothing. Wagner was right. Still, he had no choice but to try it.

When Koepp reached Friars' Close, he was elated to find Gwen on duty at the administration office. She was close to the Merricks; if anyone could be counted on to see that Karen got a look at the contents of his envelope, she could. The young woman smiled without warmth at him and walked to the chest-high counter that separated them.

''Are Dr. and Mrs. Jaroff in?'' he asked. He knew she kept a log of the comings and goings of the project's planners. She consulted a clipboard which had been lying on a desk. ''They're about. Probably at dinner in the refectory.'' ''Refectory'' was a term he hadn't heard since his seminary days.

''And the Merricks?''

''Karen's in her office. Paul is traveling to Chicago tonight. He left about an hour ago. You can go back to Karen's office if you like.'' There was a suggestion of a smirk on her features.

''No, that's okay. I want to talk to the Jaroffs now. When is Paul due back?''

''He's doing an interview on public television tomorrow,'' the girl said. ''He's also going to discuss the situation here with some colleagues, so he won't be back until the day after tomorrow."

"I may be back later," Koepp said. "Perhaps you could help me track down some other residents if I need them?"

"Of course. How is the investigation going?"

She inadvertently had given him an opportunity to put a little more bait on the hook; at the risk of overplaying his role, he said, "We have new evidence. If it pans out, we'll be able to make an arrest in a couple of days."

With that he departed for the "refectory."

He found both of the Jaroffs eating dinner, but at separate tables, true to the collegiality of Friars' Close. Dr. Jaroff looked annoyed when he noticed Koepp and didn't respond to his visitor's cheery greeting. Koepp, mindful that the sociologist had been criticizing him throughout the investigation, savored the man's irritation. Despite his hostile expression, Jaroff agreed to meet Koepp in half an hour in his home. Koepp poured himself a cup of coffee and sat at a table alone. He waited a few seconds after Jaroff departed, then followed the gaunt figure to his condo. Koepp had two objectives for this visit: he needed to kill some time to establish his presence at the co-housing complex; and he intended to find out what happened the night that Neil Erickson and Jaroff had borrowed Phil Merrick's tape recorder.

He attacked the second assignment as soon as they were seated in the den. "Dr. Jaroff, I'd like you to tell me about that tape you listened to a couple of weeks ago." To avoid any verbal fencing, he added, "The night Neil Erickson and you borrowed the Merrick boy's tape recorder."

Jaroff permitted himself a faint, fleeting smile. "So you found out about that? We had a meeting with a man named George Dietmeier at his hotel. He's the grant administrator for the Grayson Foundation."

Koepp wrote the name in his notebook. "What was he doing in the area?"

"He came from Boston to investigate charges Erickson had made against Dr. Steiner." Jaroff crossed his arms on his chest, but this time his posture didn't convey resistance.

"And the tape was evidence to support those charges?"

"Yes."

"And the nature of those charges?"

Jaroff chose his words carefully. "Perhaps we'd better back up a bit," he said. "Neil taught some science lab classes here for a few months. He was a good teacher, but he began to come to us—the Planners—with some unfounded accusations that Dr. Steiner represented a threat to the children. A sexual threat. It was conjecture. He never was able to offer any real proof to substantiate his charges. We told him to bring hard evidence or cease making accusations. When he didn't, we fired him."

"And Dr. Steiner didn't know about any of this?"

"No, nobody wanted to confront him because we had no real evidence. Ironically, Dr. Steiner pleaded Neil's case when we said he had to go. Issac had recommended him in the first place, so it was doubly ironic."

"But the tape was real evidence?" Koepp suggested.

"Yes," Jaroff said. "Neil had once worked for Issac, doing some kind of statistical analysis for one of his projects. They were also friends, played chess and that kind of thing. Somehow Neil had gotten hold of tapes Issac had made of therapy sessions with a few female patients. He sent them to Dietmeier, who came out here to discuss what to do about Issac and the project."

"And?"

"I listened to the tapes and agreed with Dietmeier that the grant could not continue unless Issac was forced out."

"The other two Planners—did they agree?"

Jaroff looked embarrassed when he said, "I couldn't let Paul Merrick hear the tape. His wife was one of the patients." He smiled grimly. "That left Elizabeth out, too."

"Yeah, I can see your point."

"Indeed. Dietmeier solicited my commitment that we'd continue the project without Issac, then told him he could bow out gracefully. Issac didn't take it well. In the end though, he agreed to announce he was leaving—"

"But he didn't do it right away," Koepp pointed out.

"No, he kept stalling. Deitmeier was furious. He didn't want to leave until he was sure Steiner had gone public. But he also wanted to keep a low profile, so the Merricks and the others wouldn't think Grayson had pressured Issac. Deitmeier was very circumspect. He would call me or he'd get Neil to call me. Issac just kept stalling—until that Saturday."

"He got a phone call from Erickson just before he was murdered," Koepp said. "What do you think that was about?"

"I'm sure Dietmeier made Neil call."

"That explains part of the riddle. Erickson lied about the reason for the call, the way it looks, but he was probably under orders from Dietmeier—"

"No doubt. Erickson's own grant application was turned down, so I assumed he was making himself useful to Deitmeier so he could get his application reconsidered. In the beginning I think he was genuinely worried about Issac doing something to one of our kids." Jaroff paused for a moment, then he asked, "What's the other part of the riddle?"

Koepp had to think for a moment before he said, "We never found the telephone message slip."

Jaroff grunted. "I can't help you with that one."

Koepp returned to his car then, staying well clear of the Administration Building. As he drove down the county road past the service station, Mary Jo flashed her lights to show him that she was ready to carry out her part of the stratagem. She must have seen the headlight signal in a James Bond movie, Koepp thought. He drove back to his apartment to

await her phone call report. Koepp felt grimly satisfied that
at last he had a plan that might end it.

THE FOLLOWING MORNING Koepp found himself teamed with
a rookie detective named Marston to investigate a jewelry
store robbery and shooting in the tony northern suburb of
Collinswood.

The shooting had a high priority because the citizenry,
while tolerant of street killings, took a jaundiced view of violent crime at shopping centers. Koepp managed to break free
from the robbery investigation long enough to call Tarrish in
midmorning. "Just checking in," he told his boss. "What's
happening?"

"Mary Jo got a call from the project. They want to know
what to do with your envelope."

"Who called in?"

"I don't know. You wanna talk to Mary Jo?"

Koepp said he did.

"I also got a call from Merricks' attorneys," Tarrish said.
"They're making noises about filing a complaint. Mrs. Merrick claims you've been interrogating her kids without permission. Tell me what happened."

Koepp explained about his encounter with Phil and Erin.
"You want me to come in?"

"Hell, no. That just gets everyone's blood pressure up. I'll
take care of it. Here's Mary Jo."

Koepp heard the clicking sound that meant his call was
being transferred to Mary Jo's extension. She came on the
line. "Got a call from that girl Gwen," she said. "The same
one I gave the envelope to last night."

"What did you tell her?"

"I acted like I was going to catch hell because you didn't
get the envelope yet. I said a uniform cop would be around
to get it." Her voice had an alien, emotional edge to it,
prompting Koepp to ask gently, "Is something wrong?"

Silence followed. "The lieutenant didn't tell you?"

"Tell me what?"

"He wants me to take a job with the Metro cops. They have an opening. He thinks I can get it if I apply for it."

This time the bird of silence roosted on Koepp's end of the line. Obviously, Tarrish planned to get rid of the temptation of Mary Jo Riley's vulnerable nubility by shipping her downtown. "What are you going to do?" he asked.

She was close to crying. "What choice do I have? If they don't want me here, what choice do I have?" Her voice broke, close to a sob. "It's because of what happened when we arrested Omsby, isn't it?"

"No, it's not, Mary Jo. That happens to everyone when they're new—me, Margaret, everybody."

She was not placated. "Oh, sure. A guy tried to give you a hard time, and you shot him twice in the heart."

Was that how she saw it? How did God see it?

"I'd think seriously about making the change, Mary Jo," he told her. "It's a political thing, it has nothing to do with what happened on the Omsby arrest, and the lieutenant is trying to do the right thing by you. Take his advice."

"But why? What did I do wrong?"

"Nothing. Listen, some day I'll explain it to you. Right now I can't." He switched to another subject. "Any other messages for me?"

"Karen Merrick called twice. She wants you to call her. Do you have her number?"

"Yes, but I'm not going to call her. If she calls again, just tell her you gave me the message. Above all, don't make excuses for me or say I've been too busy. I want her to realize that I'm deliberately not calling her."

"Okay."

"When did you get an officer over to Friars' Close to pick up the envelope?"

"About an hour after they called, about ten or ten-thirty."

"And you got the envelope to Kalmbach in the lab right away?"

"Yes," Mary Jo said. "Russ is kinda ticked at you because he doesn't like this—whatever it is. He's going to check the lab report for prints, though. He'll call me as soon as he knows whose prints are on the report. Do you care about the envelope?"

"No," Koepp said. "The envelope doesn't matter. I just want to know who gets inside it to look at the fingerprints."

"That's all Russ thought you were interested in. He's got a set of Mrs. Merrick's prints from Margaret. She printed everyone you talked to the day of the murder." Mary Jo made a brave effort to laugh. "Russ says Margaret is a pain—but thorough."

Koepp promised he would call back soon. Then he added, "Don't fight the system, Mary Jo. Take the Metro job."

It wasn't fair, but he was giving her the best advice he could. He was not about to tell her that she had to go elsewhere because she was exciting the passions of her superior. A practical concern was that she might file a formal complaint and destroy Tarrish's career as well as her own. And from an ethical standpoint, he was hardly in a position to criticize his boss, not after getting involved emotionally with a suspect.

She'd go in the end. As she put it, what choice did she have? What choice did any of them have? If his crazy plan fell apart, he'd be looking for a job in Metro himself.

HE NEVER had a chance to call Mary Jo again until after her shift ended. But when he arrived back in the squad room, he found a note inside a number ten envelope marked "Confidential." The note said: *Two sets of prints inside; one unidentified, one belonging to Karen Merrick.*

He crushed the note and held it up triumphantly. She went for it, he thought. He tossed the note into the wastepaper basket under his desk. There were two call-back slips from

Karen's attempts to reach him. He threw those in the waste container as well.

Of the day-shift detectives only he and Milt Farmer remained, although both of them had been relieved. Milt stood up at his desk and started to put his sport coat on.

"Want to go out for a beer?" Koepp asked.

Farmer looked surprised. Then he said, "Sure."

They went to O'Malley's, a popular watering hole for county cops about a block and a half from the Safety Building. It was a bar with an 1890s motif, including ornate brass chandeliers and fine wood paneling which had once adorned a now-defunct Presbyterian church. The current owner of O'Malley's, Vito Gianelli, took immense pride in the paneling, both because of its innate beauty and because of its ecclesiastical origins.

A handsome mahogany bar, appliquéd with padded stools, thrust out from one end of the room. Booths lined the holy walls of the establishment. All of them were occupied, so Koepp and Farmer circulated around the room, looking for an invitation to join somebody in a booth. Pete Marston, Koepp's partner for the day, was having a beer with Margaret; they invited the new arrivals to sit with them.

Koepp sat next to Marston so he could face Margaret. He knew she seldom frequented the place and then only with the stockbroker, whatever the hell his name was. He wondered if the pair had had a falling-out.

"How are things at Friars' Close?" she asked, forcing a smile; all she could manage was a suggestion of one. He had kept her informed about his doctored fingerprint report, which made it easier for him to update her in their verbal shorthand; he didn't want anyone else in the department to know what he was doing. "Karen Merrick has been trying to reach me by phone. Her prints are on the lab report."

This time his partner managed a satisfied grin. One of the things he liked about Margaret was her genuine satisfaction in other cops' successes. In this instance her pleasure was undoubtedly enhanced by the knowledge that it was Karen Merrick who was falling into his snare.

Farmer ordered a martini. Koepp asked for Scotch on the rocks. They listened to a resumption by Marston and Margaret of their discussion of the shopping mall shooting. A pregnant woman, an unlucky passerby, had been struck in the head by a stray bullet. She had died on the way to the hospital. The two younger officers obviously were angry about the killing, which was a healthy sign; you needed anger to keep going on a boring, routine investigation. Often it was the only thing that sustained a cop. They spent a few minutes unloading their job-related frustrations, then began to criticize Chief Vorhees's new exam protocol.

Suddenly, Margaret leaned across the table toward Koepp and whispered, "Speak of the devil!" He turned to look toward the bar. He could see Karen's head as she walked along the booths on the far side of the room. In another thirty seconds she was standing next to their table. Margaret nodded the faintest of acknowledgements. Koepp glanced up long enough to say, "Mrs. Merrick." Then he went back to looking at Milt Farmer, who was sitting opposite him with his eyes locked on the new arrival.

"I'd like to talk to you," Karen said. She was wearing a brown raincoat; he could see tan slacks below the coat's hem.

"There's only one thing I want to hear from you," Koepp said. "If that's what you're here for, then we can talk."

Almost immediately he regretted his harsh response. He was bullying her in public, in what was already an awkward situation for her. He had the right to send her to prison, but not to humiliate her.

Although she said nothing, her eyes flashed with hurt or anger. He couldn't be sure which. She had tied a print scarf over her dark hair, which had the effect of making her face seem smaller and younger than usual. The phalanx of backs along the bar provided a backdrop that also somehow diminished her stature. She reminded Koepp, as she stood with her hands on the edge of their table, of the girl in Manet's *The Bar at the Folies-Bergère*. The coloration differed—Karen's browns in place of Manet's blues—but the subjects' faces were identical: sadness, fatigue, the expectation that the only human response would be confused indifference. Her calmness, the confidence she had exuded so often in the past had deserted her; she had been reduced by the ordeal to the point where her desperation was exposed.

Koepp rose and put his hand on her arm, gently prying her away from the table. She offered no resistance as he led her slowly through the crowd of standing patrons who clogged the aisle between the bar and the booths. There was no place to take her for privacy except back to the street.

Outside, the air was dank. An ominous east wind prophesied the coming of a rainstorm and tried to draw attention to itself by raising dust and scraps of newspapers out of the gutters. A dog was barking several blocks away. They could hear it plainly despite the heavy automobile traffic on the street. They turned instinctively to the right, away from the wind.

"Perhaps you should go back to your friends," she said in a reedy voice.

"Where is your car?" he asked. He grasped her arm more firmly, feeling protective.

"I took the bus. There weren't any pool cars available."

"Mine's across the street." He steered her to the corner, waited with mounting uneasiness for the light to change and led her into the Safety Building parking lot. It started to rain. When he reached his car, he unlocked the passenger side first and held her arm while she climbed in. He sat in the driver's seat.

"I'm sorry, Ray. I truly am sorry that you're involved, that you had to be the one. I hope you'll believe that."

He stared ahead at the cycles of pink that appeared in a hundred beads of water on the car hood when a neon car wash sign ignited. Rain pattered in sympathetic cadence on the automobile roof. Normally he liked rain in the spring; tonight it annoyed him. He was aware of the scent of perfume, of her tense stillness in the seat next to him, of her constricted energy. All the while he had no idea what she was up to or what she hoped to accomplish. For some reason he was sure that she was not going to make one last tearful appeal; even in a crisis she couldn't resort to the conventional. She waited for a long time before she realized he wasn't going to say anything.

"Are you planning to arrest my husband?" she asked at last.

"Yes. Tomorrow, as soon as he gets back."

"How do you know I won't call him and warn him?"

"I expect you will. It won't matter. He can't get far, and it would be a mistake for him to try."

"He wouldn't run. Paul could never do anything like that. He would never do that to Phil and Erin."

"Tell me about Paul."

She turned to look at him in surprise. He couldn't see her face, but the movement of her head betrayed the emotion. "What do you want to know?" she asked.

"Your daughter said that you were going to get a divorce, but that now you've changed your minds. I think that happened in the hotel in Forest Junction. How did he manage to get back in your good graces?" Even though the question degraded them both, Koepp was glad he had asked it; curiosity often triumphed over good sense.

"How strange that you should think that," she replied softly. "He took *me* back into his good graces. At least to the extent that he was still able to. I was not a good wife to Paul. I could never give him the only thing he really wanted. By the time we were married there wasn't any warmth left in me. Red took that away."

"Is there any now?"

"Not for Paul. At least not yet. But our children need us. And maybe there's still hope." Karen laughed grimly. "At the age of forty-one I learned something very incredible. I learned that I'm capable of loving a man. For me that's a significant achievement."

Don't say anything else, Koepp thought in rising panic. Don't try this, please. I won't be able to handle it. He realized then that she had said something else.

"I'm sorry—"

"I asked what evidence you had to arrest Paul."

"You know about the fibers of his sweater on Steiner's shirt. I'm sure you also know that Paul knew Omsby wanted to kill Steiner, yet he admitted him to the community anyway. There's more."

"Paul's fingerprint on the knife?"

"So you looked inside the envelope that arrived last night?"

"You knew I would. I suspect you even concocted the whole thing, from beginning to end. I know that report is phony. Paul never touched the knife. He found the body. That's all."

"The only way you could be sure is if you did it."

She ignored that charge completely. "If you persist, it will come out in court that you doctored the knife."

"You're wrong there, Karen. When a latent print is dusted, the contours of the skin show up. A piece of lift tape is applied, and the print is transferred to a lift card. The technician notes on the card the location from which he lifted the print. Russ Kalmbach has Paul's prints from microdisks in the computer room. All he has to do is put one of those prints on the lift card and say that it came from the knife handle."

"That's perjury. He could go to jail for falsifying evidence."

"He didn't the last time." Now that he was committed to the lie, he felt almost relieved. Lying got easier with practice. "A rapist named McGruder. He was convicted last summer—about July, I think. Have your lawyer look into it. Russ will perjure himself if he thinks that it's the only way we can convict the guilty. He believes your husband is guilty. I've convinced him. Paul is going to prison."

"But you know he isn't guilty."

For the first time, her voice was constricted with genuine fear. Koepp could sense that it was going to work, yet he felt no satisfaction, no sense of winning. Something in his insides was drying up.

"I don't know any such thing, Karen. One of you did it. I know Russ will testify that he got the print from the knife because he already agreed. If Paul is guilty, then he gets what he deserves. If he's innocent, you've got a moral dilemma."

"You'd let an innocent man go to prison?"

"I'd let a man who might be innocent go to prison. Would you let a husband you knew was innocent go to prison? You're the one with the bigger problem."

"I can see this was a mistake." She pulled down on the door handle and started to climb out of his car. But Koepp reached across and yanked the door shut. "I'll take you back. Maybe before we get there you'll tell me the truth." But she choose not to speak to him again in the half hour it took to drive to Friars' Close.

# EIGHTEEN

IT WAS A measure of Koepp's desperation that he went back to O'Malley's after he dropped Karen off. It was a measure of Margaret's curiosity that she was still there, waiting for him. Marston had disappeared, having been replaced by one of Russ Kalmbach's lab technicians, a gangling young man from Iowa or Nebraska who was always setting up betting pools around the Safety Building. He wore glasses and a perpetual expression of pained incredulity beneath a crown of unruly blond hair. He was a clever mathematician, one of those curiously annoying people who was capable of doing vast sums in their head with remarkable speed and unerring accuracy. His skills had made him suspect as a betting pool organizer, and his trade was reported to have fallen off during the recently completed NCAA basketball tournament. He was trying to entice Margaret into betting on a Bucks-Hawks game, evidently without much success, judging from her bored expression.

Although Margaret clearly had been waiting for news, she didn't question him when he sat down. The mathematician looked disappointed once he realized that Koepp intended to stay. After a while he said good night and drifted off toward the bar in search of high rollers, particularly those as yet unacquainted with stories about his math skills.

"He'd make book on the end of the world," Koepp said. "And skim salvation off for himself."

"Where is—you know?"

"You know and I came to a fork in the road." She didn't sound devastated. More like relieved.

"I'm sorry."

"There's no need to be."

"What happened?"

"He couldn't deal with my being a cop, for one thing," Margaret said.

"And the other things?"

"They aren't any of your business," Margaret answered in a flat tone. "Ray, let's talk about something else. Did Mrs. Merrick give you a tearful confession?"

"No. But she says her husband is innocent. She maintains his prints couldn't be on the knife. I told her Russ Kalmbach will lie on the witness stand. I don't know if she believes me."

"The arrow points at her then." If she felt any elation in having been right about Karen Merrick's guilt, she had the grace not to let it show. "I think she'll crack. She looked bad tonight, really stretched out."

A piano player took up his post and began to play some songs from the thirties. A crowd gathered around him. Koepp ordered another Scotch. Margaret waved the cocktail waitress away and continued to nurse a stein of beer; the beer looked flat, like it had been setting there a long time. Some of the patrons began to sing along with the piano player, an ascetic, thin man of indeterminate age who was said to be a high school band director during the day. Good cheer and camaraderie oozed through O'Malley's. Koepp ordered more drinks, searching for the sharper mentality and duller senses that presaged alcoholic euphoria. Soon the quality of the singing seemed to improve, the lights glowed with a wonderful cheery color, and Margaret's wan beauty took on a mysterious aspect he hadn't noticed before. They joined the crowd beside the piano, stopping to laugh whenever they couldn't remember the words, which was often.

The other revelers were uncommonly pleasant and well mannered, Koepp decided. He put his arm around Margaret's waist, felt her tense, then relax. Someone mentioned Cole Por-

:er, but the musician had embarked on the theme from *Exodus*. It was dramatic, but sad. Koepp wanted happy music. He only liked sad music when he was happy.

The atmosphere began to get blurry; people looked like they were tangling together and he was aware that Margaret was talking to him. He smiled encouragingly even though he couldn't quite understand what she was saying. Or maybe he couldn't hear her. At any rate there was no comprehension, only a warm, muzzy sensation of being talked to by a woman who liked him. He wanted her to know that he appreciated her kindness.

"Do you know what I like about you, Margaret? You're straight ahead. You don't play mind games with other people." He was very pleased at how successfully he had explained that. And how clearly.

Margaret smiled up at him, understanding. He was surprised how short she looked standing next to him. He had always thought she was much taller than Karen. Now he saw that she and Karen were almost the same height. This also pleased him. He was glad that she looked shorter tonight than she usually did. He became vaguely aware that she had removed his hand from her waist and had taken his arm in both of her little Karen hands. No, he thought, *Margaret.* Margaret's hands. They were working their way slowly through the crowd toward the door, which probably meant that they were leaving.

"Margaret, another brew for you?" He liked the poetic sound of that so much that he said it again.

"I have to drive," she said, continuing to steer him through the tangle of people. He knew when the blast of rain struck him that he was outside again, on the same street where he and Karen had walked a month or a year ago. After what seemed a long time, he felt Margaret—or was it Karen?—shoving him into a small red sports car. He couldn't seem to get his enormous bulk into the front seat and protested, "I can't get in, now that's a sin, but I could if you could make me thin.''

He laughed hysterically; anything that rhymed made him laugh. God, he loved rhyming. Rhyming was something you could depend on. Not like people, who always let you down sooner or later. "People are bastards, partner," he said. But she wasn't there. Neither Margaret nor Karen. He was in the car by himself.

After a while one of them materialized—he wasn't sure anymore which one—and bent over to unlock the door on his side. He thought this was her car, so he couldn't understand why it took her so long to get into it.

She must have managed somehow because he realized that he was at his apartment and was trying to get out of the tiny, tiny car. "I'm stuck," he cried, panicked. She kept pulling on his arm, though, and after a while he popped out like a cork coming free of a bottle of champagne. The ground was undulating so badly that he had to put each foot down when the next wave of asphalt came up to meet him. It took a long time to navigate to the front door. She was there. She was helping him.

Then she was sticking her little hand into each of his pockets, trying to find his apartment key. He couldn't help. He didn't know where the damned thing was. Anyway, he liked having her sticking her hands into his pockets. He was starting to become aroused. He giggled. She was bent over, trying to insert the key into the lock. Then the huge, majestic door swung inward toward the black cave beyond.

"Open sesame," he cried. It was truly marvelous the way she had solved the riddle of the door. She led him into his bedroom, removed his coat, his sport jacket, his tie, and finally, after pushing him onto the bed, his shoes. He looked up into her enigmatic eyes, saw the lopsided smile. He wondered what she had done with the print scarf as he reached for her. But she eluded him.

"Sleep here tonight," he invited.

"Ask me again when you're sober," the woman said.

Then she was gone. He was alone once more.

KOEPP'S FIRST sensation as he regained consciousness was that he was freezing to death. His second sensation was that he would die of thirst before hypothermia dispatched him. He chose thirst and reached for his blanket. It was gone. In the act of reaching he had made the mistake of moving his head; it felt as if it would fall off his trunk. Some arteries in his neck and head throbbed relentlessly in cadence with ancient Scottish bagpipes. Fortunately, he didn't feel nauseous, which he had long since discovered was the sole advantage of drinking Scotch.

He opened his eyes slowly and saw Margaret standing beside his bed, stripped now of the dual personas that had bedeviled him the night before. Some of it came back to him. She had brought him home. Most of his clothes were still on. Apparently she had taken his key with her and had returned to roust him.

She was a fabulous, loyal partner, he decided.

"Better get your carcass out of there, Sergeant," she said. "You're going to make us late for work."

Loyal, yes, but also tough. Very tough.

He tried to comply by first sitting up. He managed it with difficulty and more pain in his brain. Margaret, gripping him by the shoulders, pulled him forward and onto his feet. She was surprisingly strong, and tall, much taller than she had been when they left O'Malley's.

"How tall are you, Margaret?" he asked.

"Five seven and change," she answered, not surprised. "Take a shower. I'll make some coffee."

After he had showered and shaved, he put on a robe and went to the kitchen. She had made orange juice from a concentrate in his freezer and some instant coffee. He gulped the orange juice from a tall glass, asked for a refill, and sipped the coffee while she poured the fruit juice. If he got enough liquid, he might be able to make it to work.

"You drove me home, didn't you?"

She nodded, smiling faintly.

"Thanks. I hope I wasn't too much trouble."

"What are friends for? You're a happy drunk at least. I made some toast for you."

She brought two pieces of buttered toast on a plate and a glass of apple jelly. When he turned away in disgust, she insisted he eat something. He tried, out of gratitude for what she had done for him the night before. He nearly gagged on the first bite; with a lot of coffee to liquify his throat he managed to get one piece down. Margaret smiled approvingly, showing for the first time a maternal side he hadn't discerned before. He wasn't sure he liked it.

Just then the phone on the kitchen wall rang. He looked at Margaret beseechingly.

"I'm not answering your phone at seven o'clock in the morning," she informed him. "Why take the pain if you don't get the gain?"

"You're only talking dirty because I'm helpless," he grunted, staring at the offending telephone. It rang again, mocking his physical incapacity. He rose slowly and lurched across the room. "La Belle Dame Sans Merci," he muttered for no particular reason.

"You don't deserve mercy, Sergeant," Margaret said. She raised a coffee cup to her lips and began to sip.

Ah, Sergeant, is it? he thought. That meant she was mad at him after all. He wondered if she read Keats.

"Hello. Koepp."

It was the lawyer he had met at Forest Junction, *her* lawyer, Everett Longworth. He apologized for the early hour, explaining that he had tried without success to call Koepp the previous evening. He had been requested by Mrs. Merrick to arrange a meeting at Friars' Close as soon as possible. Would it be convenient for Sergeant Koepp to meet Mrs. Merrick and himself about eight-thirty in the Administration Building?

Koepp said it would be. He hung up and wended his way back to his chair. Margaret, seated on the opposite side of the counter, watched him with a small, triumphant smile on her full lips. "Lady Macbeth?"

"Her lawyer."

"A meeting?"

"Yes, at Friars' Close in an hour."

"La Belle Dame Sans Merci," Margaret said.

"I KILLED Issac Steiner," Karen Merrick said.

She was sitting across the conference table from Koepp and Margaret, next to Everett Longworth, who appeared much less distinguished at this early hour. Koepp guessed that the lawyer might have had a bad night. Maybe he had gotten tanked at a bar like O'Malley's.

Karen seemed to be waiting for something to happen. Unlike her attorney, she looked calm and well rested. She wore a cream-colored blouse, a black skirt, and a black-and-gray hound's-tooth blazer. Too severe for her, Koepp thought, but appropriate under the circumstances. She was quite lovely, despite her paleness and the deathlike opacity of her eyes.

"Tell us how you killed him, Karen," Margaret said.

"I stabbed him with a butcher knife from the kitchen."

"No. We know that. Tell us what you did before you killed him. What did you do afterward? How did you hold the knife? When did you decide to kill him?"

"Karen, I have to warn you—"

She held up her hand to stop the lawyer from interrupting. "It's all right, Everett. I know what I want to do. I'd hated Issac for years, for what he did to me, for the way he debased me when he was supposed to be treating me. The day of the art fair my husband came to my office from the meeting the

Planners had with Issac. He told me what had happened, how the two of them had scuffled. I went to Issac's room on the second floor, but he wasn't there. Then I came back downstairs and went to the kitchen for a knife. I thought he might be in the computer room. He was.''

''What made you think he'd be there?'' Margaret asked.

''He went there to escape sometimes,'' Karen said without hesitation. ''Lots of us hide from people behind our PCs.''

''Go on.''

''I stood outside the door of the computer room. I asked for permission to come in to talk to him. He said he knew what I wanted. He also said it wouldn't do me any good. I went in. When he stood up and turned around, I stabbed him. I kept stabbing him. To make sure.''

Koepp remembered Margaret's observation that Steiner's body was well away from the axis between his PC and the door. The position of the corpse didn't quite fit with Karen's description of her attack.

Margaret reached into her handbag and brought out a short, collapsible umbrella. She laid it on the table in front of Karen. ''Pretend that's the knife. Show us exactly how you used it.'' Karen gripped it overhand and made several downward thrusts. The angle of her hand was consistent with the entry wounds in Steiner's body.

Margaret motioned for her to sit down again. She retrieved her umbrella and put it back in the handbag. ''Why did you go to his room without the knife if you intended to kill him?'' Margaret asked.

''I hadn't thought about killing him at first. I was angry and upset. When I saw he wasn't in his room, it made me stop and think. I realized that he would never listen to reason. He didn't care about anyone but himself. The drugs proved that. I begged him to stop selling that poison. I threatened to turn him in, but my husband Paul always begged me not to. We had terrible fights about it. Paul was afraid of something

Issac knew about him. He thought Issac would use it to get revenge if we reported him.''

"What did he have on Paul?"

"I don't know."

"What did you do after you stabbed him?"

"I went back to Issac's room. I had found the door unlocked on my first trip, so I knew I could get in. I washed the knife in the bathroom—''

Margaret interrupted. ''In the bathtub?

"No, in the sink—the washbasin."

Koepp thought with churning emotions that only the murderer could know that for sure. Or, she could have guessed; the chance of being right was fifty percent.

Margaret resumed her questioning. ''What next?''

"I took off my blouse and washed it in cold water. There was a lot of blood on it. Then I went to my office, where I always keep a sweater. While I was there I got a phone call from Elaine, who was running a charity raffle in the parking lot of Building D. She said she needed some more raffle tickets and would send Ina Jaroff over to get them. I took a roll out of the safe and went to intercept her. I didn't want Ina to come into the Administration Building for fear she'd be the one to discover—Issac. She's so hysterical. She insisted I look at some paintings, so I had no choice but to go out with her. I was wearing the sweater to cover up the wet blouse, and I had the knife inside a rolled-up magazine. When we got to the bridge I stopped to pretend to tie my shoe. While I was kneeling, I let the knife slide through a space between the boards into the creek. That's what Roman saw. When I got to my own building, I threw the blouse in a clothes dryer and put on one just like it. After that, I came back here. As soon as I got inside I met my husband, who had just found Issac's body. I was the one who went back and closed the door to the computer room. I told him to recall the meeting. After that I went to the lounge and found Mrs. Kusava."

"She wasn't there the first time you went, is that right?" Margaret asked.

"Yes. I waited for about fifteen minutes for my husband to find Elizabeth and Leon, then I suggested that she take the Planners' group some refreshments. She found some soft drinks, as I recall."

"What time was that?" Margaret asked.

"About three-ten or three-fifteen."

"What did you do next?"

"I went back to the computer room to open the door so someone would see what I had done." She paused for a moment to cough demurely into a handkerchief. Longworth gallantly offered to go to the kitchen for a glass of water, but she told him it wasn't necessary. She resumed her confession with the same icy control she had exhibited from the start. "I didn't want to be the one who 'discovered' the body. I also didn't want any of the leaders involved. While I was by the front entrance, Charlie must have come in the west door and passed the computer room. As I recall, I met him returning from the direction of my office. He told me that—well, what he had seen. I sent him back to get the ice and told him not to tell anyone but to go about his business like nothing had happened. Then I went back to my office and called the police. You know the rest."

Margaret sat quietly, watching Karen, and thoughtfully digested what she had been told. She seemed to be satisfied that what she had heard was consistent with the evidence previous witnesses had given them. Koepp was surprised that she apparently had not noticed the one odd discrepancy; Karen's failure to say anything about her daughter Erin. Then Koepp remembered that Margaret had been on the plane to Ann Arbor when Tirquit/Omsby had mentioned to Milt Farmer and himself that he met Karen, Ina, and Erin in the corridor after finding Steiner's body. He was about to question Karen about Erin. But something stopped him. He remembered a statement

Dr. Syrk had made: Erickson had asked her to talk to one of the Friars' Close children.

The detectives went into the hallway to confer. "The way she says she killed him leaves the position of the body unexplained," Margaret noted.

"And her motive?"

"She had good reason to hate him, and this place is very important to her. She might kill to protect it."

Margaret obviously thought Karen's story held together. Except for leaving her daughter out of the narrative, Karen had given a plausible account.

"She didn't hesitate about where the knife was rinsed off," Koepp said.

"She could have guessed right," Margaret countered. "But she came back with the right answer so quick. If she had to guess, it would have taken her a moment to come up with an answer. Should we take her in?"

"Not yet. I want to make a quick phone call. In the meantime, make her go through it again. Maybe she'll contradict herself, or get creative."

Margaret nodded. "Face it, Ray. She killed him."

"You're right, I'm sure, but I still want to make that phone call to Dr. Syrk. Humor me. Make her go through it again." Koepp walked to the purchasing agent's office and dug a phone directory out of a desk drawer. He dialed the university hospital and asked for Syrk, the colleague of Steiner's they had interviewed early in the investigation. "She's on rounds," a female voice informed him.

"Have her call Sergeant Koepp as soon as she's free. Tell her it's important I talk with her right away." He gave her the general number of Friars' Close, then he went to the office to tell the person on duty where he would be when his call was returned. For once Gwen was not there. Instead, he was greeted by a chunky, brown-haired girl he assumed was

Elaine. She promised to come and get him as soon as Dr. Syrk called.

When Koepp got back to the conference room, Karen was well into her narrative the second time. After a few minutes it was obvious that the second version was identical to the first. She even used many of the same phrases, the same inflections. Either she was reciting the truth or she had rehearsed her story to perfection. She never looked at Koepp when he came back into the room, nor did her eyes leave Margaret's face until she reached the end of her confession. Again, she made no mention of her daughter.

The second confession concluded, Margaret looked expectantly at Koepp. Her expression conveyed that her opinion had not changed. As far as she was concerned the case of Issac Steiner's homicide was solved.

Koepp could see little point in delaying further. "Karen— Mrs. Merrick—we're going to take you to headquarters. You're under arrest for the murder of Issac Steiner."

"I'd like to get some things together."

"Of course. Detective Loftus will go back to your apartment with you. I'll bring our car around."

"Sergeant," Longworth said, "I'd like to take Mrs. Merrick to the Safety Building in my car if you don't mind. She obviously has no intention of escaping prosecution."

Koepp paused for a moment. Finally, he said, "Okay, you can drive ahead of us." Both women rose.

"My children don't know what's happening," Karen said, looking down at Koepp in an accusatory fashion, as if this oversight were his fault. Or perhaps he saw accusation where none existed. Arresting officers often felt guilty about sending their fellowman to prison; justice didn't always make it less cruel.

"When is your husband going to be back?" Koepp asked.

She glanced at the gold watch on her slim wrist, then mentally calculated for a few seconds. "In about an hour and a

half," she said. "But he'll go directly to the university. He
has a lab class."

"I can leave a message for him to come back here right
away, or we can intercept him at the airport."

"No, that won't be necessary. Just have him paged. Elaine
can do it. Tell her he's on the Mid America flight from Chicago that gets in at eleven."

Koepp promised he would do so.

Then the two women departed. Koepp and Longworth
stood together in the conference room a few moments longer,
unsure what to do, suddenly and inexplicably irrelevant. In
silence they strolled out to the reception area, where they entered the office through a side door. Elaine was on the telephone, so Longworth sat down on a secretary's chair to wait.
Koepp walked across the room to stand in front of the bank
of windows facing the tiny, bucolic valley that bisected the
property. Karen and Margaret, their backs toward him, were
crossing the footbridge. As they ascended the walk on the
opposite side of the creek, a slight figure emerged from Building C and ran toward them. Koepp recognized Karen's daughter Erin.

He heard Elaine say good-bye to her caller and hang up the
telephone. Then he was aware of a hushed conversation on
the other side of the office between the girl and the attorney.
He was probably giving her instructions about paging Paul
Merrick at the airport. Koepp paid little attention to their conversation because he was preoccupied by the three figures on
the walkway. Margaret and Karen had been joined by Erin.
The mother and daughter were engaged in an intense discussion when suddenly the youngster lunged at Margaret and
tried to strike her with her clenched fists. His partner backed
away, fending off the ineffectual blows with her forearms.
Even at this distance Koepp could see that Margaret was surprised by the aggressiveness of the attack. Karen managed to

intervene and pulled the girl against her. For a moment they hugged each other fiercely.

Just then the office phone rang.

He heard Elaine say, "Yes, he's here. Just a moment."

Reluctantly, Koepp gave up his vigil and went to the phone. Elaine handed him the receiver. The caller was Dr. Syrk from the university. Koepp reminded her that they had talked about Dr. Steiner.

"I remember you, Sergeant Koepp," the woman said.

"On the day when we talked to you and Dr.—"

"Abrams," she said helpfully.

"You told us how Dr. Steiner made fun of psychotherapy, how he talked about the vulnerabilities of female patients."

"I remember that," the psychiatrist said.

"You also told me on the phone that Erickson wanted you to examine one of the Friars' Close children. Did he tell you if the kid's problem involved Dr. Steiner?"

"I'm sorry, Sergeant." Dr. Syrk said. "I can't comment on that. It would be nothing more than slander."

"Is it also slander to say that Steiner was a dealer?"

"No. Everyone knew about the cocaine. It was an open secret, if you know what I mean."

"Was Steiner using drugs to seduce kids?"

"I've told you. I won't disclose that. It would be very unfair to—"

"Do you know Dr. Paul Merrick? He teaches at the university."

"Of course. He's in the sociology department. Quite well known in his field, I understand. He was an associate of Dr. Steiner's as a matter of fact. They were joint recipients of several research grants, I believe." Koepp's impatience had begun to fester; he didn't need a recitation of Merrick's academic credentials.

Frustration caused him to try to gain his ends by shocking

her. "Dr. Merrick's wife has just been arrested for Dr. Steiner's murder," he said.

She listened to this revelation in silence. Koepp could hear her breathing heavily. And more rapidly. I might be right, he thought.

"I must know why Erickson was concerned, Doctor. It's essential to our investigation."

Again there was only silence at first. Then the woman said hesitantly, "Dr. Merrick's daughter had been admitted here for treatment, for psychotherapy. Her regular physician was a woman, Dr. Mapes. While Dr. Mapes was on pregnancy leave, another member of the staff naturally treated some of her patients."

*"But what did Erickson say!"*

The woman's calm demeanor had abandoned her. "I'm coming to that," she said in a tight voice. "Dr. Merrick always took the girl home after her therapy. One day Mrs. Merrick came for her daughter because Dr. Merrick was out of town. Mrs. Merrick found out that her daughter had a session with Dr. Steiner. She reportedly became very upset."

"Go on."

"Neil thought Steiner had seduced one of the children, a girl. After the incident with Mrs. Merrick, I concluded he had been talking about the Merricks' child."

After Dr. Syrk hung up, Koepp stood still for a moment with the phone clamped against his ear, immobilized by shock. He tried to digest the implications of what he had just heard.

Was Karen trying to protect someone? Or was her motive staring him in the face for the first time? Or was the answer the same for both questions?

The attorney said something as Koepp, fully energized again, strode grimly out of the office. Koepp ignored him.

Ina Jaroff was approaching the front door of the building from the opposite direction, her arms filled with parcels. She saw him headed determinedly toward the glass door; with surprising dexterity she stepped off the sidewalk to let him pass. Something in his face must have warned her, just as it caused an elderly man with a cane to pause and wait on the opposite side of the footbridge. Tony Divito, driving a large riding lawn mower along the serpentine path of the creek, brought his machine to a stop and watched Koepp's progress with an open mouth.

By the time he reached the top of the grade and the sidewalk that ran along the length of Building D, he had brought his anger about her lies and deceptions under control.

But a small maggot of fear had begun to slither up his spine.

KOEPP ENTERED the building and knocked on the door of the Merricks' home.

A muffled voice responded, but none of the room's occupants came to open the door for him.

He knocked again, harder. Again nobody came. He grasped the knob and cursed softly when it failed to turn. But he heard a strident cry inside, some unnatural sound, the sound of violence. With his .38 now gripped in both hands, he stood back about three feet, cocked his right leg and sent it crashing against the heavy door. He heard wood splintering inside, but the door remained in place. Once more he raised his leg and kicked straight ahead. This time it gave way.

With the door partially ajar, the shriek of pain and terror struck him with pointed fury. He pushed the damaged door out of his path and ran down the narrow corridor which led to the living room. He heard the swishing sounds of movement across a thick carpet, and a second scream, not of terror or pain, but of frenzy.

His momentum had carried him well into the large room before his eyes had a chance to transmit the essential ugliness of the scene to his brain. Margaret, with one hand on the arm of the sofa for support, was backing toward the picture window opposite the apartment door. The side of her blouse was drenched with red, in startling contrast to her ashen features. Part of her body was screened from Koepp's view by a crouched, menacing figure which stalked her with one arm raised high. The arm had a simian quality about it because it was elongated grotesquely by the blood-drenched implement it wielded.

Koepp took an involuntary step back, colliding with someone—Karen, he realized at once—who gasped as he raised his gun. In that instant it seemed that Erin would make her attack over the back of the sofa. Instead, realizing her victim was a little out of reach, she moved to the right to circle behind the couch.

*"Freeze!"*

For the first time the girl acknowledged his presence. She coiled so only her face was turned toward him. Koepp looked into her eyes and saw their murderous opacity. A cobra's eyes. The eyes Issac Steiner had been looking into the afternoon he died.

Koepp's mind reeled with the effort of connecting this creature with the child he knew.

He tried to sight over the barrel of his .38, but the revolver's muzzle moved shakily back and forth. She was standing in such a way that Margaret's slumping form was directly behind her. Koepp moved to his left so he could change the angle and get Margaret out of the line of fire.

Erin turned her back on him and looked for Margaret, who had slumped to a kneeling position with only her head visible above the back of the couch. The scene had an eerie familiarity to it. He saw Roman Weber's contorted body lying like a rag doll on the cabin floor. He remembered the panicky features of Charlie Tirquit as he dragged Mary Jo.

Once again fate had taken charge. If Erin went for Margaret, he'd have one chance to stop her. If he missed, the knife would strike again, fatally. Or he would kill a thirteen-year-old. His only hope was Karen. Karen would disarm Erin as she had disarmed Charlie.

He waited for her to act, to appear from behind him and soothingly speak to her daughter. But a quick glance revealed her immobilized by fear, staring at his gun.

With a pitiable groan, Margaret disappeared completely from his sight. This made her position even more precarious. Now Erin could dive to the floor to attack and Koepp wouldn't have a clear shot. He'd have to fire into the back of the couch and hope that he hit his target.

He had to divert her attention from Margaret, keep her focused on him. "Drop the knife, Erin. *Drop it!*"

The girl hesitated. For the first time, she appeared unsure of what to do next. Her hesitation caused Koepp to act instinctively, to move toward her. She fixed her attention on him. He moved a step closer.

"Drop the knife," he commanded more gently.

She raised the knife behind her, getting it in throwing position.

Koepp reasoned coolly that he was justified now in shooting her. But he could not squeeze the trigger.

With snakelike quickness she drew back her arm and hurled the knife at him. The weapon struck him with its haft end, caroomed off and bounced into the wall behind him.

Koepp dove for the girl and seized her by a wrist.

She offered only feeble resistance. In a moment she was encircled by her mother's arms. "Oh, Erin, Erin, oh, my beautiful Erin."

Koepp swept up the knife, shoved it into the pocket of his jacket, then went to Margaret's aid. She lay motionless on her back with her eyes open. He crouched next to her. She was breathing, but only with great difficulty. Her color had a frightening bluish cast. She winced each time she drew a breath. He eased her onto her side so he could see the back wound. Judging by its location, he guessed the blade had pierced a lung. He talked to her, trying to coax the look of terror out of her eyes. She was losing an incredible amount of blood. He took the knife out of his pocket, revolted by having to touch it, and slid it underneath the sofa. Then he shifted his wallet and badge from his jacket breast pockets to hip pockets in his trousers. The jacket, rolled lengthways and pressed against the wound, seemed to staunch the flow. How much blood loss before a person went into shock? Karen and her daughter huddled together in the center of the room. For a moment he and Karen looked at each other in silence. Then Koepp shrieked, "Call 911, you stupid bitch!"

LIEUTENANT TARRISH joined Detective Sergeant Koepp in the waiting room outside general surgery at County General Hospital shortly after noon. His face was pinched with worry. Koepp imagined that his own features mirrored his supervisor's perfectly.

"How is she?" the lieutenant asked with an unnatural, affected briskness.

Koepp shrugged. "She's been in there a long time," he said. "In the ER they said she was in shock and had lost a lost of blood. But they said she was stable. They haven't talked to me since."

Tarrish grunted. Then he said, "I called her brothers. They're flying in as soon as they can make connections. I've got a car standing by to pick them up at the airport." He stripped off his suit jacket and tossed it carelessly into a chair, which Koepp interpreted to mean that he was going to stay to the end. "It's always worse when a woman cop gets it. I suppose that's chauvinistic, but I can't help it. It's more— obscene. Yeah, that's it, obscene. You know?"

Koepp nodded.

"By the way," Tarrish said, "Chief Voorhees put you back on the regular homicide rotation."

Yesterday that would have meant a lot to Koepp. Now, with what had happened to Margaret, it wasn't important.

The room filled up with people, then emptied when residents and nurses came by with cryptic messages from time to time. Others came to replace them. Koepp got up after a while and walked to the window, where he stood looking down at the parking lot and the grove of woods which separated the hospital from Roosevelt Boulevard. Traffic was heavy.

It was in the window that he first caught sight of her, an insubstantial reflection approaching him from the side. "How is she?" Karen asked.

He told her what he knew, then introduced her to Tarrish. The lieutenant surveyed her with interest from top to toe. Koepp saw that he was disappointed by the reality of the woman he had heard so much about.

"I'm responsible for this—not Erin. I didn't believe it would happen again. But Erin needed me so desperately and Margaret was taking me away from her. I'm so sorry."

"We know that, Mrs. Merrick. Everyone makes bad judgements about their kids," Tarrish said. Koepp was surprised by Tarrish's response; it was close to forgiveness.

They waited together in silence, Koepp and Karen standing, Tarrish slumped in a chair. After twenty minutes, a youthful-looking resident in his rumpled green scrubs sought them out, with some assistance from a hospital volunteer.

His message was less discouraging than Koepp had expected. "The knife punctured her lung," the young doctor said. "It caused a hemopneumothorax to develop—"

"In English, Doctor, please," Tarrish said.

He smiled in that indulgent way that doctors mastered during their intern year. "An air/fluid level is visible in the pleural space on the upright chest X-ray. It's caused by bleeding into the pleural space—that's the area between the lining of the lung and the chest wall."

"What are you doing about it?" Koepp asked.

"We've inserted a chest tube into the pleural space to drain the blood and aspirate air," the doctor replied. "She's having surgery now to repair the laceration."

Tarrish was losing patience. "What then?"

"The chest tube will be connected to suction for a few days until the lung is reexpanded. Then some rest. She's not going back to work for a while."

"But she will be back?" Koepp asked.

"Definitely. Her surgeon is excellent. She's in good health and young. She'll recover fully in time."

Koepp's relief was so intense he felt a little dizzy. He noticed that Tarrish was grinning foolishly. Grabbing his jacket, the lieutenant rushed out of the room to spread the good news.

Koepp and Karen were alone, facing each other.

"Did you believe I killed Steiner?" she asked quietly.

There was a long silence. Koepp finally replied, "Do you believe I trump up evidence to get convictions?"

Karen smiled her crooked smile and sighed. 'I keep thinking that if I had returned the knife to the kitchen everything would have been different."

"Why didn't you?"

"I had just changed Erin into some clothes I got from her dad's apartment—white tee and jeans—who can tell one from the other? She was numb, but I got her cleaned up in Steiner's apartment and was taking her home when Ina Jaroff grabbed me."

"In the downstairs corridor?"

"Yes. She insisted I approve of two watercolors she wanted to buy for the dining room. I couldn't get away from the silly woman, and I couldn't walk around with a knife wrapped in a copy of *Mother Jones*. I sent Erin home and dropped the knife in the creek when I had the chance."

"How long has Paul known about Erin?" Koepp asked.

"Since that night in Forest Junction," she answered, looking away from him toward the picture window. "I was angry

that he had left her alone with Steiner. I didn't tell him then
what Steiner had done to me. He learned about that the next
day—when you talked about the money I paid him. I suppose
we were both at fault. We didn't trust and confide in each
other. Our daughter is going to pay the price.''

Erin was not the only one, Koepp thought unhappily. Despite everything, he pitied her. In a few days he'd contact her
lawyer and explain to him about the position of Steiner's body
in relation to the door and personal computer. It suggested
that Steiner might have been stalking the girl when she tried
to deliver the phone message. Perhaps the lawyer could use
the information to support a self-defense plea.

"I hope someday you'll forgive me," Karen said.

"You don't need my forgiveness," he said. "You need
forgiveness from the Entity you don't believe in."

She stiffened and turned to leave. "Erin is at the children's
detention center. Her father's with her. I should get back
there."

Koepp waited at the window for her to emerge from the
hospital. He watched her, so tiny and indistinct at this distance, as she went to the lot. She seemed to have forgotten
where she had parked. She walked back and forth aimlessly
for a while, which reminded Koepp of the movements of an
insect or a small spider.

She looked very insignificant. And isolated.

Koepp returned to the nurses' station and asked when he
could see Margaret.

# A DOUBLE COFFIN

## GWENDOLINE BUTLER

### A COMMANDER JOHN COFFIN MYSTERY

**Former British Prime Minister Richard Lavender still knows when things need handling quickly and discreetly. Lavender's father was a serial killer. And the ex-PM wants to put matters right, nearly three-quarters of a century later. Hence the summons to Commander John Coffin of London's Second City police.**

**But when a journalist investigating Lavender is murdered, past and present collide, proving what Coffin already knows: that the past never disappears—it's buried, only to resurface in shocking and menacing ways.**

*Available May 1999 at your favorite retail outlet.*

Look us up on-line at http://www.worldwidemystery.com          WGB313

# DEATH
## OF A DUSTBUNNY
# CHRISTINE T. JORGENSEN

A STELLA THE STARGAZER MYSTERY

When Elena Ruiz disappears,
five-year-old Steven Holman is convinced
that a vampire has taken his nanny.
Stella the Stargazer, astrological adviser
to the lovelorn, is certain there are no
vampires, and she also knows that
Elena wouldn't walk away from her
charge. Only Steven has the clues to
her disappearance. So Stella has taken
over Elena's job temporarily to find
her friend.

Between comforting the boy and
trying to put her own haphazard life
in order, Stella discovers a trail that
leads to monsters of a very human sort....

*Available May 1999 at your favorite retail outlet.*

Look us up on-line at: http://www.worldwidemystery.com

# The
# AUDUBON
## *Quartet*
## RAY
## SIPHERD

## A Jonathan Wilder Mystery

Artist and bird lover Jonathan Wilder is eager to
view four newly discovered works of legendary
painter John James Audubon, purchased by
friend and art philanthropist Brian Ravener.
But at the first showing, notorious art critic
Abel Lasher declares the Audubon Quartet to
be fakes.

Hours later, Lasher is found murdered and
Ravener is arrested. Anxious to help his friend,
Wilder dives into the world of high art, where
powerful collectors play for high stakes....

*Available May 1999 at your favorite retail outlet.*

Look us up on-line at: http://www.worldwidemystery.com       WRS311

# PATRICIA TICHENOR WESTFALL

**A MOLLY WEST MYSTERY**

# MOTHER OF THE BRIDE

Even a seasoned list ma
like Molly West can get
jitters, especially when
her daughter announces
she's getting married in
two months—and worse,
that the wedding will be
Civil War reenactment.

Then a bridesmaid finds
skeleton in a cave where
escaped slaves used to
hide on the Underground
Railroad. But clearly the
human remains aren't tha
old. And as Molly starts
digging, she discovers
something old…somethin
new…and something
very deadly.

*Available May 1999 at your favorite retail outlet.*

Look us up on-line at: http://www.worldwidemystery.com        WPTW